THE
IMPERFECT
MURDER

A list of titles by James Patterson appears
at the back of this book

JAMES PATTERSON
& J.D. BARKER

THE
IMPERFECT
MURDER

CENTURY

CENTURY

UK | USA | Canada | Ireland | Australia
India | New Zealand | South Africa

Century is part of the Penguin Random House group of companies
whose addresses can be found at global.penguinrandomhouse.com

Penguin Random House UK,
One Embassy Gardens, 8 Viaduct Gardens, London SW11 7BW

penguin.co.uk

First published in the UK by Century 2025
001

Printed and bound in Great Britain by Clays Ltd, Elcograf S.p.A.

The authorised representative in the EEA is Penguin Random House Ireland,
Morrison Chambers, 32 Nassau Street, Dublin D02 YH68

A CIP catalogue record for this book is available from the British Library

ISBN: 978–1–529–94481–5 (hardback)
ISBN: 978–1–529–94482–2 (trade paperback)

Penguin Random House is committed to a sustainable future
for our business, our readers and our planet. This book is made
from Forest Stewardship Council® certified paper.

THE IMPERFECT MURDER

THEN

CHAPTER ONE

Log 10/18/2018 18:58 EDT

Transcript: Audio recording

[Detective Declan Shaw] Maggie Marshall?

[Voice unidentified] Yeah. Fourteen years old. Student at Barrett's Academy. She went—

[Shaw] I know who she is. We've all had eyes out for her since the Amber Alert. Transcriber, for the record, Maggie Marshall was reported missing two and a half days ago by her mother. Last seen leaving school, and she never made it home. She's been all over the news. The whole city's looking.

Has she been touched or moved in any way?

[Voice unidentified] No. That's exactly how she was found.

[Shaw] Electrical repair team found her?

[Voice unidentified] Yeah.

[Shaw] Where are they?

[Voice unidentified] We're holding them at Eighty-Sixth Street.

[Shaw] Central Park Precinct?

[Voice unidentified] Yeah.

[Shaw] Okay, give me a little space. [*Clears throat.*] We've had rain the last three nights. She's lying in the mud about a foot off the northeast exterior wall of Blockhouse in Central Park. Severely bloated and discolored from exposure. Same shoulder-length brown hair as in the photo circulated. Do you have positive ID?

[Voice unidentified] We found her backpack in the bushes over there. Student ID card inside, and her name is written in a few of the textbooks. It's her.

[Shaw] We'll confirm ID back at the ME office, but high probability this is Maggie Marshall. Aside from her left sock, she is naked from the waist down. I have eyes on her jeans, other sock, and shoes, all discarded randomly about four feet from her body. Left sock is still in place. Her underwear is

twisted around the base of her left foot. The
ground immediately around her has been
severely disturbed. Even with the standing water, maybe because of it, I can see
deep indents on either side of her where
it's clear he stood over her. There are also
trenches approximately six to eight inches
in width both on her sides and between
her legs. They appear to be marks left by
our unsub's knees. There are obvious signs
of struggle — kick marks and gouges in the
mud and dirt around her feet and hands,
almost like . . . almost like she tried to dig out
from under him.

[*Twelve seconds of silence.*]

I can see clear bruising around her neck consistent
with a single hand — right — about the same
size as mine. Thumbprint begins about one
and a half inches to the left of the hyoid
bone with the other four fingers rounding
the right side. He used a single-hand grip.
There is another large bruise directly above
her navel, giving the impression he held
her down with his knee. Additional bruising visible on the undersides of her wrists.
If he strangled her with his right hand, he
most likely pinned both her hands above
her head with his left hand as he did it. It's
clear from the surrounding ground she put
up a struggle, but she didn't stand much of

7

a chance. Both eyes are bloodshot. Petechiae in the right supports strangulation. This is an isolated spot, but why the hell didn't anyone hear her screaming? She must have screamed. [*Sniffle.*] Upon closer examination of her hands, her fingernails are caked with dirt from clawing at the ground. It's possible she scratched her attacker, but retrieval of trace may prove to be problematic. We've got a mess of footprints. We'll get elimination prints from all first responders and the crew that found her; maybe we'll get lucky.

[*Nine seconds of silence.*]

Where's that backpack?

[Voice unidentified] Over here.

[*Shuffling.*]

[Shaw] Transcriber, confirming for the record we've got a student ID in the front flap of the backpack for Barrett's Academy reading "Margaret Marshall." Three textbooks inside, got some math homework, and a paperback copy of *Little Women* by Louisa May Alcott. Library card being used as a bookmark at page ninety-seven also reads "Margaret Marshall."

[Voice unidentified] Detective, you'll want to see this!

[*Shuffling. Eighteen seconds of silence.*]

[Shaw] [*Shouted but muffled.*] Hey, get a few pictures of this before we move it. Up close and at a distance to establish proximity. Get these tracks around it too... [*Unintelligible, then muttered.*] Goddamn rain. We've got a Citizen watch. Old. Tan face with a tachymeter bezel. Brown leather stitched band. Looks like the top pin broke. Fell off the owner's wrist. It's a windup and still ticking, which means it was lost recently. Surrounding tracks appear similar, possibly the same as the ones around Maggie. Fresher, though. With the rain, less than twenty-four hours old.

[Voice unidentified] You think your guy came back?

[Shaw] Maybe he came back to move her or some-thing. Could be he just wanted to revisit. They do that. Based on the tracks, looks like he stood here and... ah, there it is. Cigarette butt. Bag that.

[Voice unidentified] Fucker stood here and smoked?

[Shaw] Looks like it. There's an inscription on the back of the watch. It says "Lucky."

[Second voice unidentified] I think I know who that belongs to.

[Shaw] You do?

[Second voice unidentified] Robert Morter. Head of park services.

[Shaw] You recognize this watch?

[Morter] Not the watch, the name. *Lucky.* We've got a guy on grounds crew who goes by Lucky.

[*End of recording.*]

/MG/GTS

NOW

CHAPTER TWO

DECLAN SHAW WAS a good cop.

Is a good cop, he tells himself.

Because until he actually jumps, he is still living in the present tense. And that's the rub, right? Anyone can find a deserted subway station; anyone can inch up to the edge of the platform and wait for the next train. But how many can actually work up the balls to launch themselves from the platform to the tracks? There is a science to it. Jump too early, and you'll end up under the train. Too late, and you're bouncing off the side. The key is to be in the air, meet the metal head-on. No pain, just lights-out.

The Eighty-First Street station is a dirty little secret known to New York's Finest. It's directly under the Museum of Natural

History on the A/B/C lines, and once the museum closes for the night, the platform becomes a ghost town. Also a suicide hot spot. Few trains stop. Most speed up as they shoot through because there is a tacit understanding among engineers: If you're going to hit a jumper (and odds of that are high at the Eighty-First), you want to do it quick.

The faint rumble of a train in the tunnel, maybe a minute out.

"Do it, you pussy. You're bleeding all over the nice white paint." Declan's voice sounds foreign to him, and the second the words leave his mouth, he gets all self-conscious about it, like talking to himself is the craziest thing in his life at the moment, like *that* is where all concerned observers should be pointing their fingers.

The blood is coming from a cut on his hand. Nothing too serious, just a scrape. But enough to make a mess of the metal pipe above his head. The one he's been holding for the better part of an hour. Without letting go, he inches closer to the edge of the pavement and stops when his shoes are half on, half off the concrete.

Declan tests the angle.

The balance.

Tenses his leg muscles.

Relaxes.

Tenses again.

Draws an oily, humid breath, lets it coat his throat when he swallows.

The train grows louder.

In his fourteen years with NYPD, Declan knows of four other cops who died in this very spot. Probably holding the same damn pipe. There's no plaque or commemorative photo on the wall, but when he closes his eyes, he can feel them standing right there with him. He can hear them quietly counting down the seconds until that train emerges from the tunnel. He can feel their hands on him, ready to give him a little shove. A little encouragement.

Ain't no thing, one of them mutters. *We got you.*

Bend your knees. Makes it easier to push off, says another.

It was the next one that got him. The next one struck him like a gut punch, because it sounded like his father.

You best be sure. 'Cause there's no coming back.

"There's no coming back from what I've done either," he tells him. His voice carries a faint echo with all the tile.

The train grows louder. The pipe, the concrete, the air — all come alive with the vibration of it.

Maybe twenty seconds out now.

Declan has very few memories of his father. He was only seven when he died in a construction accident over on Forty-First. One that wouldn't have happened if the foreman hadn't been pushing everyone to put in double hours to hit some ridiculous deadline nobody gave two shits about all these years later. His father lost his footing — that's what they told him and his mother. Would he have slipped if he hadn't been on fifteen straight hours? Not his father. No fucking way. Declan can barely picture the man's face anymore, but his voice . . . his father's voice, that thick Irish brogue — it's as clear today as it was when Declan was a kid.

You don't run from your problems, boy. You grab 'em by the fucking throat.

"Pops, you don't know."

A drop of blood falls from his hand, hits Declan's cheek. He wipes it away and catches a glimpse of the small tattoo on the skin between his thumb and forefinger: *MM*.

"Sometimes you dig a hole and there's no climbing back out."

Lights visible now.

The train just beyond the tunnel bend.

Ten seconds.

Every muscle in Declan's body goes tense. His fingertips are electric. Every sound, smell, and color are amplified.

Seven.

When the train rounds the corner, it's moving so fast it has no business staying on the tracks, but somehow it does. Sparks fly. There's a harsh screech. Declan's eyes find the engineer and a moment later the engineer spots him, and for that quick instant, their gazes lock. Declan tells himself he looks stoic, hard. Resolved. But in truth, he can't hide his fear any more than the engineer can.

Three.

The world slows.

The engineer reaches for the emergency brake. His fingers curl around it. But he doesn't pull. They both know it's too late for that.

Two.

Declan closes his eyes.

"Sorry, Pops."

One.

CHAPTER THREE

DECLAN'S PHONE RINGS.

In the instant it takes for his brain to process that, the train screams by at a mind-bending speed followed by a rush of air that nearly sucks him from the platform in a whirlwind of dust. It's his grip on the pipe that keeps him from tumbling over the edge and maybe under the ass end of one of the cars, maybe not, certainly not into the sweet spot at the train's nose, and that deduction—which he comes to in a millisecond—is enough for Declan to push off from the pipe, swing back, and drop awkwardly to the ground against a support pillar.

The train vanishes.

The sound fades.

Drenched in sweat, Declan sucks in a sharp breath. Every

fiber of his body is screaming. Protesting. This isn't the first time he's tried to jump tonight, it's the fourth, and he knows the next train will arrive in under seven minutes. He'll regroup and get it right. Declan is many things, but a failure isn't one of them.

His phone gives another shrill ring and vibrates in his pocket. He fumbles it out and glances at the display—his partner, Jarod Cordova.

Declan clicks Decline.

At sixty, Cordova is twenty-four years older than Declan and three short years from forced retirement. While most cops slip into low gear for this phase of their career, Cordova seems to view the ticking clock as some sort of personal challenge—how many jackets can he close before they slap an imitation-gold Apple watch on his wrist and buy him a one-way ticket to Boca Raton? Because their current workload isn't enough for him, he's gotten in the habit of taking cold-case files home and working them in his spare time. These late-night calls usually mean he's at his kitchen table elbow-deep in yellowed paperwork and wants to talk something out.

Nope.

Not tonight.

Declan's got a full dance card.

Five minutes until the next train.

He's brushing the dust from his jeans when his phone buzzes again. This time it's a text:

Pick up, you shit!

When the phone starts to ring again, he has half a mind to chuck it against the far wall but decides not to. Sometimes it's better to rip off the Band-Aid. He thumbs the side button.

"Look, man, I'm a little into something right now. Can this wait?"

Cordova's scratchy voice comes back at him. "Where are you?"

"Busy."

"Busy where? You near the Upper West Side?"

Declan glances around the empty subway station. At the dirt and grime. The streaks on the ground around him left by his shoes, his fingers. There's a poster on the wall opposite for a new shark exhibit coming to the museum next month. The date grabs him — *next month.*

He swallows.

"Declan, you there?"

"Yeah, sorry."

"Call came in. Sounds like a B and E gone bad."

The clock at the far end of the platform reads 9:52 p.m. "Sounds like someone else's problem."

"Got at least one dead with shots fired at the responding officers. Your name came up."

"Came up how?"

"I don't know the details, but LT wants us there. How fast can you get to two eleven Central Park West? The Beresford."

Four minutes until the next train.

He doesn't have to do this.

He doesn't have to do a damn thing but get back up on the edge of the platform and count to a little over two hundred and —

Cardova says, "You need me to send a car for you?"

Somewhere behind Declan, a woman giggles; the sound echoes off the subway tiles. A moment later, two twenty-somethings come down the steps from the street. Pretty girl in a slinky black dress leaning heavily on a guy in a sports coat, jeans, and Birkenstocks, both of them drunk. Probably looking for a little privacy. Evidently, neither one is happy to see him standing there, because they quickly turn around and stumble back up the steps.

Life goes on.

Declan blows out a defeated breath and looks down at the scrape on his hand. Pink and ugly, but no longer bleeding. "I'm in the park. I can be there in a few minutes."

"Take the Central Park West entrance. You want the tower apartment. I'll meet you. Move."

CHAPTER FOUR

BY THE TIME Declan ascends the steps to Eighty-First, the drunk couple is gone and he is no longer shaking. The anxiety is still there, though. It's bubbling beneath the surface of his skin, looking for a way out. It's not until he catches sight of the Beresford building that he's able to focus, get his head in the game.

Less than a block away, the twenty-two-story Beresford looms over Central Park West like some patriarch of old New York. Built in 1929 in the Renaissance style, it's one of the most prestigious and luxurious apartment buildings in the city. The limestone exterior is adorned with gargoyles, dragons, and floral patterns, from the oversize doors at street level to the three towers at the top. A modern-day castle. The building screams *money*.

You will never live there, his father had told him about a year before he died. They'd been on the bus, heading home from the Irish fair at Coney Island. His mother was sleeping. One of Declan's few memories of the three of them together outside their cramped apartment. *You're ever lucky enough to set foot inside, it will be to clean up the shit of someone who does live there. You remember that, because folks like that got a way of making their shit sparkle. Make you think you want to clean it up. You do it, there's nothing wrong with honest work, but don't let them trick you into thinking you belong. That happens, and they own you.*

The doorman at the Central Park West entrance spots Declan coming up the sidewalk, catches sight of the badge on his belt, and has the door open before he's even under the canopy. "You know where you're going?"

"Tower apartment." Declan steps by him, crosses the ornate lobby, and presses the elevator call button as his phone starts ringing again. This time, it's not his partner.

"Assistant District Attorney Carmen Saffi," Declan says. "What can I do for you?"

"You're responding on the Beresford call, right?"

How the hell did she hear so fast? "Just entered the lobby. Heading up."

"Any press there yet?"

"For a B and E? Why would the press show for that?"

"They will. I need you to handle this with kid gloves, Detective," Saffi says. "She's a friend of the mayor."

You mean a donor to the mayor's campaign, Declan thinks. *Isn't that what you meant to say?*

The elevator doors slide open and Declan steps inside, presses the button for the tower. "Kid gloves, got it."

"I'm serious, Declan. There'll be a lot of eyes on this. We don't want a negative narrative."

"In the elevator, Saffi. I'm losing you. Try back in —" He hangs up.

When the doors open, Declan steps out into a wall of cops. Six uniforms standing in a cramped foyer with their thumbs up their asses staring at a closed door at the opposite end of the hall. Cordova somehow beat him here. His back is turned, phone attached to his ear. Tense.

Sergeant Jorge Hernandez spots Declan and frowns. "You fall asleep in an alley, Dec? You look like shit."

Declan runs his fingers through his tousled dark hair. His hand is shaking again. He shoves it in his pocket. "Next time you call, I promise to wear your favorite lipstick. You wanna tell me why I'm here?"

Hernandez nods at the far end of the hall. "Woman in the tower apartment comes home to find her door jimmied and her husband dead. Calls 911. Says whoever did it might still be in the apartment. My guys show, and she fires a round at them when they try to come through the door. Tells them nobody comes in but you — 'Detective Declan Shaw, Detective Declan Shaw.' She says it over and over again. Fucking loony tunes. She's lucky nobody returned fire."

Hernandez and Declan came up patrol together. When Declan went for his detective shield, Hernandez opted to go for his stripes. Unlike Declan, he's married with four kids at home. Rumor has it his wife is pregnant with number five. Even though no one's come out and said anything yet, the whole force knows. Hernandez has a terrible poker face, is a shitty liar, and is the last person you'd ask to keep a secret.

When he's holding something back, Declan has no trouble reading him. "What aren't you telling me?"

Hernandez purses his lips. "Something about this ain't right."

"She fired at responding officers. No shit, something ain't right."

"That's not what I mean," Hernandez tells him. "The shot was a reflex thing. My guys ID'd themselves, then came through the door hard and loud and startled her. I think her finger was just on the trigger. She jerked; it went off. High and wide. She wasn't aiming at them. But that's not what I mean." He gestures at one of the patrol officers. "Marco, give Detective Shaw your vest and radio. Apparently, he's forgotten how to properly respond to a crime scene."

"I'm off the clock," Declan mutters, donning the gear. "If her shooting at you isn't the problem, what is?"

"You'll see."

This isn't Declan's first rodeo. He knows what Hernandez is getting at. "Husband's dead, you think she did it, and the B and E is bullshit? Insurance grab or something?"

"Wouldn't be the first time." His voice drops low: "She's covered in blood. You just find a body, you don't look like that."

Cordova, still on the phone, is pacing now, his face red. When he catches sight of Declan, he gives him a frustrated nod, turns away, and mutters something that sounds a lot like *Roy Harrison,* that IAU prick. Declan doesn't want to know what that's about. Internal Affairs climbed on their backs after Maggie Marshall, and it doesn't matter that they haven't found anything; those fuckers won't let go. Harrison has IAU digging through all Declan and Cordova's closed cases, looking for who the hell knows what.

Declan shakes it off and steps up to the apartment door, Hernandez behind him. He reaches for the borrowed microphone clipped to his shoulder, locks it in the transmit position, then says, "You copy?"

Hernandez adjusts his earbud and nods. "Loud and clear."

"Be ready to come in behind me."

Hernandez frowns at the officers crammed in the foyer who are caught up in nervous chatter. "How 'bout a little quiet, gentlemen? Look sharp."

Cordova ends his call; the others go silent.

Declan asks, "What's her name?"

"Denise Morrow."

Hernandez says it like it should mean something to him.

Declan reaches for the Glock on his hip and unfastens the leather safety strap. He doesn't take out the weapon, though. With a hooked finger, he gives the door a gentle knock and speaks in the calmest voice he can muster: "Mrs. Morrow? This is Detective Declan Shaw of the NYPD. I believe you requested me?" When she doesn't respond, he twists the knob. "I'm coming in. Hold your fire."

CHAPTER FIVE

AS HE OPENS the door, Declan steals a quick look at the lock and jamb. It's clearly been jimmied; there are scrape marks all around the otherwise pristine brass. The jamb is scuffed and dented, like someone shoved a wide screwdriver in the small space and tried to pry the door open. There's blood too. Not much. Like whoever did this scraped a knuckle or something.

Hernandez is right.

It's all wrong.

If a perp on a B and E knows how to pick a lock, he doesn't try to pry the door open. If a perp pries a door open, there's no need to pick the lock. You don't do both. You don't pry a door open with a screwdriver either. You need something more formidable, like a pry bar. And when you use that, you make a mess—the jamb cracks, sometimes the door. You gotta bust up enough to get the dead bolt past the strike plate. That didn't happen here. None of it. The scrapes in the brass around the lock are too wide, probably from the same screwdriver. Definitely not a lockpick. Picks are narrow, pointy. Even the blood makes no sense. What self-respecting perp wouldn't wipe it away? Maybe some meth-head looking to score wouldn't think of that, but someone doing a B and E in a building like this? It all looks superficial. Staged. Someone took a screwdriver and roughed up the doorjamb, then made some scratches around the lock.

Declan glances at Hernandez, and the man's nodding his head, silently mouthing, *See what I mean?*

Yeah, Declan thinks. *I see.*

He clears his throat. "Mrs. Morrow? It's me, Detective Declan Shaw. I'm coming in. I'm alone. Don't shoot."

Drawing a deep, calming breath, Declan steps into the apartment. He gently closes the door behind him, sealing out the other officers. His mic is live; he knows they can still hear him.

He's in a large foyer surrounded by marble—floors, walls, all of it marble. A table sits by the door; on it is a brass plate filled with keys next to a large empty vase. There's a coatrack off to the side. Silk flowers are scattered on the floor. On the wall, an alarm panel is flashing red. Tripped earlier, but silent now. Probably timed out.

He finds Denise Morrow at the end of a short hall off the entryway. She's sitting on the floor, her back pressed against the wall. Her knees are pulled tight against her chest, held there by her arms in an almost childlike hug. A .38 dangles loosely from the fingers of her left hand. What he can see of her white blouse is stained crimson; her black pants are wet with it too. She's gently rocking, the softest of whimpers slipping from her lips.

A man is on the floor, his dead face frozen in a mix of panic and fear, his chest a bloody mess from multiple stab wounds.

The knife is on the floor between the two of them, marring the otherwise pristine white marble with blood.

Declan speaks softly, disarmingly. "Is this your husband?"

It takes a moment for her to respond, like the words reach her on a delay. She bobs her head, the movement barely perceptible.

Declan lowers himself to a crouch and checks the man for a pulse he knows he won't find, then reaches over the man's body for the gun. "How about you give me that?"

She seems to shrink back farther, like she'd become part of the wall if she could, her grip tightening on the weapon. In a soft, urgent voice, she says, "I think they're still here. I heard something from the main bedroom."

Declan follows her gaze past the kitchen to a dark hall. He seriously doubts anyone is still in the apartment. Aside from her and her husband, he's fairly certain nobody has been in the apartment period, but he's not about to chance it. He whispers, "Do you mind if I bring in some officers to conduct a search? I'll stay here with you." Nodding at the gun. "You'll need to give me that, though. They won't come in if you have it. Think you can do that? You don't have to move. You can stay right there if you want. Just give me the gun. You're safe now. I promise."

He holds his hand out again.

For a second, he thinks she's going to protest, but she reaches out and sets the weapon in his hand.

Declan pops the cylinder and empties the bullets into his palm. He slips them into his pocket and tucks the .38 under his belt behind his back. Then he reaches for the radio clipped to his shoulder and pretends to push the transmit button, knowing full well Hernandez and the others are already listening. "This is Shaw," he says. "Send in two officers to conduct a room-by-room. Potential perp still on-site. I'm with Mrs. Morrow. She is no longer armed."

He half expects to hear *Copy*, then realizes they can't respond as long as he's locked in transmit mode. When he lowers his hand, he hears the apartment door open behind him, followed by the shuffle of shoes on the marble. He doesn't take his eyes off Denise Morrow as they dart by his right side and disappear deeper into the large apartment. "This will just take a moment."

Declan tries to get a read on her, but she appears to be in shock. She doesn't seem to want to look at her husband, which is understandable. Right now, Declan doesn't want her to. Looking at him might snap her out of it, bring on emotion. Emotion is unpredictable. Nobody wants unpredictable. Then he notices something else—her makeup is perfect. Not a single mascara streak from tears. No snotty nose from crying. No odd coloration in her cheeks; they're not pale, flushed, or otherwise. What kind of woman (in shock or not) finds her husband stabbed to death and doesn't shed a tear?

He stands and gets a better look around. There's a floor-to-ceiling bookshelf on his left, and he spots something odd there too—there are ten copies of the same book. A dozen more of another title. The entire shelf is like that, maybe a hundred books in all, but most of them are the same four or five titles. He pulls a hardcover at random and flips it over, finds Denise Morrow's photo on the back. "This is you?" More of a statement than a question. "You're a writer?"

Another soft nod.

The bio under her photograph reads *Denise Morrow is the* New York Times *and international bestselling author of numerous true-crime thrillers, including* The Bronx Ripper *and* The Devil of Hell's Kitchen. *Her titles have been translated into over thirty languages and can be found in more than 150 countries worldwide. She resides in New York City with her husband, David, and their cat, Quimby.*

Declan lowers the book, gives the body a quick glance, then meets her eyes. "Do you know who might want to hurt David?"

She sucks in a deep breath, and for a second Declan thinks the tears might come, but there's nothing.

Not a damn thing.

CHAPTER SIX

THE TWO OFFICERS tasked with securing the apartment return, their weapons holstered. Declan knows one of them, a heavyset guy with a strawberry birthmark on his neck. Estes. The other guy's name tag reads ORTEGA.

They motion for Declan to come over.

"Give me a second," he tells Denise Morrow.

Speaking low, Estes says, "Nobody here. We found the door off the main bedroom standing open, but it leads to a private terrace. We're in the tower. There's no place to go. No fire escape. No secondary rooftop in jumping distance."

"What about other terraces?"

"These apartments are all oversize. They got high ceilings. Next terrace is a good twelve to fourteen feet down. Could be done, but this ain't no Marvel movie. Maybe with some sort of gear, but—"

"Go down there and check it out anyway. The one in the penthouse too," Declan tells them. "They ask what's going on, just say there was a report of an intruder in the building. Not a word about Mr. Morrow here. Got it?"

Estes nods.

"Anything seem out of place to either of you? Missing? Tossed?"

Ortega shakes his head. "Nothing. No open drawers. Jewelry laid out nice and neat on the dresser looks untouched. Computers and stereo still here. Either we got an incompetent burglar, or this is the neatest B and E I've ever seen."

Estes adds, "Maybe your perp came in for something specific. Maybe the mister was some kind of target. Or..."

Or Mrs. Morrow cashed in her hubby's chips. It's impossible not to think it.

When they start for the door, Declan tells them, "Send CSU in. I want to get this on L-Tron before anything gets moved."

"You got it."

Declan returns to Denise and drops to a knee again. "Did you leave your terrace door open? The one off your bedroom?"

She shakes her head.

"The apartment is clear. There's nobody here, but they found your terrace door open. I've asked them to discreetly check with your neighbors. See if anyone jumped or exited from adjacent apartments."

Her large brown eyes drift to the floor, then back to him. "Okay," she manages. "Can I...can I get up now?"

"I'd like a medic to take a look at you before you move. Just to be sure you're all right," he says in his most reassuring voice. "It will only be another minute."

A CSU tech dressed in a white protective jumpsuit steps into the room and begins setting up a tripod with an odd-looking camera fixed to the top.

"This is called an L-Tron. It will capture a three-D rendering of this room," Declan says. "Once we have that, we can revisit this space exactly as it is now should we need to do so."

Like at trial, his mind mutters. *A 3D image of Mrs. Morrow sitting here on the floor covered in blood next to her husband's dead body with the murder weapon between them will do nicely when it comes time to prosecute this.*

"Ready, Detective," the CSU tech tells him.

"Please remain perfectly still, Mrs. Morrow. This will only take a moment. We'll be right outside the door."

"You...want me to stay here?"

"It's important we preserve the scene. It will just take a second, I promise. I'll check on that medic for you. Try not to move."

Declan and the tech quickly exit the apartment and close the door. The tech presses a series of buttons on the remote and studies the screen as images begin flooding in. In under a minute, the camera captures every inch of the room. Once it's run through the software back at the precinct, they'll be able to zoom in on anything with incredible detail. Circle around. Go up. Down. Declan does not miss the days of flat photographs. "Run images in every room. Get the terrace off the main bedroom too. Who do you have taking samples?"

Another woman dressed in an identical jumpsuit raises her hand. "That would be me. Kim Diaz."

Declan glances at the L-Tron monitor, Denise Morrow centered on the screen. He's half hoping she'll do something incriminating when she thinks nobody is watching. Stash something. Reposition something. The guilty ones can't help themselves. But she's not moving, and he knows he's got a ticking clock. He's left her there too long as is. He turns back to the CSU tech. "Diaz, you said?"

She nods.

"I want you to get some help and process every inch of that woman as quickly as possible. Get samples of all the blood. Anything under her fingernails. In her hair. Get it all. She's part of this crime scene. I want everything. We may not get another chance. The second she lawyers up, we're behind a wall."

"Understood."

Declan quickly scans the remaining uniforms huddled around the elevator, lands on Lori Hunter. "Hunter—you're with us. I need a female officer as a witness."

Declan grabs a pair of latex gloves and glances back at Cordova—who's on the phone again. Declan tells Hernandez, "When he finishes with his girlfriend, can you tell him to talk to the doorman and maybe pull security footage? We need to get a timeline together."

"You got it."

Back inside, Declan finds Denise Morrow still frozen on the floor. He gestures toward the CSU tech. "Mrs. Morrow, this is the medic I mentioned," he lies. "She's going to check you for any injuries. We're also going to need your clothing. She'll help with that too. Is there someplace private you can change other than your main bedroom? If the person who hurt David exited that way, it's best we stay out until my team has had a chance to gather any evidence."

"There's a guest room."

"Good." Declan nods at Officer Hunter. "Lori here will go with you too. Keep you safe. You need anything at all, you ask her, okay?" As he reaches out a hand to help her to her feet, Declan catches movement out of the corner of his eye. In a flash of gray and black, something heavy drops from the top of the bookcase and slams into his head. Sharp claws dig into his scalp. Declan grabs a fist of fur, yanks, and tosses the largest cat he's ever seen halfway across the room. The cat lands on his feet, gives Declan a disdainful glance, and scrambles away, disappearing somewhere near the kitchen.

"Quimby," Denise Morrow says in barely a whisper before starting down the hall, followed by the officer and CSU tech.

"Quimby," Declan repeats, tentatively touching his scalp with the back of his gloved hand, thankful to find no blood. Shaking it off, he takes out his phone and opens the department's transcriber app, clicks the record button, and turns back to the body on the floor. Time to go to work—

"Transcriber, this is Detective First Class Declan Shaw of the NYPD Twentieth. It is Friday, November tenth, 2023. The time is twenty-two eighteen. Current location is two eleven Central Park West. Apparent homicide of one David Morrow..."

CHAPTER SEVEN

TEN MINUTES LATER, when Declan clicks off the transcriber app, he finds Cordova standing behind him, a glum look on his face.

Declan slips his phone back into his pocket. "Do I want to hear what that business with IAU was about?"

"You do not," Cordova tells him. "I wish I didn't have to hear about it either. I'll fill you in later." He glances around. "Where is she?"

"Guest room with CSU and Hunter."

Unlike Declan, who's in a T-shirt and jeans, Cordova is wearing a sports jacket, matching pants, and a tie. Old-school NYPD. The man has even been known to wear a fedora, although he catches shit for it. They're four hours off the clock, but he looks freshly shaven. Fucking Cordova. The notebook he pulls from his breast pocket is new; Declan doesn't have to see it up close to know that. Cordova keeps a stack of them on hand and starts fresh with each case. "David Morrow. Thirty-nine years old. Cardiologist over at Mercy. Brought in seven hundred and ninety thousand last year before taxes, which is about two hundred K higher than the average for New York. Seems aboveboard; he's just good. Brings the hospital a lot of out-of-state business. Married to Denise Morrow, writer, wed sixteen years ago. They own this place as well as a lake house in the Catskills. No mortgages. No outstanding debt. At least that we've found. I've got the folks in financial digging deeper." He takes a few tentative steps closer and stops several paces from David Morrow's body, letting out a low whistle. "We've got ourselves an overachiever. How many stab wounds you count?"

"Six obvious. Maybe more. Tough to say with all the blood," Declan says. "Best I can tell, the assailant clipped the heart a couple of times but kept going. Maybe he didn't go down, or the attacker was in some kind of rage. This is telling, though." He kneels and, using the tip of a pencil, turns Morrow's left palm toward Cordova. "Not a single defensive wound. Nothing on the other hand either."

Cordova considers that, then looks down the hall to the front door. "That's, what, at least twenty feet?"

"Twenty-three. I measured."

He knows what Cordova is thinking. It's the condition of the lock; he keeps going back there too. If (and it's a big *if*) someone tried to pick it, he didn't succeed. It's possible David Morrow heard him trying, maybe opened the door, surprised the guy. But in that scenario, the altercation would have happened near the door, not twenty-three feet away. There would be a high probability of defensive wounds, and David Morrow has none. The theory doesn't track.

"He knew his attacker," Cordova mutters.

"You think?" Declan stands, jerks his thumb toward the back bedroom. "Come on, Cordova, it's clear what this is."

"Doesn't mean we don't have to prove it."

"She was covered in blood."

"She'll say she tried to revive him."

"She hasn't shed a tear. Her makeup looks damn near perfect."

"They make waterproof makeup. You haven't heard the 911 call yet. She sounds plenty upset there. That's what the jury will hear. What they'll remember when they go to deliberate. She'll get some expert to testify she was in shock when we got here. They'll explain it all as some form of break, detachment."

"Whose side you on?" Declan frowns.

"I'm just pointing out what we'll be up against as this thing progresses."

Declan isn't in the mood to go down the what-if rabbit hole. Cordova tends to approach these things like he's playing chess—he maps out his opponents' next three moves and thinks through some counter. The problem with that is most of those moves never happen and he ends up wasting time and energy on nothing. Best to keep him on task. "What did the doorman say? You pull the cam footage?"

Cordova nods and flips a page in his notebook. "This is one of the most private buildings in New York. It's technically three different buildings, three separate sections, each with its own lobby. You can't get from one section to the other from the inside; you have to go down to street level, exit, and reenter at the appropriate lobby. The lobby you entered when you arrived serves only a handful of apartments, and her nearest neighbors are in Switzerland until the end of the month. David here got home at four forty p.m. Nobody else comes up until the wife gets home at nine twenty p.m." Cordova's face goes grim. "She dials 911 at nine thirty-one p.m., eleven minutes after she passed through the lobby, and first responders arrive at nine thirty-seven p.m. That's a full seventeen minutes of the wife's time unaccounted for. It takes two minutes tops to get here from downstairs. If she killed him and staged all this, she had fifteen minutes."

"That's plenty of time," Declan tells him. "Her story just doesn't jibe. Even if someone got in here and she stumbled into a robbery gone wrong, no way she waits eleven minutes to call for help, says the perp is still inside, then sits here and waits for us to show...come on. This is about as clear as it gets. She got home, killed him right here, mucked up the door and lock, opened the terrace door, and dialed. That's the only thing that makes sense." Declan gestures to the bookshelf. "You know what she does for a living, right? True-crime author. Hell, with that pedigree, she should've done a better job of staging."

Cordova takes a long, hard stare down the length of the apartment, past the open kitchen and living room, toward the bedrooms in the back. Muted light streams in from floor-to-ceiling windows that offer sweeping views of Central Park. "Place like this goes for…what? Ten million? Fifteen? That her motive, money? They have no real debt, remember."

Behind them, the apartment door swings open. A wiry little man pushes past Hernandez and steps inside. His ratlike eyes quickly take in Declan and Cordova, the body on the floor. Then he actually has the balls to remove his coat and hang it on the rack. Hernandez grabs him by the shoulder and tells him, "You can't be in here!"

He twists out of Hernandez's grip. "I got a call—"

Declan gets between him and the body. "And you are?"

"Geller Hoffman. I'm…a friend."

Declan has never met the man, but he knows the name. Hoffman is one of the city's most prominent defense attorneys. The squirrelly little fucker is notorious for putting criminals back on the street, providing they can afford him. Just last week, he made headlines for defending John Cornelli in a racketeering case brought by the feds. The mobster should have gone away for ten years, minimum. Instead, he got six months in a federal country club. Cordova knows who he is too; it's all over his face. "Who called you?"

Hoffman gestures toward the flashing panel on the wall. "The alarm company. I'm on the Morrows' security list. When Denise and David didn't answer, they tracked me down." He takes another step forward and freezes. "Christ, is that David?"

Cordova points. "I need you to step back."

Hoffman doesn't move. "Where the hell is Denise? Is she okay?"

"She's fine," Declan tells him. "They're processing her down the hall."

Hoffman's eyes narrow. *"Processing her?"*

Before anyone can stop him, he goes stomping through the apartment, shouting her name.

CHAPTER EIGHT

BY THE TIME Declan catches up with Geller Hoffman, he has the guest room door open, and his face is bright red. "What the fuck are you people doing?"

Naked, with her back to them, Denise Morrow is standing next to the bed, her arms outstretched. The two female CSU techs are hovering around her. Diaz is running a swab down the length of Morrow's arm, and the other is busy brushing the woman's hair, capturing trace. The bed is covered in gear—open cases, a black light, various solutions. Morrow's clothing has been bagged and tagged along with multiple samples. At the sight of Hoffman, Officer Hunter quickly rounds the bed and stands between him and Morrow, one hand extended, palm up, the other resting on the butt of her gun. "Back up! Now!"

Hoffman turns to Declan. "Who gave you permission to do this?"

"She didn't decline," Declan fires back.

"Did she specifically say yes?"

"You need to get back into the hall before you get yourself arrested for interference."

He ignores him. "Denise, did you give them permission to touch you?" She doesn't answer, so he steps around Officer Hunter and goes to her. When he sees her face, he appears horrified. "She's practically catatonic! What the hell is wrong with you people? Somebody get her some clothes!"

Hunter looks at Declan, who nods. From one of the black cases on the bed, she retrieves a package of hospital scrubs.

Hoffman snatches them from her hand. "All of you, out. Now." When nobody moves, he twists and stares down Declan. "Has she been charged with a crime?"

"Not yet."

"Then get your people out of this room. Do you have any idea how many of her rights you've violated? *Do you even care?*"

Declan isn't about to get pushed around. He turns to the two CSU techs. "Did you get everything you need?"

They both nod.

Hoffman waves at the collected samples on the bed. "None of this will be admissible if you try to pin whatever happened to David on my client."

"Your client?" Declan meets his beady little eyes. "If Mrs. Morrow has retained counsel, we haven't been told about it."

"Consider yourself told. I want to speak to her alone. Now." Before Declan can object, Hoffman nudges Denise Morrow into the bedroom's en suite and closes the door behind them. Clicks the lock.

"You believe that guy?" Declan asks Cordova.

"Hoffman could be a problem."

"This case is open-and-shut. He can't do a damn thing for her."

Cordova doesn't reply to that. He looks at Lori Hunter, then nods at the bathroom door. "Keep an eye on those two." To Declan, he says, "There's something you need to see."

He leads Declan back down the hall, past the living room and a formal dining room to an office off a shorter hall behind the kitchen. Large space, at least twenty by thirty, with a wide window looking out over Eighty-First. Built-in bookcases on all four walls. The books are neatly arranged, not in alphabetical order but by color. A mix of fiction and non-fiction. Everything from Charles Dickens to Grisham to world politics to socioeconomic texts. Many of the books have yellow Post-it notes sticking out the top, flagging marked pages or passages or who knows what. Declan has never been much of a reader; he is more of a movie guy.

An antique cherrywood desk polished to a high sheen sits in the center of the room. The top is bare except for a laptop and a neat stack of paper in a black wire tray. That's what Cordova is interested in, and when Declan steps close enough to read the top sheet, he understands why.

"This must be her latest book," Cordova says, picking up the stack and thumbing through the pages.

"No shit," Declan mutters, unable to look away from the title.

The Taking of Maggie Marshall
Incompetence in the NYPD

By Denise Morrow

"You said she asked for me on the 911 call."

"She did. Kept saying your name over and over again. You'll hear it."

"If she's looking at Maggie Marshall, why would she ask for *me?*"

Cordova doesn't get the chance to answer that. From the other room, someone shouts his name.

They go back to the large foyer, where four CSU techs are busy processing David Morrow. The ME is here now too. The shout came from Lori Hunter near the front door, where they find Geller Hoffman back in his coat and attempting to guide Denise Morrow out of the apartment. Hernandez is blocking their path.

Declan has had enough of this guy. "Where do you think you're going with her?"

"I'm getting her help."

Denise Morrow's gaze is fixed on the floor. Her lips are moving but without sound, as if she's lost in some silent conversation with herself.

Declan isn't buying it. The more he sees, the more this feels like some bullshit act. "Is she injured in any way? Does she need to go to the hospital?"

"She's traumatized."

"If she doesn't need to see a doctor for immediate medical care, we're taking her to the precinct for questioning."

Hoffman twists his scarf around his neck. "She came home to find her husband dead on the floor and a possible intruder in her apartment. She's lucky to be alive. *She's the victim here.* Why are you treating her like a suspect?"

"Her role in all this has yet to be determined."

"You're stretching, Detective. I've seen this before. Some half-assed investigator gets a theory in his head, and the blinders go on. He gets so obsessed, he looks at nothing else. The product of a simple mind." Hoffman licks his lips. "What's your educational background, Detective? When I dig into that, what am I going to find? I seriously doubt you're a scholar. My money is on a GED and some community college. Probably couldn't stick it out long enough to get a degree and decided to become a cop instead. That what I'm going to find?"

Declan feels the blood rush to his face, and he takes a step closer.

Cordova's hand settles on his shoulder. Declan starts to say something, but his partner cuts him off. "We're all just doing our jobs here, Counselor. No reason to get personal. We'll give Mrs. Morrow a ride to the precinct, where we can talk this through. You're welcome to follow. The sooner we learn all the details, the sooner we can get this resolved."

As Cordova speaks, Hoffman's eyes don't leave Declan. He actually draws closer, cranes his neck up to look him in the eye. Then he tells Denise, "I'll be right behind. Don't say a fucking word to anyone."

CHAPTER NINE

STUDYING THE SMALL observation monitor two doors down from the precinct interview room, assistant district attorney Carmen Saffi taps the end of her pen against her lips. Declan, next to her, nurses a cup of tar-black coffee from the break room. On the screen, Denise Morrow is sitting at the aluminum table, her hands in her lap; her attorney is in the chair beside her. He keeps looking up at the camera. When he speaks to her, he does so in whispers.

"Geller Hoffman just happened to show up?" ADA Saffi asks Declan.

Although it's approaching midnight, Saffi looks as sharp as she does in the courtroom—gray pantsuit, hair and makeup perfect. She's the same as Cordova, married to the job. It's like the two of them sleep standing up in their Sunday best, ready to roll at a moment's notice. Like they wait for it. Unlike Declan, who knows he still stinks of subway and despair. "The Morrows' alarm was tripped. He said the monitoring company called him," he tells her.

"Seems odd to have a defense attorney on the call list, doesn't it?"

"Said he's a family friend."

"What do you make of their body language?" she asks. "Something seem off to you?"

Declan has picked up on that too.

Denise Morrow is an attractive woman — a bit on the odd side, but attractive. She has that mousy thing going on. With the black-rimmed glasses and her hair swept up, she makes you think of a sexy librarian or a teacher from some '90s rock video. It's like she knows she's attractive and purposely tries to dial it back. Even now, sitting in an interrogation room wearing borrowed scrubs, she's striking. Every guy who passed her in the precinct hallway turned to get a second look. Declan flashes back to Geller walking in on Denise Morrow naked when she was being processed — *he* didn't give her a second look. He didn't give her a first look. *He went out of his way not to,* Declan thinks. *Not out of respect — that squirrelly fucker doesn't know from respect. It was something else.* Declan got the feeling that seeing Denise Morrow naked was nothing new to Geller. He got the feeling that Geller and Morrow were intimate and going out of their way to conceal it. Her husband was just found dead. *She's traumatized,* Geller said, yet he didn't do a damn thing to comfort her. For her part, Morrow gave no indication she needed or wanted comforting. None of this was typical. While it might mean nothing, it also might mean something.

Cordova knocks twice on the door frame and steps into the small room; he's clutching a computer printout. "We've got life insurance, but not exactly what I was expecting."

ADA Saffi frowns. "What does it say?"

"Joint policy. They took it out three years ago. Pays out five million for natural death, eight million for accidental."

Declan whistles. "There's your motive."

"I agree. It would have been a fantastic motive if Denise Morrow hadn't canceled the payouts on David six weeks ago. Would have been one hell of a motive."

"What?" Declan snatches the paper from him and scans the text. "Says here she terminated all coverage related to David but left hers."

"That's what I just said."

Saffi's frown deepens. "So she dies in a home invasion, he gets eight million, but he dies, she gets zero?"

Cordova nods.

"And she changed that six weeks back?"

"When she paid the premiums for the year."

"You saw that apartment," Declan says. "She doesn't need the insurance money. This woman is smart. She knows we'd see insurance as motive, so she took it off the board. Don't forget, she writes about this sort of thing for a living."

"Oh, I didn't forget." Cordova smirks. "I've been looking at that too. There's something I want you to watch, an interview she did for her second book, *A Mother's Burden*. The book's about Michelle Bacot. Remember that case?"

Saffi does. "Bacot killed her husband when she learned he was molesting their thirteen-year-old daughter. Made it look like an accident—pulled the ladder out from under him when he was cleaning gutters around the house. Jersey City, right?"

Cordova nods. "I found this interview on YouTube. I'm skipping the preamble nonsense and starting at the eight-minute mark." Holding his phone between them, he plays the video.

"The jury didn't take any pity on her, though, right? I mean, Bacot is serving twelve years. Hardly the perfect crime," the interviewer says.

The camera flashes to Denise Morrow. She looks a little younger, and her hair is longer, but she's otherwise the same. "She didn't get caught; she turned herself in. It wasn't the police that got her, it was the guilt. She had saved her daughter, but she couldn't live with what she'd done. Even with the understanding her daughter would be raised by someone other than her if she surrendered, the guilt ate her up until it outweighed everything else."

"So you take guilt out of the equation, and Bacot is a free woman today."

"Exactly."

"The perfect crime," says the interviewer.

"There were no witnesses. People fall from ladders all the time."

"Not once did she report her husband's activity to the police. That's why the jury convicted. Maybe if she'd filed a complaint, gone on the record, and proved the system failed her, the jury would have shown some leniency."

"If she had filed a report, created that paper trail, the police would have had reason to suspect her when her husband died. The fact that she didn't report the crime is the reason she would have gotten away with it," Denise says.

"If not for the guilt."

"If not for the guilt."

"Why do I get the feeling that if you were in Michelle Bacot's shoes, you'd be a free woman today?" the interviewer says.

"If I had been in Michelle Bacot's shoes, not only would I be free, my daughter would be sitting here next to me, not an ounce of guilt between us."

Cordova stops the video, and a heavy silence falls over the room. He slips his phone into the breast pocket of his jacket. "I checked with Murdock at CSU. They covered every inch of that apartment and found no sign of an intruder. The only prints on the main bedroom's terrace door belong to the Morrows. No unknowns in or out on security footage. Neighbors and doorman saw nothing. Break-in appears staged. Sometimes you gotta call it what it is."

Saffi's gaze goes back to the monitor as she takes this all in. Finally she says to Declan, "Remember how I told you to handle this with kid gloves?"

"Yeah."

"Be ready to take the gloves off."

CHAPTER TEN

DECLAN AND ADA Saffi go in; Cordova stays in the observation room. He's got a few more calls to make and doesn't want to crowd the room. Backed into a corner, Morrow is liable to clam up, and that won't do anyone any good.

Declan doesn't expect the truth—they never tell the truth—but he and Saffi know she'll feed them a story, and once they have her on record with a story, they can punch holes in it.

Declan closes the interview room's door and holds up his half-empty coffee cup. "Are either of you thirsty?"

Hoffman glares at him for several seconds, then turns to Saffi. "Do you have any idea how many civil rights your detective has violated in the past two hours? Before we leave here, I want to see him up on disciplinary or my first stop tomorrow morning will be a filing against this precinct!"

Hoffman has actually found time to change. He's in a fresh Armani suit, a pale blue shirt with a white collar, and a sleek dark tie perfectly knotted.

Saffi brings in several folders, including the one containing the insurance information. She drops them on the table and sits. "Calm down, Geller, your nostrils are flaring. It's not a good look for you."

Carmen Saffi is anything but a pushover.

Holding back the smirk that desperately wants to come out, Declan tells Hoffman, "I'm doing you a damn favor. I'm here because your client asked for me. I've been off the clock since six. Saffi or my LT want someone else on this, I got no problem going home and getting some sleep."

"Sit, Declan." Saffi waves at the empty chair beside her. "It's a little too late at night for a pissing match. Both of you need to put it to rest so we can get to the bottom of all this."

Geller's frowning. "My client didn't ask for you."

Declan takes out his phone and scrolls through his texts with Cordova until he finds the 911 call. He hasn't heard it yet but presses Play anyway. Denise Morrow's whispered voice fills the room:

"My...my husband...somebody stabbed him! God, he's... somebody stabbed him. I think they might still be here!"

"Ma'am, can you confirm your location? I have two eleven Central Park West."

"Yes."

"What apartment?"

"Tower number two."

"I've got officers en route. Is your husband responsive?"

"Responsive?"

"Awake? Breathing?"

"I think they're still here!"

"If you feel you're in danger, you should exit the apartment immediately and wait in the lobby or on the street for officers to arrive."

"No! I can't leave my husband."

"Is he responsive?"

"I have a gun. I can't leave him."

"Ma'am, if you're in danger, you need to get out."

Sudden intake of breath. "Detective Declan Shaw."

"Excuse me?"

"Declan Shaw! Detective Declan Shaw!"

Declan's not sure what to make of that. When he looks up from the phone, Denise Morrow is staring at him; the others are too. Before he can say anything, Morrow speaks in a low voice:

"I don't even remember making that call."

And this is where ADA Saffi shines—in the disarm. She reaches across the table and places her hand on Morrow's. "Of course not. Who could expect you to in a situation like that? I can't imagine what that must have been like. Let's just take this one step at a time, okay? We're right here with you. You found your husband when you came home?"

Denise Morrow nods.

"Where were you prior to that?"

"Tribeca. I was giving a talk at a bookstore."

"Which bookstore?"

"Mysterious Bookshop on Warren Street. If you call Otto, he can confirm."

"Otto?"

"He owns the store."

Hoffman says, "Otto says there were sixty people in attendance, not including employees. I confirmed with him about twenty minutes ago."

"You called him? This late?"

"With good reason."

Declan can tell Saffi doesn't like that. The last thing they need is Hoffman getting ahead of potential witnesses. Sixty percent of any good prosecution is controlling the narrative, and the other forty is dumb luck. She lets it go for now and asks Morrow, "What time did you leave for the bookstore?"

"Seven fifteen."

"Did you drive?"

"No, I took a cab."

"And your husband was . . ."

Morrow purses her lips. "David was in the kitchen making a sandwich when I left."

"Did you lock the door when you left?"

"Always."

"In a building like that?"

"Especially in a building like that. The Andersons in fourteen C were broken into last year. Two years before that, there was a home invasion in eight A. I love the Beresford, it's an incredible place to live, but it makes you a target. And I've had fans appear out of nowhere too. They just show up on my doorstep. So we always keep the door locked."

"Anyone recently just show up?"

Morrow considers this, then shakes her head. "The last one was about four months ago. A sweet senior lady. About six months before that, there was a young guy. They were harmless. I signed their books, let them take a few photos, and they left, so—"

Hoffman interrupts. "My client's talk was widely advertised. There's a good chance whoever broke in knew she'd be out and expected the apartment to be empty. David . . . David surprised them."

Saffi doesn't acknowledge that, most likely because she knows it's bullshit and doesn't want to go down that rabbit hole. She returns her attention to Morrow. "You caught a cab to the bookstore at seven fifteen p.m. What time did you arrive there?"

"About twenty minutes to eight."

"Did you keep the receipt?"

"I don't keep paper. I used my credit card, though. Easy enough to confirm."

Hoffman raises a hand. "For the record, we're not authorizing you to check credit card records. You want that, you'll need a warrant."

Morrow frowns at him. "Geller, don't be difficult. I have nothing to hide. Let them check it if they want to."

"Yeah, Geller," Declan says. "Why make it hard for us? She has nothing to hide."

Saffi clears her throat, keeps her focus on Morrow. "What time did your talk begin?"

"Eight o'clock. I was up there for about thirty minutes, and I signed books and answered questions until nine. I didn't want to be out too late, so I left right after that."

"Another cab?"

She nods. "I was home in maybe fifteen or twenty minutes."

"Anyone see you?"

"Hank, our doorman. I went up and..." She goes quiet, closes her eyes, and draws in a deep breath. Nearly twenty seconds slip by before she speaks again. "Sorry...I just...until just now, I couldn't really recall this."

"It's okay, take your time," Saffi tells her. "Let it come back."

Morrow licks her lips and slowly continues. "When I went to unlock the door, my key didn't work right. It got stuck. Then I saw the scratch marks around the lock and realized something was wrong. I...I twisted my key a few times until it finally grabbed and I opened the door. Something felt...wrong. I don't know how to explain it. The air just felt heavy. I knew David was home, but the space felt unoccupied. That's crazy, right? It sounds crazy when I say it out loud. And listen, I don't go in for that supernatural nonsense. That's not what I'm saying. There was just something wrong—that's the only way to put it. David is...was...cautious, and he kept a gun in his nightstand and another near the front door, hidden in the bottom of a vase of silk flowers. I dumped the flowers from that vase and grabbed the gun the moment I came through the door. I didn't see David, not right away."

"We found blood on the door frame. Was that there when you went in?"

Morrow's gaze drops to the table. Her brow furrows slightly

as she struggles to recall. "Not that I remember, but everything is very...hazy. At that point, I was so worried about David, I didn't notice much of anything." She shakes her head. "I should have been paying more attention."

"It's okay," Saffi says quietly, then prompts the woman to continue: "So you entered the apartment..."

Morrow nods. "I found David at the end of the hall leading off our foyer. He wasn't moving. I...I went to him and...he was covered in blood. Blood was everywhere. Then I remember I heard a sound deeper in the apartment, a thump. Like someone was walking in the dark and hit something." She raps the table with her knuckles. "I think that's when I called 911."

"You think you did or you know you did?"

"I don't remember."

"Did you check David for a pulse? See if he was breathing?"

"I don't remember."

The room goes quiet for a long moment. Saffi reaches across the table, lines up the corners of the folders in a neat stack. Pulls them closer. She opens the top folder and reads something, shielding the text with her hand, then closes it. When she leans back to Morrow, the concern that filled her eyes earlier is gone, replaced with a flash of ice. Declan has seen that look before and never wants to be on the receiving end of it. It's go time. "Mrs. Morrow, security footage has you arriving home at nine twenty p.m. You didn't dial 911 until nine thirty-one. That's eleven minutes. It takes a minute or two to get to your apartment from the lobby. The actions you just described account for maybe another minute. What were you doing for the remainder of that time?"

Morrow says nothing.

"What aren't you telling me?" Saffi says.

"Nothing. I told you everything I remember. I'm sorry. I don't remember."

Saffi leans closer to her. "I think we need to cut the bullshit, so I'm going to ask you a very simple question: Did you kill your husband?"

CHAPTER ELEVEN

MORROW DOESN'T EVEN hesitate. "No."

Saffi doesn't let up. "First responders arrived at nine thirty-seven p.m. That's *seventeen* minutes after you arrived home. Did you let them in? No. Instead, you fired a round at the door. Forced them to stay outside. You didn't let a single person into your apartment until Declan got there, and he didn't go in until a little after ten. That gives you more than forty minutes. What exactly were you doing during that time?"

"I don't remember."

"You claim there was an intruder. You're obviously an intelligent woman. Why stay in that apartment with a possible intruder for forty minutes?"

"I don't remember."

"Were you struck? Did you hit your head?"

Hoffman raises a manicured hand to silence Morrow before she can answer. "I think we're done here. This was a home invasion that went bad. Nothing more." He starts to rise.

"Sit," Saffi tells him. "We're hardly done." She shuffles through her folders, settles on the third in her stack, and opens it. It contains a series of photographs. "Sit," she tells him again.

Hoffman hesitates, then lowers himself back into his chair.

Saffi slides the photos across the table to Morrow along with a blank notepad and pencil. "Those are shots of every room in your apartment. Every table, drawer, and countertop. Go through and make a list of everything out of place. Anything missing."

"Right now?"

Saffi leans back. "I'm not in a hurry."

Morrow looks to Hoffman, who nods reluctantly.

There are close-ups of jewelry. A drawer containing at least a hundred thousand dollars' worth of high-end watches. Purse and shoe collections large enough to stock a shop on Fifth Avenue. Photographs of artwork, televisions, sound systems, the handgun found in David Morrow's nightstand. A closed safe, apparently untouched, in the closet of the main bedroom. Morrow flips through the pictures three times before finally sighing. "I don't see anything."

Hoffman says, "We've already established David surprised the intruder. He fled through the main bedroom. It's obvious he didn't get a chance to take anything. He was understandably spooked after finding David and *stabbing* him."

Saffi ignores him. "So, for the record, nothing missing or out of place?"

"Don't answer that," Hoffman tells Morrow. He glares at Saffi. "You can't expect my client to make that determination from photographs alone. We need to do a proper walk-through of the apartment. This was a break-in gone wrong. Nothing more."

Saffi lets out a huff. "That's your story?"

"Yes."

Her eyes don't leave Hoffman's when she says to Declan, "Detective Shaw, you reviewed the security camera footage, correct?"

"My partner and I did, yes."

"What time did David Morrow get home?"

"Four forty p.m."

"Between four forty p.m. and when Mrs. Morrow got home at nine twenty p.m., how many other people went up to that tower apartment?"

"Zero."

"Not one?"

"Only nine other people entered the building through that lobby, the one you have to go through to get to the Morrows' tower apartment. All of them were residents, and we've accounted for their whereabouts. Nobody went up to the tower."

"You're sure?"

"The building is quiet. Exclusive. There is very little foot traffic."

"What about a service elevator? Stairs? Other access?"

"The stairwells all have cameras. Nobody used the stairs. Lobby cams capture the service elevator for this part of the building, and nobody used that either."

"So nobody went up to that tower apartment except Mrs. Morrow here?"

"Correct."

"And nobody left either?"

"Not unless they knew how to fly."

If Hoffman is rattled by this, he shows no sign of it. "My client did not kill her husband."

Saffi shakes her head, removes another photograph, and slides it across the table.

Hoffman goes red. "Is that necessary?"

It's an eight-by-ten glossy taken from the L-Tron footage: Denise Morrow covered in blood on the floor next to the body of her husband, the knife between them. "How do you plan to explain this to a jury?"

"She clearly tried to revive her husband. What you're looking at is transfer."

"The pattern isn't consistent with transfer; any layman can see that. In fact, our experts are confident it's not transfer, it's spatter resulting from stabbing someone."

"You know that can be argued."

"I asked your client if she checked her husband for a pulse, breathing, tried to revive him in any way, and she said no."

"She said she didn't remember. That's not the same thing."

"The ME places time of death between eight thirty and nine thirty p.m.," Saffi continues. "Detective, you said nine people entered the building between four forty and nine twenty. How many of those were after eight thirty, within our TOD window?"

"None."

"Only Mrs. Morrow, right? Nobody else."

"Yep."

Hoffman says, "You do not want to go down this road, Carmen."

Saffi says, "Forty unaccounted-for minutes. No other possible suspects based on security cams. That's damning."

"You have no motive."

Declan's phone dings with a text from Cordova. He has to read it twice because it sounds too good to be true. When he shows it to Carmen Saffi, a sly smile crosses her lips. She tells Hoffman, "Oh, we have motive. We have one hell of a motive. Your client should have checked her husband's pockets."

CHAPTER TWELVE

"ALL RISE," THE BAILIFF says in a booming voice. "Court is now in session. The Honorable Judge Ronald Berman presiding."

Freshly shaved and in his best suit, Declan stands up from his seat in the second row behind the prosecution bench, Cordova beside him. After reading Denise Morrow her rights and formally charging her Friday night, they'd spent the weekend in Saffi's conference room locking down their case. And it is tight. The courtroom is packed, standing room only. Sketch artists are busy scribbling; the hall just beyond the double doors is lined with reporters. Both the *Times* and the *Post* ran stories above the fold in their Sunday editions yesterday.

Judge Berman steps from a side door and settles behind the bench. "You may be seated."

The bailiff says, "Case number 1930502, Your Honor, *State of New York versus Denise Morrow.*"

Saffi stands again. "Carmen Saffi for the prosecution, Your Honor."

From the table on the far right, Geller Hoffman rises, the shine of his suit catching the overhead lights. "Geller Hoffman for the defense, Your Honor."

Denise Morrow is sitting at the table beside Hoffman in an orange prison-issue jumpsuit. No makeup. Her hair is pulled back in a ponytail, which accentuates her features. She's not wearing her glasses, and Declan can't help but wonder if she really needs them. They don't allow contacts in jail, but she's not squinting. Maybe she's one of those people who wear glasses like they're some fashion accessory.

Judge Berman scans a sheet of paper, frowns, and looks at Hoffman. "Counselor, your client has been charged with murder in the first degree of her husband, one David Morrow of two eleven Central Park West. How does she plead?"

"Not guilty, Your Honor."

This brings on a rumble from the courtroom, quickly silenced by a cold look from the judge. Berman studies Denise Morrow for a moment, then scribbles on the paper. "So noted." He turns to Saffi. "Does the prosecution wish to be heard on the issue of bail?"

"Yes, Judge," Saffi says. "The State asks that the defendant be held without bail pending the trial. Mrs. Morrow was found hovering over the deceased with the murder weapon close at hand, demonstrating zero remorse. Blood on her clothing and the murder weapon are a match to the victim."

Hoffman rolls his eyes. "My client tried to revive her husband, Your Honor. As anyone would."

Saffi adds, "Her statement, which was given to police in the presence of myself and her attorney, contradicts that, Your Honor. Furthermore, the defendant prevented authorities from entering her apartment. She fired shots and held them off with a pistol for more than forty minutes. She also staged the scene in an attempt to frame this as a break-in."

"This *was* a break-in," Hoffman snaps. "My client arrived home to find her husband dead and someone in her apartment. The gunplay was purely defensive. The police have homed in on Mrs. Morrow with complete tunnel vision. They haven't bothered to look for other suspects."

"Building security cameras place *only* Denise Morrow and her husband in that apartment. No strangers. There are no other suspects because nobody else was there. She did this, Your Honor."

"My client had no reason to want her husband dead. They were deeply in love. She gains nothing financially. Their marriage was sound. To claim she murdered her husband is absurd."

Judge Berman asks Saffi, "What's your motive, Counselor?"

"Their marriage was hardly *sound*, Your Honor. We have reason to believe David Morrow was having an extramarital affair."

Again, the courtroom erupts with chatter. Phones out, the handful of reporters who made it in quickly type out messages, each hoping to scoop the others.

Judge Berman raises his voice: "As a rule, I prefer not to have anyone arrested for contempt before ten a.m., but I'm willing to make an exception if you people can't keep it down." When the room is quiet again, he nods at Saffi. "Continue."

She retrieves a photograph from her briefcase and holds it up. "We found condoms in David Morrow's pocket, Your Honor."

Hoffman waves that off with a soft laugh. "Condoms are hardly motive for murder. If they were, half the boys in high school would be on a bus to the clink every prom night."

Unperturbed, Saffi produces three copies of a stapled document. She hands one to Hoffman and explains the contents as she walks another copy to the judge. "This is an interview Denise Morrow did with *People* magazine six years ago where she candidly discusses suffering an ectopic pregnancy." She goes on to explain. "The fertilized egg implanted in her fallopian tube and wasn't discovered until the tube ruptured—a life-threatening condition that required immediate surgery. During that surgery, the bleeding became so severe that an emergency hysterectomy had to be performed. This means, Your Honor, that Mrs. Morrow is unable to get pregnant." Saffi lets that sink in as she returns to the prosecution table. She continues, raising her voice slightly, "What reason could her husband possibly have had for carrying condoms? Nothing other than an extramarital affair. Clearly, Mrs. Morrow learned of his affair and in a fit of rage killed him, then tried to cover up her actions with some half-baked story."

For the first time, Hoffman appears shaken, but he's not willing to give up. "Mrs. Morrow has no criminal record, no history of violence, and is not a flight risk."

Carmen Saffi goes in for the kill. "Mrs. Morrow is a well-known author with substantial resources. She writes true crime—she knows how to set a crime scene, as evidenced by her attempt here. Two of her books revolved around identity theft, and another chronicled how a man named Frank Abagnale managed to elude authorities for decades. She has the means and know-how to vanish. Mrs. Morrow can't be allowed to walk out of this courtroom. We will never see her again."

Judge Berman takes another look at Denise Morrow, who has remained silent through all this. There's a crack in her otherwise stoic demeanor, but she's doing her damnedest to hold it together. Apparently Hoffman hasn't told her that at moments like this, she's supposed to cry. Declan's pretty sure she'll figure it out in time for trial. She seems like a quick study.

The judge turns to his computer, then turns back to Saffi. "Grand jury meets this Wednesday. Is this case on their agenda?"

"Yes, Your Honor."

He gives a soft nod. "I'm going to withhold bail pending that outcome. We'll reconvene on Thursday; I want to see if they're willing to indict before I consider bail." He gazes at Morrow, then reaches for his gavel and brings it down with a hard *thwack*.

THEN

CHAPTER THIRTEEN

Log 10/18/2018 22:41 EDT

Transcript: Audio/video recording (body cam of Detective Declan Shaw)

[Detective Declan Shaw] Uniforms in position?

[Detective Jarod Cordova] We've got two on the
alley out back, another watching the stairs.

[Shaw] Transcriber, we're at the registered address
for one Ruben Lucero, aka Lucky to his
coworkers at the park. He's a member of the
grounds crew. A watch believed to belong
to him was found near the body of Maggie
Marshall. We obtained this address from his

employment records. Lucero has a sheet and
is a registered sex offender. [*Pause.*] We go
on my mark. You ready?

[Cordova] Yeah.

[*Three knocks.*]

[Shaw] Ruben Lucero, NYPD. We'd like to speak
to you. [*Eleven seconds of silence.*] Ruben
Lucero! Open the door!

[Cordova] You hear that?

[Shaw] Yeah. He's in there. Ruben Lucero!

[Radio] I've got him! Came out a window! He's on
the fire escape!

[Shaw] Shit! Go, go, go!

[*Loud bang—door breached?*]

[Radio] He's going up! I repeat, he's going up. Heading for the roof!

[Shaw] NYPD! Fuck. I'll go this way—head back
down, track him on the ground. [*Running.
Rattle of metal. Climbing fire escape?*] I've
got eyes on him! He's on the roof. Heading
east! Lucero, stop right there! Shit, he just
jumped! Fucker's fast! He's on the next roof
over! East! East! I'm following. [*Loud thump.*]
Stop, damn it! [*Loud thump.*]

[Cordova] Anyone see them?

[Shaw] We're one building over! [*Heavy breathing.*]
Rooftop door is locked from the inside. He
just tried it and ran off when it wouldn't
open. Get up here—I'm tracking him
around HVAC, but I've got no visual. I don't

think he's — [*Multiple thumps. Struggle.*] I got
him, get up here!

[Cordova] On my way!

[*Struggle. Unintelligible sounds.*]

[Shaw] I got him! Hurry up!

[Radio] Coming up the stairwell!

[Shaw] Stop squirming. Give me your hand, now!
Other hand! Stop fucking squirming! NYPD.
You're under arrest!

[Lucero] Get off me, man. I didn't do nothing!

[*Detective Shaw reads Miranda rights.*]

[Lucero] I didn't do shit!

[Shaw] Then why'd you run?

[Radio] At roof level. There's a dead bolt on this
door. Code enforcement will love that.
Declan, we're coming out. Hold fire.

[Cordova] You see him?

[Radio] Affirmative. Suspect in custody. Assisting.

[Cordova] I'm on my way up.

[Shaw] We got this, Jarod. Secure his apartment. I'll
meet you there.

[Cordova] Understood.

[Lucero] I need a doctor. I think you broke my arm.

[Shaw] Your arm's fine. Sit up. Hey, nice watch.

[Lucero] I ain't wearing no watch.

[Shaw] No shit. I said sit up. Watch him. I'm gonna
check his pockets.

[Lucero] Fuck! I told you, you broke my arm!

[Voice unidentified] Shit, Declan. I think you did.
That's bone, right? Sticking out?

[Lucero] Stop moving it! It fucking hurts! Get me a
       doctor!
[Shaw] Tell me about Maggie Marshall.
[Lucero] Who?
[Shaw] You know who. The girl in the park.
[Lucero] You gonna let him do this? Take me to a
       hospital! Get this fucker away from me.
[Voice unidentified] Should I call a bus?
[Shaw] In a minute.
[Lucero] Fuck in a minute! This hurts! Get the cuffs
       off me!
[Shaw] So you can run again?
[Lucero] It's ten o'clock at night, and you come
       busting down my door. What the hell I'm
       supposed to do?
[Shaw] You recognize this girl? [*Silence.*] Look at the
       picture! You recognize her?
[Lucero] Fuck you. Get me a lawyer.
[Shaw] Thought you wanted a doctor. Tell me about
       the girl, then I'll get you both.
[Lucero] I don't know who that is. Ow, fuck! Let go!
       Let go my arm!
[Shaw] Stop resisting.
[Lucero] I ain't resisting! You all just saw what he
       did!
[Voice unidentified] I know he knocked on your
       apartment door, and now we're on the roof of
       the next building over because you ran. That
       sounds an awful lot like resisting to me.
[Lucero] I think I'm gonna be sick.

[Voice unidentified] That is bone for sure. Went right through his shirt.

[Shaw] Go ahead and call that bus. I'm thinking maybe we should push it back in and tape the wound. I'd hate to see him bleed out while we're waiting. Just a little push and—

[Lucero] Aw, fuck! Stop! Don't!

[Shaw] Tell me about the girl.

[Lucero] I don't know no girl!

[Shaw] You hold his arm, I'll push the bone back in. On three. Ready?

[Lucero] No! Stop! No! I don't know her—I just seen her!

[Shaw] Seen her where?

[Lucero] She cuts through the park sometimes. Lots of kids do!

[Shaw] Where exactly did you see her?

[Lucero] Comes in from Fifth on the north end and cuts across near the hill.

[Shaw] That's awfully specific. You follow her?

[Lucero] Fuck. I really need a doctor. I'm gonna pass out.

[Voice unidentified] Oh, there he goes.

[Shaw] Lucero! Wake up! [*Eight seconds of silence.*] Wake up! [*Unintelligible mumbling.*] Get him downstairs and wait for the bus. If they can't patch him up, take the ride to Memorial. Stay with him. As soon as he's ready for transport, I want him at the Twentieth.

[Voice unidentified] The nurses will ask how the
     arm got broke.

[Shaw] Tell them the truth: He resisted. I was forced
     to tackle him to get him to the ground, and
     he landed wrong. You saw that, right?

[*Response unintelligible.*]

[Cordova via radio] Declan. You need to get over
     here.

[Shaw] On my way.

[*End of recording.*]

/MG/GTS

NOW

CHAPTER FOURTEEN

IN THE CAFETERIA-LIKE meeting room of Rikers Island, Denise Morrow sits at the aluminum table with her hands in her lap, her fingers twisting and turning over each other like she's kneading a pound of dough. She doesn't want to touch *anything*. She doesn't want to breathe the air. Every time she inhales, the stale scent of vomit and urine buried beneath years of bleach fills her nostrils, and it's all she can do to keep from throwing up and adding to whatever came before.

The floor is pale green, the walls dull yellow, with doors and random pieces of furniture in purple. Looks like a day care decorated by a mad clown.

She doesn't belong here.

This is a bad dream.

She *will* get out and make things right.

It's that last line she keeps repeating in her head like some kind of mantra. She can't help wondering how many other people in this room, this place, are telling themselves the same.

Led into the room by a female guard large enough to wrestle a bear, Geller Hoffman spots her and smiles, showing his perfectly capped white teeth.

"How you holding up?" He takes the seat next to her and unbuttons his suit jacket.

"How do you think?" And this comes out angrier than she means it to. None of this is his fault, and taking it out on him isn't going to help. She draws in a deep breath and shifts gears. Time to plead. "Please get me out of here."

"I'm working on it."

She says, a hitch in her voice, "I didn't do this. You *know* that."

Geller glances at the surrounding tables, nearly all full. The large guard who brought him here is standing against the wall not five feet away. She's not hiding the fact that she's watching them. She's close enough to hear them. Probably reporting back to someone. Maybe the warden. Maybe the police. Maybe both. Geller gives Denise a perturbed glance. "I tried to get us a private room, but the next one isn't available until tomorrow at three. I didn't want to wait that long before coming to see you."

Denise feels a pang in her chest. "How's Quimby?"

"He's doing fine. I took his food and treats from your apartment but they rushed me out, so I had to leave his automatic feeder and his water-fountain thing behind. I picked up some dishes and a litter box at the pet shop."

"Is he eating and drinking? He's had his fountain since he was a kitten."

Geller places his palms down on the table between them, an attempt at reassurance. "Don't worry. He's drinking. He did turn his nose up at first, but I watched him, and after a while he seemed to accept the temporary change in amenities and went slumming at the peasant ceramic dish. You know you spoil that cat. How's anyone supposed to cat-sit for you?"

She pulls at the orange fabric by her collarbone. "Well, I wasn't planning on signing him up for sleepaway camp, Geller. When I travel, I get a cat-sitter to check on him so he doesn't need to leave home. He likes his feeder and his cat bubbler. He likes his bed and his tree and—oh, no. What kind of litter box did you pick up?"

Geller looks bewildered. "The plastic-box kind?"

"And is he using it?"

"Of course. I would have noticed if he selected a different toilet option. Why, what does he use at your place? A gold-plated cat throne with a warm-water bidet?"

Denise swats his hand. "Quimby is my boy. Some women have children; I have Quimby. And no, he does not have a cat bidet. Though I wouldn't deny him one if I thought he'd use it."

"Well, perhaps you can upgrade his can when you're back home. For now, don't worry, I'm taking good care of him. You have my word."

"Speaking of that, how long do you think they're going to keep me here?"

"You heard the judge. With the grand jury convening Wednesday, our next shot to get you out will be Thursday. We need to prep for that."

"Thursday," she mutters. That feels like a lifetime. She's already been here for three days. "You don't understand what it's like...I can't..."

"We'll get you out," he insists.

The promise feels hollow, and she wonders how many times he's said those four words to clients. Denise reminds herself she's not a client, she's a friend. She's a *close* friend, and there is a world of difference.

Under the watchful eye of the guard, Geller retrieves a pad and pen from his briefcase, scribbles in the top corner to get the ink flowing, then says, "Can you think of anyone who might want David dead?"

"It was a break-in. I told you that." She eyes the notepad. "Can I have a sheet and something to write with?"

Geller looks to the guard, who nods. He tears off the top sheet, finds another pen, and slides both over to her. "I understand it was a break-in, but with nothing taken, we need to consider other options. I got a look at the police report, and they mentioned that David had no defensive wounds. Given how far back in the apartment you found him, there's a very good chance he let his attacker in and walked the guy down that hall before he turned on him. That indicates someone who was known to him. We need to give the police someone other than you. Can you think of *anyone* who had a problem with your husband?"

"No."

"Think."

"He never mentioned anyone. I suppose there could be someone at the hospital, but David rarely talked about work when he was home. He did in the beginning, but all the sleepless nights started to take a toll, so about four years ago he decided for the sake of his mental health to leave the hospital at the hospital."

"Okay, so is there someone I can talk to there? Mercy, right?"

Denise nods and thinks about that for a second. "Try Jeffery Varano. He runs the cardiology department. He and David are friends. He'd know." She hesitates, then mumbles, "*Were* friends."

Geller Hoffman has never been big on emotion. He offers her his facsimile of a sympathetic glance, then makes a note of the name and goes quiet for a long time.

"What is it?" she asks.

"The condoms are a problem for us," he says in a low voice. "Can you think of any reason David might have had them?"

Denise closes her eyes for a moment. When she opens them, she doesn't answer but writes a sentence down on her paper. Geller reads it aloud. "'A criminal's best asset is his lie ability.'" He frowns. "What the hell is that supposed to mean?"

She looks down at the words as if she's seeing them for the first time. "Sorry. When I get stuck while I'm writing, I jot down puns. It's just this trick I learned. Writing words, *any* words, helps me think and makes more words come. Like opening a valve."

"Puns aren't going to get you out of jail, and condoms in your husband's pocket could keep you here, so let's try and focus. Was he cheating?"

"Give me another sheet of paper."

He does, and she begins writing again. Writing fast. A list of at least thirty items. When she finishes, she slides it over to him.

"What's this?"

"Things that could be missing from my apartment."

Geller's gaze shifts to the guard; she shakes her head. He slides the list back to Denise. "I'm going to push for a walk-through. Once we do that, we can create a real list."

"The police are treating me like a criminal. *They're* lying, so why shouldn't I?"

"Because you don't have to. The truth—"

"Is doing a shitty job of setting me free."

Geller rolls his eyes. "How about we stay on task. Was David cheating?"

Denise glances at the guard, who's gotten closer. She's looking at them like she's watching her own personal soap opera. Lovely. "Not that I know of," she tells Geller.

"If he was—and I understand this is hard for you—any idea who it was with?"

She shakes her head.

"Can you think of anyone who might have seen something?"

"No."

"Friends? Neighbors? Coworkers?"

Again, she closes her eyes. It's hard to say this. "David wasn't sloppy. He was meticulous. If he was having an affair, no one would have known unless he wanted them to. Including me. He wouldn't be so careless."

"Let's look at this from a different angle. How about someone who can testify your marriage was solid?"

Denise thinks about that for a second, then shakes her head again. "You know how much the two of us work. Our schedules don't leave much time for socializing. He's always at the hospital, and when I meet new people, I feel like they're interested in me only because I'm a little famous. We keep our circle small." She forces a grin. "I don't suppose you can testify? You know us better than anyone."

"I'm afraid not," he tells her. "What about your housekeeper? Maybe she saw you two hugging? Kissing? Laughing together?"

Denise runs through her recent memories, then says, "No. Martha is like a ghost when she's there. With the language barrier, she and I have never been close."

"That doesn't mean she didn't see anything."

"I don't think she likes me much," Denise admits. "Look, David and I were married for sixteen years. I'm not going to tell you it was all roses and sunshine. Things got particularly ugly after I had the emergency hysterectomy, and for a long time I resented him, but we got past it. Did I occasionally want to pick up something heavy and swing it at his shins? Sure, and I don't doubt I drove him batshit with my own unlovable quirks. That's how it goes. We were a team, though."

Geller doesn't look at her directly when he asks his next question. "Were the two of you . . ."

"Fucking?"

Geller's cheeks flush. "Yes."

"Yes. He had no complaints. I kept him fed and happy. At least twice a week."

The guard looks away with that one. Good to know she has some boundaries.

On the opposite end of the room, there's a flash of orange jumpsuit. A lanky inmate covered in tattoos gets to her feet and lunges at another inmate who just entered the room, a burly beast of a woman with a partially shaved head. The two of them stumble, roll across one of the tables, and drop to the ground in a tangle of limbs. The guards are on them fast. There are several shouts. The crackle of a stun gun. Then they're pulling them apart.

Denise watches all of this in absolute horror. She turns back to him. "Geller, you've got to get me out. I don't belong in here with these wild animals."

"I will." He rests his hand on top of hers and gives it a gentle squeeze. He doesn't pull away until the large guard returns and tells him to, and even then, he waits several more seconds. "But first, you need to tell me everything you know about Detective Declan Shaw."

CHAPTER FIFTEEN

THE EVIDENCE LOCKUP for the Twentieth Precinct is located in the basement of 120 West Eighty-Second. When the elevator doors open, Declan finds Officer Moody in the cage, a sandwich in one hand and a crumpled Lee Child novel in the other. He grins up at Declan with coffee-stained teeth and mayonnaise on his cheek. "Saw you on TV. You looked like shit."

"We can't all be pretty like you." Declan steps up to the window and nods toward the back. "Has IT been down here yet to process Denise Morrow's laptop?"

"Not that I've seen."

"When'd you get on?"

"Been here since eight."

"Buzz me in."

Moody takes another bite of his sandwich and nods at a clipboard resting on the counter at the window. "Sign the sheet."

Declan scribbles down his name and badge number and steps over to the door. There's a loud buzz, and it clacks open. "Where is it?"

Moody sets his sandwich down, wipes his hands on his uniform pants, and pecks away at his computer. The keyboard is stained with years of grime. "Row six, shelf thirty-four. Looks like they got seven boxes for Morrow—you want number five."

Moody may not be big on personal hygiene, but he keeps the evidence room as organized as a librarian with OCD. The box is right where it should be, sealed like the others. Declan makes quick work of the tape with his pocketknife and finds Denise Morrow's computer, a MacBook, on top. He takes it out, sets it on the shelf to his right, mashes down the power button until the familiar Apple logo appears, and goes back to the box while it boots up. The box is filled with the contents of Morrow's desk—press clippings and the printed-out pages of the book she's currently working on. The cover sheet stares up at him.

The Taking of Maggie Marshall
Incompetence in the NYPD

By Denise Morrow

Fucking bitch.

Declan doesn't want to go there, but hell, the fucking bitch.

Who does she think she is? He did his job. Put the guy away. He wonders what the book's title would be if Maggie had been her daughter. He flips through the pages, and there are a lot of them, three or four hundred at least. Some notes handwritten in the margins. Spelling fixes, punctuation. Not much in the way of edits. He had hoped she was only at the beginning stages of the book, but this looks like it's close to the finish line.

Under the manuscript are dozens of newspaper clippings covering the case, the trial. There's some notes on those too. One of the articles is titled "Detective in the Maggie Marshall Case Under Internal Investigation," and if that isn't bad enough, Roy Harrison's name is written in the top corner of the clipping, a phone number below that. It's not the prefix they use for their internal extensions, which means it's probably his cell. Harrison is an asshole, but would he talk to the press? To some woman writing a book? Probably. Maybe the two of them got together and compared notes. Chatted over coffee. Cordova never did tell him why Harrison had called him that night at Morrow's apartment; maybe there's a connection. He makes a mental note to ask him when he gets back upstairs.

On the shelf, the MacBook plays a short tune and the screen fills with Denise Morrow's desktop wallpaper. No password, just right in. Trusting woman. Declan runs a quick search and locates the file for the Maggie Marshall book. The same folder contains about a dozen subfolders, several hundred files. Information on him, the crime scene, Ruben Lucero. He retrieves a USB drive from his pocket, plugs it in, and copies everything. When he finishes, he opens the iMessage app and keys Harrison's phone number into the search box. Nothing comes up.

He doesn't find anything when he searches for keywords like *Lucero* and *Declan* either. He thinks, then tries *Cordova*. Nothing. It's not until he tries *Anatomy* that anything comes up. That brings up a single one-line message. Declan reads the sentence half a dozen times, swearing under his breath. There's no name linked to the phone number that sent it, no other messages from that number, just the one text, but it's enough.

You step in it and you're gonna leave tracks, Declan's father's voice mutters from someplace in the back of his mind. *Best you're wearing someone else's shoes.*

Declan didn't leave tracks. Other than Cordova, nobody knew. So who the hell is this? He takes out his own phone, snaps a pic of the text. He considers deleting the message entirely but knows that will do no good. Morrow clearly read it. There's nothing he can do about that. He needs to understand what she did with the information once she had it. Exactly how bad is this?

Declan's phone rings. Cordova. "Yeah?" he says.

"Can you meet me at the morgue? We've got a problem."

CHAPTER SIXTEEN

THE CITY MORGUE is just off First near Bellevue. Declan catches a ride with a uniform and gets there in under twenty minutes. He finds Cordova waiting for him in the lobby on the third floor, a grim look on his face.

"What is it?"

Cordova shakes his head. "You need to hear it from Martinez. He's waiting for us."

He leads Declan through the double doors to the lockers outside the autopsy room, where they both quickly pull scrubs on over their clothing and head inside. Oscar Martinez looks up as they step into the frigid room. He's tall and lean, with short-cropped black hair, the slightest gray around his temples betraying his age. Cordova is always telling him if he dyed it, he'd shave off ten years and could pass for someone in his mid-thirties. Martinez is quick to point out he's seen his share of dye jobs, plastic surgery, and cosmetic dentistry cross his table, and pretending you're younger than you are does little to fool the Grim Reaper when he comes knocking.

Martinez isn't alone in the autopsy suite. He gestures to his right and says, "You know Kim Diaz from CSU, right?"

"Sure. She collected samples at the Morrow apartment."

Kim is wearing a mask and a green surgical cap to tame her long brown hair. Declan would like to believe she's smiling beneath that mask, but the subtle lines around her eyes suggest she's anything but happy.

Martinez says, "I wanted her here to help explain all this."

On the table between them is David Morrow. His body has been washed. The large Y incision in his chest has been stitched closed, and the stab wounds are clearly visible—ugly pink lines on pale flesh. Declan counted six at the scene but missed two others. Eight in total.

"This was a brutal attack," Martinez tells him. "The strikes occurred in quick succession, almost like someone was in a blind fury. Typically I find at least one shallow wound, since most people tend to hesitate with the first one or they realize that far more force is necessary than they'd expected, but I don't see any of that here. Best I can tell, your killer buried the blade to the hilt with each thrust and did it so quickly, your victim had no time to react. Overall, maybe four seconds elapsed, if that. Both lungs are punctured, but I believe this is the wound that actually killed him." He points to one slightly to the left of center on Morrow's chest. "Your killer either got lucky or knew where to put the knife because he came in at an angle right here between the third and fourth rib. Perfect positioning. He hit the heart and followed that up with this one, directly into his aorta. Morrow was dead before his knees buckled. Certainly before he hit the ground. All of these wounds were inflicted by a right-handed assailant."

From a wheeled aluminum table, Martinez retrieves an evidence bag and sets it to the side of David Morrow's chest. Declan recognizes the knife in it from the crime scene. The blood has dried to a crusty black tinged with a dark rust. Martinez pokes the bag with his index finger, turns it slightly. "This is a common chef's knife. Eight inches long, two inches wide at the hilt, tapered to a point with a smooth cutting edge." He pauses for a moment. What he says next makes no sense: "It's not the knife that killed this man."

Declan feels his stomach tighten. "You're kidding, right?"

Cordova mutters, "I wish he were."

The blood rushes to Declan's face. "How is that possible? Look at it—we found it right next to the body!"

Martinez taps the evidence bag again. "It's too long and too wide to be your murder weapon." He points at Morrow's chest. "The knife that did this is one inch wide—half the width of this one—no more than five inches long, and has a serrated edge. Nothing like this blade."

Declan tries to wrap his head around this and can't. "But the blood on the knife came back as a match for David Morrow?"

Martinez, Cordova, and Kim are all quiet.

"What? Don't tell me..."

"The blood *type* was the same as Morrow's, A positive," Kim Diaz says. She shuffles her feet nervously. "But the DNA came back this morning and it's conclusive—the blood on that knife didn't come from David Morrow."

"How is that possible?"

Kim clearly has no idea. "It gets worse. The blood on Denise Morrow's clothing is a match to the blood on the knife, but it didn't come from her husband either. We didn't find a drop of her husband's blood anywhere on her. Her prints aren't on anything useful—not on the knife, not on the body."

This isn't happening. No way. "This has to be some kind of lab screwup," Declan fires back. "Someone got the samples wrong. Contaminated them. Mixed them up. Something. How can that not be his blood? Hell, she was right on top of him! The knife was right there!"

"The lab ran everything twice," Kim says. "I stood right there the second time and watched every step. There's no mix-up. It's not David's blood."

"So whose blood is it?"

"Unknown."

"Is it Denise Morrow's?"

Kim shakes her head. "We ruled her out with an exclusion sample."

Declan does a slow lap around the room, returns to the autopsy table, and looks down at David Morrow. "Run it all again," he says softly. "All of it."

"It won't matter," Martinez tells him.

"Run it all again," Declan repeats, trying to hold back the anger brewing in his gut. "Nothing personal, Martinez, but I want someone else to weigh in on the knife too. You've got to be wrong."

"I'm not," he replies. "Neither is Kim." He peels off his latex gloves, drops them in a biohazard bag. "That knife, the blood — none of it belongs to your crime scene."

CHAPTER SEVENTEEN

"ORDER! ORDER!" JUDGE Berman bangs his gavel against the block on his desk for the third time. There's enough force behind it, ADA Carmen Saffi wouldn't be surprised if it snapped in half. He is out of patience. She's never seen him so angry. "Bailiff, I want the reporters out! Now! I gave them a chance to sit quietly, and they blew it. They can listen through the door like everyone else."

The time to avoid a media circus is long gone. By Sunday morning, the New York papers had the story; the local television networks ran with it that night. By Monday, while they were in Denise Morrow's initial arraignment, the story went national, with coverage on all the morning shows. The 24/7 news channels pounced that afternoon. In the following days, a million Nancy Grace wannabes flooded the internet putting in their two cents. Then late yesterday, someone at the county morgue leaked their findings, adding gasoline to an already roaring fire. Saffi wants to string up Declan and Cordova, but the truth is she's just as responsible for this mess as they are. Hell, she still thinks Morrow did it. The woman has yet to show a single sign of remorse. The smug, indifferent expression on her face now as she sits quietly at the defense table does nothing to make her look innocent.

Saffi spent the past three days reading Denise Morrow's books, every last one of them, and came to a single conclusion—Denise Morrow is playing them. The woman has made a career writing true crime. She's studied not only some of the world's most infamous killers but those who were wrongly accused. More important, she dissected the police work on all those cases. In her books, she showed an uncanny ability to get in the head of everyone involved—not only the accused, but the victims and the investigators. She knew their methods. Their weaknesses. Their strengths. She took some of the most complex scenarios and broke them down into the simplest terms so they could be understood by the layman. She's smart, educated. The fact that they found her the way they did should have been a red flag. She has the know-how to conceal a crime, but instead, she sat herself down in the middle of the mess and waited for them to point their collective finger at her. Hell, she let them take pictures! She made herself look guilty, knowing none of the evidence would stick. Knowing they'd look like idiots. Knowing—

"Counselor? You still with us?"

When Saffi looks up, Judge Berman is staring at her.

"I asked you a question."

"Sorry, Your Honor. Can you please repeat that?"

"What happened with the grand jury yesterday?"

"I filed a postponement of one week."

Geller Hoffman puts up an exasperated hand. "You can't expect my client to sit in a cell while the State licks its wounds." He holds up a folder containing the medical examiner's findings. "In light of this new information, we'd like the court to revisit bail."

Saffi points at Morrow. "She was covered in blood, Your Honor!"

Hoffman makes a show of shaking the folder. "Not hers. Not the victim's. The State doesn't even have a murder weapon. What it does have amounts to nothing more than a random kitchen utensil found at the scene. My client's prints aren't even on it."

"Nobody else was near that apartment at the time of death. Nobody but the defendant. Security footage proves that. We believe the blood belongs to the victim and there was a lab error. We need time to retest."

Hoffman shakes his head. "Your Honor, this is what I mentioned the last time. It's clear my client didn't do this, yet the prosecutor's office and investigating officers are laser-focused on her. They haven't looked at a single other person. They have no theories. They have...nothing."

A copy of the ME's report is open on Judge Berman's desk. He has the data from CSU too. He flips through it all again before turning to ADA Saffi with a sigh. "A grand jury would toss this, and you know it. Obviously, that's why you asked for more time, but Mr. Hoffman is right—you can't keep his client in a cell while your team attempts to patch the extensive holes in your case." He closes the folder and slides it off to the side. "I'm setting bail at two hundred and fifty thousand, and that's generous; it should be zero. You need to drop these charges and issue an apology."

Saffi swallows the lump in her throat. "The State requests the defendant surrender her passport with bail. For reasons previously stated, she is a flight risk and has the means to disappear."

Geller Hoffman rolls his eyes. "Your Honor—"

Judge Berman cuts him off. "It's not unreasonable to ask your client to stay in the country as the police investigate the murder of her husband. Suspect or not, she needs to remain accessible. She will surrender her passport as a condition of bail, and it will be promptly returned to her if the State drops these charges or the grand jury fails to indict." He frowns at Saffi. "You've got one week. Get it together, Counselor."

CHAPTER EIGHTEEN

DECLAN GLARES AT the television in the squad room, unable to look away. If he could somehow reach up through the screen, grab Geller Hoffman by his perfectly knotted tie, and yank him through, he would. Hoffman is standing on the courthouse steps (no doubt on a milk crate or two) preaching to the throngs of press and court lookie-loos like some messiah come down from the mountaintop to spread the word. Denise Morrow is at his side, no longer in the orange jumpsuit. Now she's wearing a conservative tan dress and an equally conservative off-white coat with a subtle floral print near the knee-length hem. Her makeup has been expertly applied, accentuating her dark brown eyes. Her chestnut hair is swept back in a loose ponytail. This carefully crafted look is meant to disarm and draw you in. And it is working, even as Hoffman rattles on; every eye is on her.

"Now that we've moved beyond this nonsense," Hoffman continues, "maybe the police will spend some time searching for the person who actually killed my client's beloved husband. Unfortunately, the incompetence they and the prosecutor's office have demonstrated doesn't exactly inspire faith."

"Oh, fuck him," Declan mutters, clicking off the television. "She fired a round at the responding officers. We should charge her with that. Keep her behind bars until we sort this out."

Cordova is at his desk, his eyes closed, thinking. He's leaning so far back in his rickety old wooden chair, it's in danger of toppling over. "She fired a round in self-defense at someone attempting to enter her home moments after she found her husband dead. If ADA Saffi was even willing to go that route, Hoffman would tear it apart. What you just saw is us losing the public's trust. We don't tread lightly, he'll crucify us in the press. You read the email from CSU?"

"Baby steps. My mind is still trying to process the term *beloved husband*. The press knows about the cock socks, right?"

"The what?"

"Baby bags. Raincoats. Jimmy caps."

Cordova opens his eyes and stares.

"The condoms we found," Declan explains. "Jesus, Jarod, expand your vocabulary. Feed your brain. It helps keep you sharp."

"I'll get right on that."

"Is anyone talking about infidelity?"

"Depends on the network. If they're Team Morrow, they've decided David had a perfectly logical explanation for carrying condoms. The conspiracy theorists are claiming we planted them. I'm guessing Hoffman put that out there."

"Well, that's bullshit." Declan nods at Cordova's computer. "What's in the CSU email?"

"They found wool on David Morrow's clothing. Trace amounts in his hair, on his skin, and in the blood surrounding his body."

"Wool? From what?"

"They don't know."

"Could be transfer from someone he sat next to on the subway. Someone in a wool coat."

"Maybe."

"Hoffman will say it's transfer from the real killer."

"Maybe." Cordova leans back, closes his eyes again. Goes quiet.

Declan has worked with the man long enough to know what's going on in his head. "You don't think she did this, do you?"

He doesn't open his eyes. "I think we need to consider that possibility. Maybe she found him, just like she said."

"Yeah, she's as innocent as O.J."

"Maybe we missed something."

Declan steps over to his desk and shuffles through the mess on top. He finds the blueprints of the Beresford and tosses them in front of Cordova. "We spent, what? Two hours going over these with Saffi? Three main lobbies at ground level, all leading to separate sections of the building. It's not really one building, it's more like three buildings with zero access to each other. To get to the Morrow apartment, you have to go through the entrance on Central Park West and take the main elevator. There's also one service elevator for that part of the building.

That's it. Doorman and cameras put only Denise Morrow there. Even if someone managed to get in or out from the terrace, like she claimed, they'd have to pass through the Central Park West entrance or scale the building from the outside. That's fucking crazy, but we checked it anyway because, contrary to what Hoffman would like everyone to believe, we're fucking thorough. Traffic cams on Central Park West give us full visual of the exterior. There's no Spider-Man on the footage. No nobody. Hoffman can claim we haven't looked for other suspects all he wants, but the truth is *we have looked* and there are none. Maybe we release *that* to the press."

"We're not releasing *anything* to the press. That's what Hoffman wants. Give a guy like that the chance to try a case in the court of public opinion, and he'll run over us. There's no rules there, only sensationalism."

Cordova's mobile rings. It's Roy Harrison, IAU. "Let it go to voicemail," Declan says.

"He'll just come down here."

"He needs the exercise. What does he want, anyway? You never told me why he called you at the Morrows'."

"It was nothing."

"It was *something*. You looked pissed."

"He was just fishing on Maggie Marshall. Same old, same old."

"Why call you at the Morrow place?"

Cordova purses his lips, says nothing.

"Jarod . . . what'd he say?"

With a sigh, Cordova tells him. "He said, 'What are the odds of your partner planting evidence on this one?'"

Cordova has barely gotten the sentence out when Harrison

sends a text: A picture of a condom wrapper. The same kind they found on David Morrow. He shows it to Declan.

"What a dick."

"Yeah." Leaning forward, Cordova loads up the security footage from the Beresford. "I'm going over this again. If Hoffman is right about anything, it's that we've got holes. We missed something." He nods at Declan's computer on the desk facing his. "IT sent over everything they could pull from David Morrow's phone. Why don't you try and track down his girlfriend? Emails. Texts. Call logs. There's got to be something there."

CHAPTER NINETEEN

DECLAN IS ON his third cup of crappy coffee and nursing the beginnings of one hell of a headache when he finally sits back in his chair and rubs his tired eyes. "This guy was either a Boy Scout or he had a burner. I've got nothing useful. His texts with Denise are the usual—'On my way home,' 'Working late,' 'Heading out,' 'Need me to pick something up?' He had a handful of other doctors he talked to, but it was all about patients. Emails are mainly from medical journals. Nothing remotely romantic or confrontational. His only friends appeared to be Geller Hoffman and a guy called Jeffery Varano. According to the website for Mercy, Varano runs the cardiology department. They had a weekly poker game on Wednesdays. Aside from that, David Morrow didn't have much of a social life. GPS data had him moving between the hospital and his apartment, not much more. If he was having an affair, he was smart enough to leave his phone behind so his movements wouldn't be tracked." When Cordova doesn't say anything, Declan asks, "Hey, you still with me?"

Cordova is lost in his screen, a frown on his face.

"Jarod?"

When Cordova speaks, his voice is soft, like he's thinking aloud, working through some problem. "The blood on Denise Morrow only matched the blood on the knife you found next to her. CSU found no trace of it anywhere else in the apartment. That means it had to be on her when she got home, right? She had to pick it up somewhere else."

"Unless the lab screwed up."

"I don't think they did." He nods at his monitor. "You need to see this."

Declan gets to his feet, stretches, and rounds the desks. The lobby security camera footage is frozen on Cordova's screen. When he presses Play, the doorman opens the door and Denise Morrow enters the lobby, crosses to the elevator, and presses the call button. She stands there for a moment, goes in the elevator, and faces forward as the doors close. The doorman is visible in the bottom corner of the screen for a few more seconds, then he heads back outside. The time stamp runs from 9:20:18 through 9:21:04 — less than a minute.

Declan isn't sure what he's supposed to see. "So?"

Cordova rewinds the video and freezes it when Denise Morrow enters the elevator and faces the camera. He picks up a pen and uses the tip to point at her image on the screen. "You see any blood?"

She's wearing a long black coat. It's buttoned at her neck and stretches down to her ankles. She's wearing black leather gloves too. "Can't see anything. She's all bundled up."

Cordova shrinks the video, moves it to the side of the screen, and opens a second window containing another frozen image of Denise Morrow. "This is from the L-Tron footage."

On the screen, Morrow is sitting where Declan found her, her back against the wall. David Morrow and the knife are on the floor. Her white blouse is covered in blood.

"So where's the coat?" Declan asks. "The gloves?"

Because the L-Tron records a 360-degree image, Cordova is able to swing the camera around until they're looking back down the hall to the foyer and front door. He zooms in and settles on a coatrack near the door; her black coat is hanging from one of the hooks. The pockets are bulging, and when he zooms in even closer, a hint of one of the gloves is visible. "I checked with CSU. They processed her coat and didn't find a speck of blood on it. Zero transfer."

"If the blood wasn't on her when she came up, then it had to be from her husband. I told you it was a lab screwup."

"It's not the lab," Cordova says. "You're going to love this." He opens a third window. "CSU ran the VR camera again when Denise Morrow was in the back bedroom, right after you finished your walk-through. They wanted to capture the scene without any people present." He circles the shot around from David Morrow's body to the door again and zooms in on the coat. "See anything different?"

"No bulge in the pockets. The gloves are gone."

"There's a very good reason for that."

After minimizing the other windows, Cordova locates two

photographs from the lobby security camera footage. On the left is Geller Hoffman when he arrived; on the right is a picture of him leaving. The long black coat he's wearing is identical to Denise Morrow's. His pockets don't look bulky when he arrives, but they do when he exits.

Declan gives a low whistle. "Bastard switched the coats."

"Yep," Cordova agrees. "How much you want to bet he walked the real murder weapon out of that apartment too?"

"Maybe David Morrow wasn't the one who was cheating."

"Denise Morrow and Geller Hoffman?" Cordova sounds skeptical.

"Geller Hoffman's not the kind of person to hide a murder weapon just because you ask nice. But if he's sleeping with her..."

Cordova considers that, then nods. "We need to learn everything we can about this woman. Every detail. I'll call Judge Thomas and get a warrant for Hoffman's apartment."

THEN

CHAPTER TWENTY

Log 10/18/2018 23:16 EDT

Transcript: Audio/video recording (body cam of Detective Declan Shaw)

Transcriber note: Video malfunction. Recording is audio only.

[Detective Declan Shaw] Transcriber, I'm entering the apartment of Ruben Lucero, aka Lucky. My partner, Jarod Cordova, is already on scene. [*Knock.*] You in here?

[Detective Jarod Cordova] Yeah. In back.

[Shaw] Pew. For the record, this place smells like ass. He's got a pest problem. Roaches. Mice.

Probably rats. I'm no expert, but I'm guessing that's because the untidy fuck has old food rotting everywhere. Pizza boxes. Half-eaten cans of ravioli. Spoiled carton of milk just sitting out on the counter. Piles of newspapers and magazines nearly to the ceiling. Clothes everywhere. Who the hell lives like this? It's a hoarder's paradise. Jarod, where are you?

[Cordova] Bedroom. Look at this.

[Shaw] Give me a second. My camera's been acting up, so I've got to describe this place for the record.

[Cordova] Mine's in the car. Should I get it?

[Shaw] No. It's fine. Happens all the time. Looks like Lucero carried his unique decorating style into his bedroom. Crap piled everywhere. More clothes. No furniture. Mattress on the floor. I imagine those sheets were white once. CSU could spend a week in here and...is that rope?

[Cordova] Rope. Handcuffs. Bucket in the corner. I can smell it from here. It's a makeshift bedpan.

[Shaw] So this is some kind of dungeon?

[Cordova] I saw a sleeping bag in the other room, balled up in the corner. I'm guessing he slept out there when he had someone in here.

[Shaw] Jesus.

[Cordova] Yeah.

[Shaw] Maybe he planned to nab Maggie. Bring her here.

[Cordova] She fought back. Something went wrong. He killed her in the park to cut his losses.

[*Forty-three seconds of silence.*]

[Shaw] Did you look at these books?

[Cordova] Not yet.

[Shaw] You know any of these? V. C. Andrews, *Vampire Academy*, John Green, Suzanne Collins, Veronica Roth, *Little Women*.

[Cordova] They're all young adult. Skews female.

[Shaw] We've got pictures between some of the pages. Cutouts from magazines. Young girls. Barely legal–type stuff.

[Cordova] Not just magazines . . .

[Shaw] Is that a Polaroid?

[Cordova] Yeah. Not porn, but girls.

[Shaw] For the record, we've got a Polaroid image of a girl, maybe thirteen, fourteen, tough to say. It's taken from a distance. She's sitting on a bench reading, seems unaware she's being photographed. What book was it in?

[Cordova] *Great Expectations*. Looks like a library book. Got a bar code on the spine.

[Shaw] Here's another. *White Oleander*. Another Polaroid inside. We need to get CSU in here to process all of them. Run the girls against the missing persons database. These books might all be souvenirs.

[Cordova] Do any of them belong to our girl? Maggie Marshall?

[*End of recording.*]

/MG/GTS

NOW

CHAPTER TWENTY-ONE

CONFERENCE ROOM.

Cordova is standing at the far end, hovering over a woman Declan vaguely recognizes. Thick glasses. Hair cut in a short bob, dyed black from a box, a coppery red visibly growing out at her scalp. Thirties.

"This is Susan Reynolds," Cordova tells Declan. "She works downstairs in community affairs. She happens to be an avid reader." His eyebrows shoot up as if to tell Declan there's more to it than that.

Declan remembers her then. Oh, boy, does he remember her. "Christmas party. You hogged the karaoke machine. Kept singing Taylor Swift."

Her cheeks go bright red. "It was actually Rihanna, but I

don't blame you for not being able to tell the difference. It wasn't exactly my finest moment."

She doesn't mention the bottle of Jim Beam she'd carried all night or the three minutes she'd spent in the copy room with Jonny Brandt. That's how he got the nickname "Three-Minute Jonny."

Cordova nods toward the door. "Can you close that?"

Declan nudges the door shut and takes a seat.

Susan produces a stack of Denise Morrow books from the canvas bag at her feet and sets them in neat piles on the table. Half of them bear stickers with raised print touting messages like *#1 New York Times Bestseller!*, *Autographed Copy!*, *Advance Reader Copy*, and *Soon to Be a Major Motion Picture!* As the impressive stack of titles grows, Declan can't help thinking of Morrow's current work in progress. The USB drive feels warm in his pocket.

Cordova pulls out a chair and sits. "Susan here is a *big* fan of Morrow's. She runs her local fan club."

"I don't *run* it, I'm just the treasurer. But I help out as much as I can."

"Help out how? What does a fan club do?"

"Mainly we work with the publishers and Denise's marketing people. Help organize local appearances. Show up when we can to support her. They send us copies of her books before they come out, and we post about them on social media. Help create buzz. That sort of thing."

Cordova says, "She was at Morrow's bookstore appearance the other night out in Tribeca."

Her face lights up. "We packed that place."

"Did she seem off in any way?"

Susan shifts in her seat. "If you're asking if she ducked out to kill her husband and then came back with guilt all over her face, the answer is no. She did not. As always, she was friendly. Attentive. She gave more or less the same talk she'd given at the Barnes and Noble on Fifth two weeks ago and at the Strand last month. Told the same stories. Made the same jokes. Just canned stuff for the paperback release of *Why Corrine Had to Die*." She studies the stack of books and taps the spine of a hardcover with that title. "That's last year's release. Her new one won't be out until March." Her shoulders slump. "Look, I was sad to hear what happened to David, but I've known Denise for nearly six years, and I'd swear on my child's life there is no way she hurt him. She's just not like that."

I've known Denise.

Those words jump out at Declan. Back in high school, he'd dated a girl who was in the Beyoncé fan club, and she talked about Beyoncé in much the same way — as if the two of them were best buds who chatted every night, had sleepovers every other weekend. But in truth, she'd met the famous singer only once, after standing in a very long line outside Madison Square Garden. Security hadn't even allowed her to take a photo.

Cordova catches it too and silently mouths, *Let it go.* Rather than call her out, he plays into it. "Because Susan is so high up with the fan club, she's sometimes involved directly with Denise Morrow's publisher and she even introduced Morrow once at . . . what was it?"

"The Academy of Art Tribeca Ball. Denise was the keynote speaker."

"Was David there?"

A disgusted look crosses her face. "Oh, he was there."

"Tell him what you told me," Cordova prods. "About David."

Susan answers in a conspiratorial whisper. "Look, everyone knows she put him through med school. You ask me, he took advantage of her. You rarely saw them together, and when they were, they weren't really *together*, if you know what I mean."

"What? Like an open marriage?"

"No. Nothing like that. Denise is loyal. Faithful to a fault. But that man was a dog. At one point during the ball, he was surrounded by women and he was not shy about flirting. He clearly didn't care who saw, and *everyone* did. A few hours in, the whole party was talking. Denise pretended not to notice. She kept smiling, working the crowd, making small talk. Thing was, she was drinking, and Denise *never* drinks. Not like that. One drink turned into two. Two turned into four. I don't know how many she had altogether, but when it was time for her to make her speech, she was slurring her words. And David had vanished. Off doing God knows what. Missed her entire talk. Half an hour later, Denise found him and they had this blowout argument near the bathrooms. Someone managed to rush them out, but not before a reporter from Page Six got an eyeful. There was a story the next day. I felt so bad for her."

Declan exchanges a look with Cordova, then asks her, "Did you ever learn where he went? Or who he was with?"

She shakes her head. "There have always been rumors, but nothing specific."

"Never about her, though? Always him?"

"Denise would *never*. She'd leave him first. Honestly, even if she wanted to cheat, I don't see how she could. The paparazzi follow her all around the city. Local celebrity and all that. She can't sneeze without three reporters writing it up. You'll find her in the society pages at least once a week."

Declan retrieves his phone and loads up a picture of Geller Hoffman. "You ever see her with this guy?"

Susan takes his phone, studies the image carefully, then hands it back to him. "Her attorney? I've seen that guy with both of them. When they do charity functions, he's usually at their table."

"What about alone with Denise?"

"She's not a cheater, Detective. And with that guy? Please. If she wanted to, she could do much better." Susan grabs a notepad from the center of the table, writes something, and slides the pad back to Declan. "Denise doesn't cook, but she's a foodie. This is a list of her favorite restaurants. When she gets stuck on a book and needs to think, she likes to walk to the theater district and take in a show. According to her website, she's seen *Wicked* forty-one times. If you want to talk to people who know her, people who regularly see her and see who she's with, I'd start with these places or down on Broadway."

Declan picks up the list. He knows most of the restaurants. A good meal at any one of them costs what he makes in a week.

Cordova flips one of the books over and sets it in the middle of the table. Denise Morrow's photo stares at them. "If she wanted to, does she have it in her to kill her husband?"

A sly smile crosses Susan's lips. "She's insanely smart. Graduated at the top of her class. If she wanted to kill her husband, she absolutely could, but you wouldn't find her hovering over the body like you did, with his blood all over her and the weapon right there. That's amateur. She'd be in Barbados or something when he died. Have an airtight alibi. Nothing pointing to her. She'd make it impossible to pin it on her."

Apparently Morrow's number one fan hasn't heard yet—it wasn't his blood. And the knife wasn't the murder weapon. Her favorite author's alibi has firmed up a bit.

Gesturing at the books, Susan continues. "Denise has picked apart some of the most complicated murders in the world, *dissected* them. She breaks them down and describes them in simple terms. She dissects motive. Everything the killer did right and wrong. Where the investigation went right and wrong. Prosecution. Every mistake by everyone involved. She hits from every angle. That's not an easy thing to do. The rumor is, for every case she writes about, she studies hundreds more. If she wanted to kill someone—went into it with that kind of knowledge behind her—do you honestly think she'd get caught?"

Declan snickers; he can't help it. "You make her sound like some kind of super-sleuth. I'd love to see her work our case-load."

"She'd clear your desk in a week." Susan waves out at the bullpen. "She's smarter than all of you."

There's a heavy knock on the door, and Lieutenant Daniels sticks his head in, looks at Declan and Cordova. "You two are on deck—female found in a dumpster off West Eighty-Third. Sounds like a stab 'n' grab."

CHAPTER TWENTY-TWO

THIS CLOSE TO the park, Eighty-Third is mostly residential. Old-money brownstones with less than half converted to multifamily. Only a handful of businesses—dry cleaner, sandwich shop, day care, a corner bodega. Unlike the corner grocery a block from Declan's apartment, the bodega here has no bars on the windows. No advertisements for lottery tickets, discount Marlboros, or two-for-one burritos. This shop's large picture window has a colorful display of fall fruit with carefully placed leaves of red, yellow, and bright orange. The alley Declan enters is sandwiched between the bodega and an antique-furniture store, and with the ivy growing across the brick, it looks more like the mouth to some secret garden than a spot to hide the area trash. The crime scene tape and two patrol cars blocking the street appear out of place—if it weren't for those squad cars and the medical examiner's van, you'd think you were on the set of some rom-com.

"Killer's gotta be a newbie," Declan says to Cordova as they duck under the tape. "The pros know better than to dump a body south of One Hundred Fifteenth. Rich folk don't stand for that."

"They're not above watching the show, though." He gestures at the windows on the opposite side of the street. "Got eyes everywhere."

Sergeant Hernandez is halfway down the alley, barking orders to a group of four uniforms. He spots Declan and Cordova and comes over. "Twice in one week, Detectives. This isn't good for property values."

Declan smirks. "Maybe it's time to talk to your broker about lightening your portfolio."

Hernandez is right, though. They're only a few blocks from the Beresford. That's two dead in less than a week. The last murder in this area before that must have been six months ago.

Cordova is still looking up at the windows. Hernandez follows his gaze. "I've got unis knocking on all those doors. I'll let you know if they get anything useful. This alley is accessible the way you came in and it opens up on Eighty-Second too, so two points of ingress."

"Any cameras?"

"Still checking." He turns and points at the dumpster. "Your girl's in there. Sanitation guys found her. Decomp is pretty bad. I'd put her at maybe five or six days."

That seems like a long time. "How often do they empty the dumpster?"

"Normally every Monday and Thursday. They said it got skipped on Monday because a delivery truck had the alley all blocked up. They don't wait around when that happens."

Declan looks at Cordova. As usual, he's wearing a suit and tie. Shoes shined to flawless perfection. Declan is in jeans and a gray henley. An old pair of Reeboks. He nods at the dumpster. "I don't suppose you want to flip for it?"

"Not a chance."

Hernandez puts two fingers in his mouth, whistles, and points at one of the uniformed officers, a kid Declan doesn't recognize. "You still got that Tyvek handy?"

The kid fishes around in a black duffel, finds a package, and tosses it to them.

Declan snatches the protective suit from the air, quickly slips it on over his clothing, tugs up the zipper, and puts on the gloves. "You're buying lunch," he tells Cordova, then steps over to the dumpster and switches on his recorder. "Transcriber, this is Detective First Class Declan Shaw of the NYPD Twentieth. It is Thursday, November sixteenth, 2023. The time is eleven twenty-three. Current location, an alley on Eighty-Third, between—" He shouts over his shoulder, "Anyone know the exact address?"

"Between fifty-nine and sixty-three," Hernandez tells him.

Declan repeats that. He peers over the edge of the dumpster, clears his throat. "We've got a female, Caucasian, possibly

Latino, tough to say with decomp. Late twenties. Multiple stab wounds to the chest and abdomen. Defensive wounds on her right hand. Thick slice down her palm. Looks like she made a grab for the knife and caught the blade. She's about halfway down. I think…" Declan shakes his head and frowns at Hernandez. "They didn't find her like this, did they? Did someone dig her out?"

Hernandez points to a pile of garbage stacked against the wall next to the dumpster. "Sanitation guys recognized the smell. They took out enough trash to confirm it was a person, not an animal, and called 911." He points his thumb back down the alley. "I've got them in a patrol car if you want to talk to them."

"Where's their truck?" He doesn't remember seeing one on the way in.

"Sanitation sent another team out to pick it up and finish the route."

Declan nods and looks into the dumpster. "I see a purse, but I can't reach it. I'm going in." Using a plastic milk crate as a step, he climbs up, swings his legs over the side, and comes down as far from the body as possible. The suit has a respirator built into the hood, but Declan isn't using it; it muffles his voice and make the recording difficult to transcribe. As the scent of decay and week-old garbage assaults him, he deeply regrets that decision. His eyes begin to water as he kneels down and carefully opens the purse. "No cash or credit cards, but they left her ID." He pulls out her driver's license and says, "Cordova? You there?"

"Yeah."

"See what you can find on a Mia Gomez." Declan stands up and watches Cordova key something into his phone.

A few seconds later, Cordova holds up the phone. "Is she one of these?"

Although the lighting in the driver's license photo is terrible, he has no trouble matching her to one of the pictures; she has the same highlights in her hair. "Third one from the left," he says softly. It's a professional headshot, most likely something for work. Brown hair rolling over her shoulders in loose waves, a mischievous look in her eyes, the slight turn of a smile at the corner of her full lips as if the photographer just told her a joke and she was trying to keep from laughing before he snapped the shot. Beautiful woman.

Cordova clicks on the picture. "Mia Gomez. Twenty-eight years old. She's a senior account exec at a company called GTS. Office is one block over on Eighty-First." He clicks through additional links. "Looks like she's active on a few social media platforms, but she hasn't posted anything in about a week. Consistent with what Hernandez said about TOD."

"I don't see her phone or the murder weapon."

"Assailant probably took both."

Declan slips the driver's license in the Tyvek suit's breast pocket and looks back down. He's standing in at least three feet of trash. "We'll need to empty this out."

"Not it," Cordova says softly.

"Detectives? We've got a lot of blood over here!" That comes from a uniformed officer standing about two-thirds of the way down the alley.

Declan climbs back over the side, and they quickly walk

over. The patrol officer is kneeling by a dark stain on the black-top. He points at some old wood pallets. "Someone stacked those on top," he tells them. "Tried to hide it."

Cordova bends to get a better look, then switches on his phone's flashlight, and the extra light brings the blood right out. He studies the nearby pavement, then slowly walks away at a crouch and stops about ten feet from where he started. "Looks like she was stabbed here, maybe tried to get away, maybe stumbled, managed to make it to where you are, then fell and bled out."

Declan looks around his feet, spots a thinner trail heading back toward the dumpster. He takes the driver's license from his pocket. "She weighed a hundred and sixteen pounds. One person could have carried her from here, but I wouldn't rule out two."

Cordova straightens up and goes oddly quiet.

"What?"

His face is slack. "Hoffman's gonna use this. You know that, right? We're only a handful of blocks from the Beresford. Morrow goes to trial, he'll say the same assailant who broke in and killed David killed this woman too."

Declan snickers. "A judge will never let him tie the two together."

"Might. Two stabbings within days. This close." He gestures at the dumpster. "Her money's gone. They're saying a burglar broke into that apartment and David surprised him...fits their narrative. I could see a judge letting that in. A judge like Berman? He would." He nods slowly. "Knowing Hoffman, he'll probably connect the two cases in the press the moment this leaks out."

Declan hates that Cordova is right. It doesn't really matter if the cases are connected; Hoffman only needs to create doubt to save his client's skin. Declan starts back to the dumpster, muttering defiantly, "I guess we better solve it, then."

CHAPTER TWENTY-THREE

DECLAN STANDS UNDER the scalding-hot water of the shower for nearly thirty minutes, scrubbing first with a wash-cloth, then a thick-bristled brush he keeps under the sink. When he finally gets out, his skin is bright pink and raw, but at least the smell is gone. After helping the medical examiner retrieve the body of Mia Gomez, he personally supervised the CSU's removal of every item from that dumpster. As he'd suspected, there was no sign of Mia's phone or the murder weapon. The press arrived about two hours in, and they were still there when he left.

Declan crosses his small apartment and turns on the

television just in time to catch a glimpse of himself, covered in grime, on the news. He shuts it off and drops down on his couch with his laptop and a cold beer in front of him. He plucks the USB drive from the corner of his cluttered coffee table and loads up Morrow's book. "Let's see what you've got."

One hour and two beers later, he mutters "Fuck me" for the third time.

Hell, she knows more about the case than he does.

It's probably seventy degrees in his apartment, and Declan is sweating.

She opens with the final day of Ruben Lucero's trial. The guilty verdict and the sentencing: life with no chance of parole. Declan's not much of a reader, but it seems like this is a smart move on Morrow's part because all the major players in the case are there—Maggie Marshall's parents, Declan, Cordova, Lucero's coworkers from the park, a handful of techs from CSU, a couple of whom worked the case on their own personal time to ensure it was tight. Even Oscar Martinez from the medical examiner's office was there that final day. His testimony comparing the shape of Lucero's hand to the bruising on Maggie's neck helped push the jury over the top. Denise Morrow worked her way around the room as the judge talked and, like a voice-over in a movie, introduced the reader to everyone. She provided casual descriptions that included just enough for the reader to get a feel for each person but not enough to be overbearing, not enough to color the image in the reader's mind. When she got to Declan, it was like she was in his head. Honest to God, it was like she read his mind, particularly right before the jury gave the verdict. She captured his inner turmoil, the pressure, the feeling of every eye in that place staring at the back of his head, but the final lines of that chapter really grab Declan by the throat.

> There was something else there. Ruben Lucero's gaze was firmly fixed on Detective Shaw, rather than the judge or even the jury, as the verdict was read. I watched Detective Declan Shaw, and it wasn't anxiety I saw behind his eyes, it wasn't fear of a potential innocent verdict — by that point, we all knew the jury had been swayed. What I saw eating away at him from the inside could only have been guilt. I'd soon learn Detective Declan Shaw had a very good reason for feeling guilty. That, too, as much as everything else, was fact.

Declan picks up his phone and starts to dial Cordova, then drops the phone and takes another sip of beer instead. Then he does what he should have done when he first opened the file—he runs a keyword search for *anatomy*.

There's no mention until chapter thirteen, then it's everywhere. Like a dog on a scent, Morrow chases, corners, latches on. It starts with the same text message he'd found at the evidence locker:

Why didn't they find Lucero's prints on Understanding Anatomy and Physiology? *His prints were on all the other books. Why not that one? Explain that!*

Denise Morrow went on to say she didn't know who'd sent the message initially, and when she finally learned who was behind it, she understood the secrecy and agreed to protect the person's anonymity. She claimed this was her first source, but she'd picked up others. She said she had no trouble finding people who believed Detective Declan Shaw had just as much to hide as Ruben Lucero, maybe more.

Fuck.

Declan looks down at his phone again. Cordova's number is still on the screen. This time he does dial.

"What the hell you thinking?" Cordova barks after Declan tells him what he found. "Unless that book has ties to the death of her husband, you shouldn't be digging around in it. Might as well draw a bull's-eye on your chest. IT pulls the logs from Morrow's computer, they'll see you digging around in there."

"It's a copy. Nobody knows. Calm down."

Cordova is quiet for several seconds, then says, "What number did the text come from?"

Declan loads the picture he took back at the evidence locker and reads the number to him.

"I'll see if I can get someone to run it quietly."

"Maybe I should do it," Declan says. "Barksdale in IT owes me."

"I'll do it. You don't want to be anywhere near this. Not with Harrison sniffing around."

Declan takes another sip of beer. "You think he sent it?"

"I don't know. Maybe."

"She was talking to him too."

"How do you know?"

"I found a phone number for him in her notes."

Cordova sighs. Finally he says, "You let me deal with this and Harrison. You stay on Morrow. She goes to jail for killing her husband, nobody will care about that damn book."

Cordova hangs up.

The apartment seems oddly quiet.

When Declan drops his phone back on the coffee table, he spots the list of restaurants Susan Reynolds gave them, Denise Morrow's favorites.

Cordova is right—there is more than one way to shut this down.

CHAPTER TWENTY-FOUR

DECLAN FINDS DENISE Morrow at the third restaurant on Susan's list, an Asian bistro called Flaming Sun that serves hibachi and sushi and is within walking distance of her Central Park West apartment. He'd learned earlier in the day that she'd already moved back in. Geller Hoffman had arranged for some crime scene cleanup company called Aftermath to come in and erase all traces of what happened to her husband. Cordova called Saffi, but she said there was nothing she could do. Her boss was riding her to drop the charges, and they couldn't keep the apartment locked down forever. Without new evidence, she had to agree to the location release. There was a bright side — Saffi also said if they managed to make the case stick, the fact that Denise Morrow moved back in so fast wouldn't play well with the jury. Not much solace, but something.

Declan isn't the only one who's found her. Two photographers are busy snapping pictures through the front window with long lenses. A reporter Declan recognizes from Fox 5 is fixing her hair as her cameraman sets up on the sidewalk.

His head low, avoiding eye contact, Declan brushes by them and goes inside. Denise Morrow is alone at a table in the back corner, glasses on, lost in a stack of pages next to her half-eaten meal.

The maître d' steps into Declan's path near the hostess station. "Sir? Do you have a reservation?"

"I'm meeting someone." Declan skirts around the man and beelines for Morrow's table.

She doesn't look up from her work until he takes the seat across from her, and when she does lift her head, she doesn't appear surprised to see him. She gives him a cursory glance, returns to the pages, and scribbles something in the margin. "What can I do for you, Detective?"

"Provide a written confession so I can get to bed early tonight."

Her face remains expressionless.

Back at her apartment, next to her husband's dead body, she'd shown no real emotion. There was no fear, anxiety, sorrow, nothing. Declan blamed that on shock, but now he isn't so sure. During his career, he'd come across his share of psychopaths — people who lacked empathy and remorse. People who had no trouble manipulating others for personal gain with little or no guilt. Always men, though.

Never women. Not once. He'd found that those people had trouble maintaining eye contact, something Denise Morrow has no problem doing. When she looks at him now, it's with laser focus, like she can see through him. Like she's learned all that's worth learning about him, has cataloged the data, and has determined the most efficient way to manage him. He has no idea if she's a psychopath, but she sure as shit is cold.

Although he's traveled less than fifty feet, the maître d' is out of breath when he reaches the table, flustered. "I'm sorry, Mrs. Morrow. He got by me."

"It's fine, Bobby. I know him." She sets her pen aside and glances at Declan. "What would you like to drink, Detective?"

"I'm on the clock."

"No, you're not."

When Declan doesn't respond to her question, she narrows her eyes and studies his face for a moment. "Get him a grasshopper, Bobby. He'll like that." She taps the rim of her own glass. "I'll take another cosmo."

Reading upside down, Declan realizes she's working on the Maggie Marshall book. The weird part is that half her handwritten notes in the margins are puns about cops:

> Honorable police officers are hard to find. Hope they
>   don't go extinct, like the tricera-cops!
> The cops found a dead cartoonist in his apartment,
>   but the details are still sketchy.
> The police investigated the murder of the crows and
>   came up with the most probable caws.

He doesn't hide the fact that he's reading. "Is this all some kind of joke to you?"

"If you know where to look, there's humor in everything. Life's too short to get caught up in the ugly parts, Detective. That's how you find yourself staring down the center of an empty Jameson bottle."

Declan's father drank Jameson. For more than a year after he'd died, Declan found half-empty fifths hidden around their apartment—bathroom, sofa cushions, cabinets. She can't possibly know that. She knows he's Irish and she's just assuming he fits the stereotype. That has to be it, right?

Their drinks arrive. Declan stares at his, a fluorescent-green concoction in a martini glass.

"Trust me," Denise says, "you'll like it." She raises her cosmo. "To New York's Finest."

Declan doesn't touch the drink. He says, "Why are you writing a book about Maggie Marshall?"

"It's an intriguing case."

"Her killer is locked up. Do you really want to stir that up? She has a family."

"So did the man you put away."

Declan nearly laughs at that. Lucero's parents were dead. His only family is a half sister who's spent most of her life in institutions and the rest on the street. When the police interviewed her, she all but said her half brother molested her when she was younger. He'd taken lewd photos of her and sold them to his friends. She hated him. Declan never saw the woman smile until the judge read the verdict and put her brother away for good. When that happened, she beamed.

Denise can tell what he's thinking. "Nobody asked you to like him, Detective, only to treat him objectively."

"Objectively, I found him to be a piece of shit." He taps her stack of pages. "What's your goal here? To get me fired? Put him back on the street?"

"My goal is to put the facts out on the street where everyone can see them, then let the chips fall where they may."

"You get Lucero out, and we pull another dead girl out of the park a month later, then what?"

She doesn't hesitate. "Then I'd expect you to do your job. Properly. If you still have your job, that is."

"There was plenty of evidence against Lucero."

"I agree. It was damning."

"Then why do this?"

"Because it wasn't conclusive."

"Do you have any idea how few of these cases are?" He tries not to raise his voice. "We don't find every murderer hovering over the body of their victim."

At that, her eyes narrow and a thin smile edges the corner of her mouth. "If you wanted an easy job, maybe you should have gone into construction."

Another dig at his father. She's clearly done her homework. Declan isn't going to bite. Anyway, he doesn't get the chance. His phone buzzes with a text from Cordova—they got the warrant to search Geller Hoffman's apartment. Unable to suppress his smile, he quickly types back, *Go, I'll meet you there.* Then he shows the texts to Denise Morrow and says, "Why don't you tell me about your coat?"

"My . . ." She settles back in her chair and tilts her head. "It's a Harlan from Loro Piana. Made from vicuña fur. David bought it for me in Milan. Generous man." She reaches back and lifts the sleeve of the coat draped over her chair. "Would you like to touch it? It's soft."

"Not that coat," Declan says. "The one you let your attorney borrow."

She smiles again and nods at his drink. "You haven't tried your grasshopper."

He leans forward and whispers, "We know you switched the coats, Denise. The knife. You think we wouldn't figure that out?" Declan sits back and takes her in. The black-framed glasses, her hair slightly tousled. Thin sweater tracing the curves of a body that clearly is no stranger to the gym. The mousy-librarian thing she wants people to see is hiding something else. Something darker. How much is an act? How much is real? There's a brilliance hidden behind the facade. Like she's tamped it down, doesn't want it to show. Why does Declan get the feeling that he's playing checkers and she's playing chess?

"It's not polite to stare, Detective."

"I'm just trying to understand you."

"Is that what you told Ruben Lucero after you broke his arm?"

Declan swallows. "You could have divorced your husband. David didn't have to die."

She raises her cosmo again. "Here's to you catching the man who did it." She takes a sip, sets the glass down, and retrieves her pen. "If there's nothing else, Detective, I really need to get back to work. I'm about a week behind schedule."

"Couldn't write in jail?"

"Too many distractions."

Declan gets to his feet and taps the top of her manuscript with his index finger. "Maybe you should practice, seeing as how you'll need to write the next one from a cell."

CHAPTER TWENTY-FIVE

DECLAN TAKES A CAB to Geller Hoffman's place because it's faster than the subway. The attorney lives on the eightieth floor of Central Park Tower, a pricey high-rise off Fifty-Seventh that claims to be the world's tallest residential building. It's located in a part of the city known as Billionaires' Row. Hoffman has money, no doubt about that, but a billionaire he is not. Declan stares up at the superstructure hoping that whatever warrant Cordova pulled will allow them to dig into the shit-knocker's finances.

"Dec! Over here!" Cordova shouts from the sidewalk. He's standing at the mouth of the parking garage, waving.

Declan walks over and frowns. "What are you doing down here? Who's up in the apartment?"

"So we get here," Cordova tells Declan as he leads him into the garage, "and Hoffman answers the door in a robe and slippers, not exactly dressed for company. I show him the warrant and he starts spouting 'privilege' this and 'privilege' that. Claims us serving a warrant on him knowing that he represents a person of interest in an open murder investigation is a violation of his client's rights. Tells us we step into his apartment and he'll have the whole case thrown out."

Declan finds that funny. "I love how Denise Morrow is a person of interest when he needs her to be, but when you put a television camera in his face, she's the victim."

Cordova ignores that. "I call Saffi and tell her what's going on, and she goes off on this rant because I pulled the warrant through Judge Thomas instead of Berman even though it's Berman's case—"

"Wasn't that the reason you went to Thomas? Keep it impartial?"

Cordova ignores that too. "She asks if I told Thomas the warrant was on an attorney."

"And you obviously didn't. Look," Declan says, "that's how the game works, right? Did Thomas *ask* you if you were serving on an attorney?"

"Nope."

"Then you're in the clear. Plausible deniability, my friend. There's no rule that says we have to go to Berman; it's just courtesy bullshit."

"Saffi tells me to start with his car while she calls the judge and figures out how to proceed. She says to get it all on camera, don't touch anything that could contain client data—no file boxes, no briefcase, nothing like that, but the car itself is fair game."

Declan kicks a loose pebble of concrete. "Your real problem is Hoffman. While you're down here dicking around his wheels, he's up there burning evidence, flushing evidence, eating evidence...he's doing whatever he can before you come through his door."

Cordova grins. "I don't care what he does. You won't either when you see this."

He leads Declan to the garage's third floor and a black BMW 7 Series surrounded by uniformed officers and CSU techs. There's something sitting on the car's trunk. Declan can't tell what it is until he gets closer, then his heart gives a hard thump. "Is that..."

Cordova beams and points to one of the officers, a young guy with red hair and freckles. "Billy there found it."

Billy shrugs and glances up at an exposed heating duct above the car. "It was right up top, wrapped in newspaper. Saw the corner sticking out. Hard to miss in here."

The garage ceilings are low—seven, maybe seven and a half feet. Low enough for Declan to reach without a ladder. He brushes the bottom of the open duct with his fingertips as he steps up to the car, his pulse thundering in his ears. Sitting in the center of a crumpled page from the *New York Times* sports section is a knife. Not just any knife, but one with a blade that's five inches long and one inch wide with a serrated edge. The blade is stained with what appears to be dried blood; the newspaper is too.

"That's it, isn't it?" Declan hears the words come from his mouth, but the blood is pounding in his ears so hard that his own voice sounds muffled. "The knife that killed David Morrow?"

"It's got to be. Hoffman must have walked it out in the coat just like we thought."

"Holy shit."

"Yeah. Holy shit."

An elevator about ten feet away dings and the doors slide open. Geller Hoffman gets out. He's changed out of his jam-jams and into a pair of khaki pants and a white button-down. One hand is pressing his cell phone to his ear and the other is pointing at Cordova. "Don't you dare touch my car. I spoke to the issuing judge and—" When he spots the knife resting on his trunk, the color leaves his face. His finger shifts from Cordova to the blade. "What the hell is that?"

"What do you think it is?" Cordova asks.

It doesn't take long for Hoffman to recover, and when he does, his angry stare moves to Declan. "You motherfucker. You seriously think you can plant evidence here too . . . *on me?* I will not only take your badge, I'll see to it you're sharing a cell with Ruben Lucero. You think I don't know what you did on that case? No way you're pulling that bullshit with me."

When he starts for the car, Cordova waves at two of the uniformed officers. "Hold him back. Park him somewhere. He doesn't go anywhere."

Cordova's phone rings. ADA Saffi. He answers on speaker, tells her to hold on a second, and shuffles to the far end of the garage with Declan so Hoffman can't hear. He quickly details what they found and where they found it. He's doing his best to stay calm, but he sounds like a kid who just discovered the latest Xbox under the Christmas tree.

"You almost fucked us going to Thomas," Saffi says. "You know that, right?"

"Berman and Hoffman golf together. Hell, they're both members of the Metropolitan Club. You think Berman would've played this on the up-and-up if we went to him?"

"Berman's an officer of the court. Same with Hoffman. Same with me. Just putting the message out there that you don't trust him could burn you on this case. He's obligated to stay objective. You don't so much as hint that you don't trust him. He can fuck you six ways to Sunday without violating the sanctity of the court. Trust that Berman will do his job, and let him do it." She goes quiet for a second, then adds, "Besides, he thinks Hoffman is a tool. Just because they travel in the same circles doesn't mean he likes him."

Declan knows Cordova did the right thing. Saffi probably does too, but part of her job is to read them the riot act. CYA.

Saffi draws a deep breath that's audible over the call and says, *"Judge Thomas conferenced with me and Berman and he amended his warrant after learning Hoffman was an attorney. He's going to appoint a special master."*

"What's that?"

"It's an unrelated attorney who will be present for the search of Hoffman's apartment and any personal belongings. They'll basically ensure you're not looking at anything that violates attorney-client privilege."

"How long's that going to take?"

"Till tomorrow. Day after at the latest."

Declan nods. They can make that work. "We're fine. We take Hoffman in and we can hold him for seventy-two hours. We keep him on ice until we're inside."

"You're not charging Hoffman with the knife. You're certainly not booking him."

"What?"

"You didn't find the knife in his car—you found it in a public space."

"Right above his car," Cordova points out. "In a gated garage that can be accessed only by residents with a key card or code."

"A public space anyone can access by walking in behind a resident's car. Look, we're not giving the press something else that has the potential to blow up, not after all that nonsense with Morrow. Process the knife. Let's make sure we've really got what we think we've got this time. Seal off his apartment and his car; Judge Thomas agreed to that much. Hoffman can slum it at the Four Seasons for a few days. Once the special master is in place, you can comb it from top to bottom."

"What about his office?" Declan asks.

Saffi goes quiet.

"Carmen? Can we search his office?"

"Thomas said Hoffman's office is off-limits unless you find something in the car or apartment. Then he'll revisit."

"This is bullshit," Declan mutters.

"This is how the game is played. Let me know what you turn up on the knife."

She hangs up, and the two of them stare at Cordova's phone.

Across the garage, Hoffman is watching them. Not only has his color returned, but his ratty grin is back. Declan says, "If he kept the coat, it will be in his office. He must have known this would happen."

"Why would he even keep it? It's probably in a landfill or a burn barrel somewhere."

Declan shakes his head. "No. He'd hold on to it. Keep it

close, like that knife. He'd want to have insurance in case Denise Morrow turns on him."

Cordova considers that, then gestures around the garage. "The knife was here. Maybe the coat is too."

Declan looks at his watch. It's twenty minutes to midnight. "How big is this garage?"

"Eight levels," Cordova tells him. "More than three thousand parking spaces with four storage closets on each floor. Rooms with HVAC too."

Big.

"It's not too late to go into construction," Declan mutters in a low voice that sounds so much like his father's, the man might be standing behind him.

"Huh?"

"Nothing. Just something that came up over dinner." Declan looks back toward Hoffman's car. "I'll radio for more uniforms. We'll start on this level and work our way out. Any luck, we'll finish by Christmas."

Cordova nods. "I'll have CSU run the knife tonight, get whatever they can pull from it. The newspaper and that duct too."

CHAPTER TWENTY-SIX

IT DIDN'T TAKE until Christmas, but it did take all night. By the time Declan and Cordova emerged from the garage, the sun was up and morning traffic was building toward rush hour.

They'd found nothing.

Not a damn thing.

Geller Hoffman was escorted to the Four Seasons. Cordova and Declan left uniforms guarding both the attorney's car and his apartment and agreed to meet back at the precinct after a shower and a change of clothes.

When Declan walks into the bullpen carrying coffee and two chocolate chip muffins (Cordova's favorite), he finds his partner already there, his eyes on his computer screen. "How the hell did you beat me? Didn't you go home?"

"I showered here. I keep a spare suit in my locker."

"Of course you do." Declan sets the food on Cordova's desk. "Hungry?"

Cordova's face lights up when he sees the muffins. He retrieves a plate, fork, and knife from his top desk drawer, delicately cuts one up, and eats as if he's at a five-star restaurant rather than in the squad room. Declan half expects him to produce a cloth napkin for his lap.

"You're a strange man, Jarod Cordova." Declan takes a large bite of his own muffin and ignores the crumbs that cling to his shirt and pepper the floor. "What are you looking at?"

"Security cam footage from that alley on Eighty-Third where we found Mia Gomez."

Cordova rewinds the video a few minutes, then clicks Play. A moment later, Mia Gomez appears on the sidewalk. She stops in front of the bodega, glances at her phone, turns and enters the alley, and vanishes off the screen. Cordova pauses the video. "That's all we've got. She goes in, never comes out. Nobody follows."

The time stamp reads *Friday, November 10, 8:21 p.m.*

Declan reaches over, rewinds the film until she's standing outside the alley again, then freezes it. "She went in with her phone, so whoever killed her definitely took it."

Cordova shuffles through some printouts on his desk and hands a page to Declan. "That's the lugs and GPS data from her iPhone. While she's standing outside that alley, her phone is back at her office on Eighty-First." He taps the screen. "What she's got there is a secondary phone."

"Burner?"

"Probably."

THE IMPERFECT MURDER

"You know anybody who carries a burner who isn't doing something they shouldn't be?"

"Nope."

Declan takes another bite of his muffin. "What about the other end of the alley? Whoever killed her was either waiting in that alley or came in from the other side."

"Probably left that way too, little good that does us. Closest camera on that side is at the corner with zero line-of-sight on our alley. Uniforms found a few other private cameras on businesses off Eighty-Third, but nothing with eyes in our direction. We find a person of interest, we might catch them on the sidewalk coming or going, but that's about it. Won't do us much good until we know what to look for."

"Has IT looked at Morrow's laptop yet?"

"Yeah, it was a bust. They said it was only three months old." Cordova loads up Denise Morrow's website, clicks to the FAQ section, and points at a line about two-thirds down.

"She buys a new laptop whenever she starts a new book?"

Cordova nods. "Says she superstitious. Thinks it's good luck. Aside from her new book and some research material, IT didn't find much else. Even her Google searches came up dry. Mainly searches about cats and Lucero. Nothing useful." He starts rooting around in his desk. "I've got a list here somewhere. Mainly just—"

"Declan! Get your ass in here!" Lieutenant Daniels's voice booms through the bullpen from his open office door loudly enough to rattle the surrounding glass. "Cordova, you too!"

Declan curses softly. "You think Saffi called him and threw us under the bus with that warrant business?"

"I don't think she'd—"

"Now!" Lieutenant Daniels bellows even louder.

When they enter his office, he tosses a newspaper over his desk, hitting Declan square in the chest. It's open to Page Six and a photo of Declan and Denise Morrow sitting at the Flaming Sun, drinks between them.

Declan swallows. "I was —"

Daniels cuts him off. "Denise Morrow and her attorney filed a complaint against you this morning. They're pressing for a restraining order. She claims you're following her. She said you threatened her. Told her not to write a book on Maggie Marshall. She said you told her you'd take her down for murder long before she gets a word in print."

"That's not what I said."

"I don't give a shit what you said." Daniels's face is bright red. "We got her attorney piggybacking on that, saying you're planting evidence, trying to frame him. Got that little shit bastard lighting up phones in IAU and with the captain upstairs. You already got Harrison all over you about that Maggie Marshall bullshit—you don't think Hoffman will take that to the networks? You back him into a corner, and he'll claw his way out any way he can. If he gets Harrison to talk to the press . . . phew." He picks up a blue paper clip, taps it on the desk. "Harrison gets on camera just hinting at what he's accusing you of, and the two of them will bury you. Harrison will do it out of spite." Daniels grabs the paper and tosses it toward Cordova. "Where the hell were you?"

Cordova raises both hands defensively but doesn't say anything.

"This is on me," Declan tells them. "I wanted to rattle her, that's all. Jarod didn't know."

From the bullpen outside the lieutenant's door, someone shouts, "LT! CSU on line three for you."

Daniels snatches up the receiver and points at both of them. "Stay here. We're not done. Daniels," he says to whoever's calling him.

His face was red before he picked up the phone. As he listens, he goes three shades redder; every line hardens. When he hangs up, he stares at Declan. "The attorney's prints aren't on the knife. Neither are Denise Morrow's. Care to guess whose are?"

"Whose?"

"Yours."

THEN

CHAPTER TWENTY-SEVEN

Log 10/19/2018 06:36 EDT

Transcript: Audio/video recording (interview room 3, Twentieth Precinct)

Present: Detective Declan Shaw

            Detective Jarod Cordova

            POI Ruben Lucero

[Shaw] How's the arm, Lucky? Looks like the docs
         at Memorial patched you up nice. Want me
         to sign your cast?

[Lucero] Fuck you. You're going down for attack-
         ing me.

[Cordova] You ran, Mr. Lucero. You resisted arrest.
    You assaulted an officer, you—

[Shaw] You made me jump off a building, you piece
    of shit.

[Cordova] Why'd you run?

[Lucero] You busted down my door and came in.
    You'd run too.

[Shaw] We identified ourselves as NYPD and
    knocked. We didn't bust in the door *until*
    you ran. It's all on tape, Lucky. Don't bullshit
    a bullshitter.

[Cordova] If you'd just talked to us, you'd probably
    be curled up in your own bed right now
    having happy dreams instead of sitting here
    talking to us.

[Lucero] Right. Get me a la—

[Shaw] You a big reader, Lucky?

[Lucero] Huh?

[Shaw] We found a lot of books in your place.
    Seems you must be a reader.

[Cordova] Budding photographer also.

[Shaw] Yeah, that too. You've got quite the eye.

[*Transcriber note: From a file box, Shaw unpacks
    numerous books and sets them on the table.
    He then opens the covers. There are pic-
    tures—Polaroids—in each.*]

[Shaw] Tell me about these girls.

[Lucero] [*Unintelligible mumble.*]

[Shaw] Who are they, Lucky?

[Lucero] Just girls. That's all.

[Shaw] Just girls. Did you hurt them?

[Lucero] No!

[Cordova] We've got CSU going through your apartment right now. Are they going to find traces of these girls? Maybe tied to that bed of yours? Handcuffed?

[Shaw] Did you take them and make them piss and shit like animals in that bucket we found? What'd you do with them after?

[Lucero] No! It's not like that!

[Shaw] It's not like that. Sure.

[Lucero] My girlfriend likes to be tied up. That's all that is.

[Shaw] You expect us to believe you have a girl-friend?

[Lucero] Well, not exactly a girlfriend. She's a pro. But she lets me tie her up. The bucket's mine. Plumbing on my toilet busted yester-day, and the super can't get up until tomor-row, so I've been using a bucket.

[Shaw] You know CSU can confirm that, right? Now's not the time to lie to us. Now is the time to come clean. You tell the truth, and maybe we can help you out.

[Lucero] I ain't lying!

[Shaw] [Gestures at photographs.] Where are these girls?

[Lucero] I don't know. I took pictures of them, sure, but I didn't touch them. I didn't even talk to them.

[Cordova] So how'd you get the books?

[Lucero] Sometimes they forget them. In the park.

[Shaw] [*Slams hand on table.*] Bullshit!

[Lucero] Okay! Okay! I took the books when they
weren't looking. I'm a groundskeeper, invisible to girls like that. They stop for water,
food, get lost in their phones, I snagged
a book. I didn't touch them! Hardly even
talked to most of them!

[Shaw] Come on, Lucky. We're not idiots. You're on
the sex offenders list. You've got history.

[*Transcriber note: Cordova produces a file, sets it on the
table, opens it.*]

[Cordova] Statutory rape. Ten years ago.

[Lucero] She was my girlfriend. I was nineteen, she
was sixteen. Age of consent in New York is
seventeen. Her parents didn't like me, so
they pressed charges to keep us apart. That's
all that was.

[Cordova] According to this, it was a repeat offense.
Year before that you were charged with the
same thing with another girl. That one was
only fifteen.

[Lucero] She was my girlfriend too.

[Shaw] Sounds like you've got a taste for young
girls, Lucky.

[Lucero] It was consensual.

[Shaw] [*Gestures at pictures.*] These too? All consensual? What do you do, pay them to go

back to your place? Let you take a few pics?
Maybe fool around a little bit?

[Lucero] No!

[Shaw] Right. It's just your *girlfriend* who likes to get
tied up.

[*Transcriber note: Cordova sets a photograph in front of
Lucero.*]

[Cordova] Tell us about Maggie Marshall.

[Lucero] Jesus! I didn't do that!

[Shaw] No? I guess we can all go home, then.
[*Slams hand on table.*] You lied to me!

[Lucero] What? No. I didn't—

[Shaw] On the roof, after you resisted arrest, after
you assaulted a law enforcement officer,
you told me exactly how she cuts through
the park every day. You told me where she
starts, where she goes out. You told me you
never talked to her.

[Lucero] I didn't—

[*Transcriber note: Shaw takes out his phone and plays a
video for Lucero.*]

[Shaw] That's you talking to her, dipshit.

[Lucero] [*Appears confused.*] That was like a week
ago. I remember now. She asked me where
the nearest bathroom was and I told her.
That's all that was.

[Cordova] If that's all that was, why did you follow
her?

[*Silence for twenty-eight seconds.*]

[Shaw] We have video of you following her, Lucky.

[Lucero] [*Voice barely audible.*] I was worried about
　　her.

[Shaw] Worried? Why?

[Lucero] I saw this man watching her. He came
　　in behind her from Fifth and followed her
　　through the park.

[Shaw] Oh, and you were just keeping her safe? Is
　　that it? Making sure some other sexual pred-
　　ator didn't pounce on your girl?

[Cordova] There's nobody else following her on
　　video. Only you.

[Lucero] I ain't lying.

[*Transcriber note: Shaw places more photographs on the
　　table.*]

[Shaw] This is Maggie dead, Lucky. Here's another
　　picture. And another. We found her right
　　where you left her, up behind Blockhouse.
　　See the bruising around her neck? That's a
　　handprint. Your handprint. You squeezed so
　　hard, the ME had no trouble pulling exact
　　measurements. He created a mold of her
　　killer's hand, his full grip. What are we going
　　to find when we compare that mold to your
　　hand?

[Cordova] You a smoker, Lucky?

[*Transcriber note: Cordova places a photograph on the
　　table.*]

[Cordova] That's the butt of a Marlboro Red found
　　right next to her body. Coincidently, we

found half a pack of Marlboro Reds in your
apartment. We'll have DNA back in a few
days. What are we going to turn up there?

[Shaw] And if that weren't enough, you forgot your
damn watch.

[*Transcriber note: Shaw sets another photograph on the
table.*]

[Shaw] Left it in the mud around a bunch of size-
eleven shoe prints I'm pretty sure we'll
match to you too. The watch has your
damn name on it, Lucky. Half the people
we showed it to on staff at the park said
it was yours. They've all seen you wear it.
You're making our job so easy on this one,
I should give you an honorary detective's
badge. Why'd you kill her in the park? We
didn't find any of these others in the park.
Did Maggie try to get away? Tell us what
happened, you tell us now, and we'll put in
a good word with the ADA. You make me do
this the hard way, and I'll crucify you.

[*Transcriber note: Cordova shows him two more photographs.*]

[Cordova] That's a knee print next to her body. This
is a picture of a pair of your jeans found on
the floor in your apartment. See the mud on
the knees? CSU tells me preliminary tests
match it to our crime scene.

[*Silence for forty-two seconds.*]

[Shaw] You know what? I'm done. Cordova, drop

this fucker in gen-pop for the weekend.
Soon as they figure out he's a child diddler,
he's a dead man. Let's save the taxpayers
some money.

[Lucero] [*Barely audible.*] Wait . . .

[Shaw] Wait? Wait why? You got something to say?

[Lucero] I found her. After.

[Shaw] Bullshit.

[Lucero] I went to clean up some branches around
Blockhouse. If I picked up mud, that's how.
The band on my watch is busted. It falls
off all the time. And yeah, I smoke Marlboro Reds. So does half the city. You found
one of my old butts on the ground where
I work? Big fucking deal. I smoke a pack a
day. Wouldn't have to look too hard to find
more. I went up to Blockhouse to clean up
from the storm and found her there. I didn't
touch her. I swear.

[Cordova] If you found her like that, why didn't you
tell anyone?

[Lucero] [*Gestures at everything on the table.*] Why
the hell do you think?

[Shaw] [*Picks up one of the books and slams it down
on the table.*] You stalked that poor girl, and
when the timing was right, you tried to
snatch her.

[Lucero] No.

[Shaw] You chased her through the woods. We have
your tracks and hers.

[Lucero] No!

[Shaw] You knocked her out and carried her to Blockhouse for some privacy, and you destroyed that poor girl. You made her final moments on this planet the most terrifying she'd probably ever experienced.

[Lucero] *No!*

[Shaw] Then you took her life. Ended her like she was just some thing you had to discard. You left her out there to rot and couldn't help going back to take another look at her a few days after. Probably got your rocks off again, you sick piece of shit.

[Lucero] I'm telling you, this was someone else!

[Shaw] Bullshit.

[*End of recording.*]

/MG/GTS

NOW

CHAPTER TWENTY-EIGHT

"CHRIST, DECLAN. HOW the hell do you live in this mess?" Stepping into Declan's living room, Roy Harrison wrinkles his nose. Using the tip of a pencil, he picks up a sock from the back of the couch and holds it at arm's length. Studies it for a second, then lets it drop to the floor. "You some kind of hoarder or just a slob?"

"I bet your apartment looks like an IKEA store and a CDC lab had a baby. All sterile and white with stickers on the furniture for tab A and slot B left over from putting that shit together. Probably keep your underwear in color-coordinated zip-lock bags. Your bunny slippers lined up nice and neat next to your bed."

"I feel like I need a tetanus shot just stepping in here."

Declan doesn't need this. Not today. "Do what you gotta do and get out, Harrison."

When his prints came back on the knife, Declan agreed to let them search his place. He had nothing to hide and knew if he said no, it would make him look bad. The thing was, he'd agreed to let Lieutenant Daniels run the search, maybe someone from the Twentieth, someone quiet, not IAU. If he'd known they'd send Harrison and friends, he would've called his union rep and squashed it. Nothing he can do about it now. Harrison showed up with three others, all IAU, all people Declan didn't know, and now they're crawling over every inch of his apartment.

"Ignore him," Cordova says. "He's just trying to get a rise out of you."

Harrison smirks. "I'm getting flashbacks to the photos of Lucero's personal shithole. The two of you must read the same decorating blogs."

There's a woman poking around Declan's kitchen, someone else in his bedroom, and a third in the bathroom. Declan can see only the one in the kitchen, and she's systematically going through every cabinet and every drawer as thoroughly as he's ever done on a scene. It's creepy watching someone else go through your stuff. When she frowns down at the dishes piled in the sink, he wants to tell her the dishwasher is busted, but he keeps his mouth shut.

Cordova pulls Declan to the side and says in a low voice, "Why don't you say you touched the knife back at Hoffman's car? Some accident. It slipped off the trunk, you grabbed it. Reflex. It happens. I'll back you."

Cordova's a good friend, but Declan can't let the man lie for him. "I didn't do anything wrong," he says. "I sure as shit didn't kill Morrow."

If the look Cordova gives him is meant to be reassuring, it's not. Seems like it's pitying.

"Roy?" This comes from the woman in Declan's kitchen. When Harrison turns, she bobs her head, signaling for him to come over. Declan and Cordova follow. She's got Declan's old knife block on the counter, the one he uses as a paperweight for bills. Apparently she braved the stagnant water in the sink and fished out all the knives among the dirty dishes. Each has been placed back in the wood block, something Declan hasn't bothered to do since the day he brought it home. The block has sixteen slots in total; seven are now filled with knives, and nine are empty. "We're missing some knives," she tells Harrison.

A grin creeps across Harrison's face.

"It didn't come with enough knives to fill it. When I bought it, half those slots were empty," Declan says.

The woman has her phone out now, the screen angled so only Harrison can see. The grin on his face widens. "You sure that's the same one? How'd you find it?"

She points to the barcode sticker on the back of the wood block. "Scanned that and brought up the listings."

Harrison looks like he might burst.

Declan fights the urge to grab the phone. "What?"

"Show him," Harrison says.

She turns and sets the phone down next to the knife block. Same set. Wüsthof. Little red logo on each handle. Declan points at the picture. "See all those empty slots? That's how it came. Half empty."

"Yeah, well, where's this one?" Harrison taps the description. "You see a five-inch serrated utility knife here? I don't. She don't."

Declan rolls his eyes. "It's gotta be in the sink." He steps around them, reaches into the sink, pulls out the stopper to drain the rest of the water, and then starts taking out the remaining dishes and piling them on the counter. His pulse quickens as he gets closer to the bottom.

"Where is it, Detective?" Harrison asks again. "Where's your knife?"

When Declan doesn't find it in the sink, he starts tugging open drawers. It's not in any of them either. He can't remember the last time he used it. It's been a while. "If it's the same one, she stole it," he mumbles more to himself than anyone. "Must have broke in here and took it."

Harrison laughs at that. "Denise Morrow broke into this shithole, stole your knife, and used it to kill her husband?"

Declan knows how ludicrous that sounds, but nothing else makes sense. He opens his mouth to argue, but Cordova tells him to keep quiet. "Not without a union rep," he insists. "Not with this guy."

That only makes Declan angrier. He pushes by all of them and goes to his apartment door. He opens it and studies the frame, hoping to find scuff marks, but there are none. Nothing on the locks to indicate they were picked or tampered with either. "She's out to get me, and her lawyer's in on it. Hoffman planted that knife where we'd find it! Must have. We know he walked it out of the apartment. They're both trying to frame me. Maybe he was in here—"

Harrison cuts him off. "Or you took the murder weapon

from the apartment yourself and tried to frame her attorney. We have no proof it was in that coat. We all know what she was writing about. Maybe you did too. Maybe you went there to put an end to it and the husband got in the way, that's why she was mumbling your name on the 911 call."

Declan's blood begins to boil. "If I killed someone, I wouldn't use my own knife, and I'd sure as shit wipe off my prints! I'm not an idiot. This is bullshit. I want all of you out of here!"

Harrison fixes him with a calm, determined stare. "Let me ask you a question, Detective. If we run your blood against what was found on Morrow's door, what are we going to find?" He nods at the cut on Declan's hand. "Why don't you tell me how that happened?"

Cordova jumps in before Declan can respond. "I think we need a union rep before anybody says anything else. Right, Declan?"

Declan wants to punch Harrison in the face, bust the man's nose open and watch him bleed, but he forces himself to nod. "Yeah, I want my rep."

Harrison doesn't seem to mind. "You're right. Let's have this conversation in an interview room back at the Twentieth. On the record. I'd hate for any of this to get misinterpreted. Wouldn't want to see a fine, upstanding detective such as yourself say or do something you might regret later."

CHAPTER TWENTY-NINE

ROY HARRISON IS sitting across the table, a smug look on his face. Declan glares at him and can't hold back anymore. "This jerk-off has been gunning for me for months! Ever since he decided I planted evidence in the Lucero case, he's been riding me. Why don't you ask him where Denise Morrow got half the shit in her book? Ask him how long he's known her. Take a walk down to evidence—his phone number is in Morrow's notes. Maybe instead of throwing the spotlight on me, you all should be looking at him. Maybe pull his financials." Declan points a finger at him. "She pay you, Roy? She pay you to hand her dirt on me? *Manufacture* dirt on me?"

Harrison doesn't even flinch. "So I'm framing you too, is that it? I'm gonna need to write all this down just to keep track—you got me, a bestselling author, her attorney... anyone else? Anyone else sabotaging your illustrious career?" He leans forward. "You're in the spotlight because you're a fuckup, Shaw. You've always been a fuckup. You're on my radar because you're a *glaring* fuckup. You can point fingers all you want, but the truth is you dug the holes, all of them. You can't help yourself, because you're not just a bad cop, you're a general piece of shit. We all know you planted evidence to secure a conviction on Lucero. You doing it again here isn't exactly a stretch. Frankly, based on your history, I'd be surprised if you didn't."

"I took a poly on Lucero and passed."

"Anyone with half a brain can fool the box."

"Yeah? Then maybe you should take one. Tell us what you fed to Morrow."

"I didn't give anything to Denise Morrow. She called me once. Asked about you. I told her I couldn't comment on an open investigation." His eyes narrow. "Unlike you, I actually follow the rules."

"Bullshit."

Declan's union rep is sitting beside him, but aside from introducing himself, the little bald man in the pin-striped shirt has barely said two words. Other than insisting on being in the meeting, Carmen Saffi hasn't said much either, but now she finally breaks in. "Detective, answer a very simple question for me so we can all get out of here. Where were you when David Morrow was killed on"—she glances down at her notepad—"the night of Friday, November tenth, between eight thirty and nine thirty?"

Oh, that's easy, Declan thinks. *I was standing on the edge of the subway platform in the station under the Museum of Natural History thinking about throwing myself in front of the B train. You know, the station where Charlie Medcalf offed himself a few months back? Yeah, that's where I was.*

When Declan doesn't answer, Saffi says, "Cordova said when he called you, it took you only a few minutes to get to the Morrow apartment at the Beresford. You must have been close."

Shit.

Declan hopes his rep will say something, but the man stays quiet. He's waiting for an answer just like the others. "I went for a walk in the park. Out near the museum. Helps me think. Wind down."

"You went... for a walk?" Harrison says, his voice dripping with sarcasm.

Saffi shuts him up with a harsh look. "Can anyone else corroborate that?"

"I was alone, if that's what you're asking. I'm sure some of the cameras picked me up."

"Just strolling in the park," Harrison mutters.

"Enough," Saffi snaps.

There's a knock at the door. A CSU tech comes in carrying a plastic case.

Saffi's eyes remain fixed on Declan. "I think we all want to clear this up, right? Maybe someone did steal that knife from your place. Just because your prints are on it doesn't mean you were at the scene. I'm willing to keep an open mind. So here's what we're going to do. I'm offering you a choice. You let me take a blood sample right now, with your consent, something we can compare to the blood found on Morrow's door *before* you arrived on scene. We do it here nice and quiet, find out what your blood type is, and maybe rule you out. Or..." She bites her lip. "Or IAU holds you on suspicion, gets a warrant, and pulls your blood anyway." She goes quiet for a second. "Declan, it's your call, but option B comes with a paper trail and a lot more noise."

"You got nothing to hide, right?" Harrison winks. The condescending prick actually winks. "You want to turn off the spotlight, here's how you do it."

They sit there in silence for nearly a minute. Finally, Declan's rep leans over and whispers, "You want my advice, I think you should do it."

Declan *does not* want his advice. He liked the man better when he kept his mouth shut.

Saffi is staring at the cut on Declan's hand, scabbed over now. "How did that happen?"

Rusty pipe back at the subway station. Caught a sharp corner when I was practicing my death dive.

"Sliced it on the back of one of those benches in the park. A screw or something was sticking out." Hell, even Declan doesn't believe that, but he can't tell them the truth. He rolls up his sleeve and tells the tech, "Go ahead."

The tech gives Saffi a quick look and she nods.

He's fast. Rubber tourniquet, quick needle prick. Less than a minute later, the tech is holding a small vial of Declan's blood and Declan is pressing a cotton ball to his arm. With an eye-dropper, the tech retrieves a small amount of blood from the vial and places four drops into separate wells on a plastic card about three inches square. "Takes about a minute," he says softly, staring down.

Declan has no idea what he's looking at, but two of the red dots go clear, the others remain dark red.

The tech says, "He's A positive."

Harrison doesn't miss a beat. "Like the blood on the door frame at the Morrow place."

Declan lifts the cotton ball on his arm. The bleeding has stopped. He tosses it aside. "The blood we found on Denise Morrow matched her husband too, until it didn't."

Saffi is staring at the tray. She says, "He's right. Run it for DNA."

The tech nods, packs up, and is gone a moment later.

"She's framing me," Declan tells them again.

"Of course she is." Harrison flicks the corner of the plastic tray, setting it spinning, and sits back. "Maybe she was hiding under the park bench when you cut your hand. Her and Hoffman."

Saffi ignores him and leans closer to Declan. "Where would she get your blood?"

Declan knows exactly where. "I donate every month—at Mercy. Same hospital where her husband worked."

Harrison huffs. "Even if that's true, it's not like they write your name on the bag. It's coded. Secured."

"She's got money," Declan says. "You gonna tell me she couldn't get it if she wanted to? This is a waste of time. A distraction. She's playing with all of us."

Harrison stubs a bony finger down on the table in front of Declan and growls at Saffi, "I want him charged. I want his badge and gun and him in a cell."

"You don't have the authority, you arrogant shit!" Declan fires back.

Saffi briefly squeezes her eyes shut and rubs her temples. "Enough, both of you. Nobody's getting charged. Not yet." She turns to Harrison. "This is no different than charging Morrow's attorney. We jump the gun again, and the press skewers us. That's bad for everyone." She turns to Declan. "Until this is sorted out, I'm going to recommend to your lieutenant that you're removed from this case." Maybe she's trying to sound soothing but it comes off as patronizing.

"Wait a minute, I—"

"You need to step back, Declan. All this is fodder for Denise Morrow's defense. It's reasonable doubt. You're not helping anyone by staying in it. You want to put her away, you need to distance yourself. Let the rest of us work."

"Let the real cops work," Harrison mutters.

CHAPTER THIRTY

"AND YOU DIDN'T hit him?" Cordova looks stunned. "Hell, I think even I would have hit him."

When they walk into Your Six, a local cop bar, the place is well on its way to packed. That's the thing about cop bars—a shift is always ending somewhere. Couple that with it being Friday night, and they'll be looking at standing room only within an hour. Declan chases two rookies away from the far end of the bar and plunks down in his regular seat. He leans back against the wall and studies the crowd. "At some point, Harrison had to be a good cop, right? You don't come out of the academy dreaming of IAU; you get lured there."

Cordova takes the stool next to him and shoves away a bowl of peanuts, sending it halfway down the bar. Declan is allergic, and the last thing either of them wants is a trip to the ER. "What, like Anakin Skywalker going to the dark side?"

"Yeah."

Cordova shakes his head. "No. I think he was always a dick. IAU just gave him purpose."

The bartender shuffles over and sets two beers and two shots in front of them. Declan catches her before she goes. "Hey, Maddie, you know how to make a grasshopper?"

Maddie is pushing sixty and she's about fifty pounds overweight, but she's still quick on her feet and quicker with a zinger. "What, is it 1955 up in here? You want I should offer free polio vaccines to whoever hasn't got one yet too?"

"You know how to make one or not?"

Maddie rolls her eyes at him. "One grasshopper coming up. I'll throw in a Shirley Temple for your partner."

She returns with a grasshopper in a martini glass a few minutes later, and when she's gone, Cordova asks, "Do I want to know?"

"You do not." Declan reaches for his shot and holds it up. "To civil service and the hazards of police work, both in-house and out."

They both drink and set the glasses down next to the beers.

Cordova's face goes pale. "Oh, hell."

Declan has seen the man put away half a dozen shots before getting sick. He's about to rib him when he realizes it's not the shot — Cordova is watching the television on the wall above Declan's head. When Declan swivels around, he catches the text scrolling across the bottom of the screen — *Dirty cop behind the murder of local celebrity's husband?* Denise Morrow is sitting on a couch with Geller Hoffman, deeply concerned looks painted across both their faces as Barbara Leyland, the talking head from Channel 2, leans closer, stroking her chin.

"Maddie, turn that up!"

While pulling a beer from the tap with one hand, Maddie fumbles under the bar with the other, finds the remote, and raises the volume.

Denise Morrow says, "You have to understand, I was in shock, I didn't remember half of this until a day or two later, and even then it only came back in pieces."

Hoffman pats the top of Morrow's hand. "We were told Denise suffered from post-traumatic amnesia, or PTA. Seeing her dead husband, knowing someone was still in her apartment…all of that was too much, and her brain basically locked down Denise's consciousness."

"To protect her?" Barbara Leyland prompts.

"Exactly. She remained conscious, awake, but on some form of autopilot. People in that state are known to act in bizarre, uncharacteristic ways. It's like sleepwalking or being under deep hypnosis. Denise was capable of simple cognitive actions, responding to verbal cues, but only in a detached manner."

Barbara Leyland nods slowly, like this is the most fascinating thing she has ever heard, then turns back to Denise Morrow. "If we play your 911 call, are you going to be okay?"

Denise swallows. "Yes."

Leyland nods to someone off camera, and Morrow's voice comes from the speaker, complete with a fancy animated graphic line bouncing with the audio and captions beneath it.

Denise Morrow: My...my husband...somebody
stabbed him! God, he's...somebody stabbed
him. I think they might still be here!
911 operator: Ma'am, can you confirm your loca-
tion? I have two eleven Central Park West.
Morrow: Yes.
Operator: What apartment?
Morrow: Tower number two.
Operator: I've got officers en route. Is your husband
responsive?
Morrow: Responsive?
Operator: Awake? Breathing?
Morrow: I think they're still here!
Operator: If you feel you're in danger, you should
exit the apartment immediately and wait
in the lobby or on the street for officers to
arrive.
Morrow: No! I can't leave my husband.
Operator: Is he responsive?
Morrow: I have a gun. I can't leave him.
Operator: Ma'am, if you're in danger, you need to
get out.
Morrow: [*Sudden intake of breath.*] Detective Declan
Shaw.
Operator: Excuse me?
Morrow: Declan Shaw! Detective Declan Shaw!

The three of them are silent for a beat, then Barbara Leyland
says, "The police say you asked for Detective Shaw."

Hoffman says, "Does it sound like she's asking for him to you, Barbara?"

"It doesn't," the reporter says. "She sounds...afraid."

Hoffman nods. "At this point, my client was fully under the influence of PTA. Incapable of proper communication. She was trying to tell them Declan Shaw was in her apartment, had killed her husband, but she couldn't get those specific words out. The best she could do was his name, and they misinterpreted."

"You actually ran him off," Barbara says, her eyes wide. "You managed to get a gun and run him off before he could hurt you too."

Denise Morrow looks down at her hands. "I...I think that's what happened, but I honestly don't remember. When I try to recall, I only get flashes, these quick images."

"But you remember Detective Declan Shaw being in your apartment."

Another quick nod from Morrow, then she wipes her eyes with the back of her hand. "It was like remembering a dream. Trying to hold water in my fist. As I came out of...the fog...as I found myself back in reality, those memories seemed so distant. Then Declan Shaw was there, standing next to me, he came through the door like nothing had happened and..."

"And my client became lost, confused, rightfully so," Hoffman explains. "This is also characteristic of PTA. In that moment, she didn't know if her memories were real, if the Declan Shaw in front of her was real or if it was all a product of her mind. Had she been clearheaded enough, she certainly would have alerted the other officers. It wasn't until days later, after she was released, that I was able to get her the help she needed. That's when the memories were retrieved. *That's* when we finally knew the truth."

"Seeing David like that..." Denise chokes back tears and squeezes her eyes shut.

Barbara Leyland started her television career on *The Young and the Restless,* playing the overly dramatic teenage daughter of one of the show's regulars. Declan knows that because Leyland talks about it every chance she gets. She tells people she knew even then she wanted more, knew she didn't want to be just another pretty face on television. She wanted to make a difference; she was born to be a reporter, not a character...blah-blah-blah. Her expression now brings to mind her early days in front of the camera. It looks as if it has been rehearsed in front of a mirror, practiced with a coach, perfected with multiple takes. She's dripping sympathy as she reaches over and clasps Morrow's hand. "David, your husband."

Denise nods. "Seeing David like that, it couldn't possibly be real—that's what I told myself. That meant none of the rest was real either. I honestly expected to wake up any moment."

"But you didn't, did you?"

Morrow shakes her head. "I didn't. I still haven't. It's...it's been horrible."

Barbara Leyland bites her lip, allows all that to sink in, then says, "I have to ask because everyone in our audience is asking themselves this—why would this detective want to kill your husband?"

"He wasn't after David," Denise Morrow says in a voice so quiet, she sounds like a little girl. "I think he wanted to kill me and David just got in his way."

"Because of your new book?"

Denise Morrow nods. "A book about *him*."

Declan grabs the grasshopper and throws it at the television. The martini glass cracks against the wall to the left of the screen, coating the paneling in green. "This is bullshit!"

"Hey!" Maddie shouts. "None of that nonsense in here!" She scoops up the remote and changes the channel to a hockey game—the Rangers are down by one to the Devils.

That's when Cordova's phone rings.

ADA Saffi.

CHAPTER THIRTY-ONE

DECLAN CAN'T HEAR Saffi's voice—the bar's gotten too noisy—but he does see Cordova's face tighten as he listens to whatever ADA Saffi has to tell him. When Cordova hangs up, he holds two fingers in the air and tells Maddie, "Another round."

A moment later, she sets two more shots and another grasshopper down in front of them, eyeing Declan. "You best keep this one off my wall." She reaches under the bar, produces a rag, and sets that down too. "And I expect you to clean up after yourself."

"Yes, ma'am."

When she heads to the opposite end of the bar, Declan tosses the rag to a rookie standing near the bathrooms and says, "Bodie, clean that up for me and I'll let you off the hook for the twenty you owe me from that Knicks shitshow last week."

The kid shrugs and goes to work wiping the wall down.

"You're an ass." Cordova doesn't bother with another toast. He swallows the shot and stares at the bar top.

"You gonna tell me what she said?" Declan asks.

Without looking up, Cordova says, "I tell you, you gotta promise me you won't overreact."

"Scout's honor."

When Cordova still doesn't say anything, Declan picks up the grasshopper and drinks nearly half. It's not bad. Tastes like mint. Low on alcohol, though. He drinks the rest, follows that with the shot, then slides his half-finished beer and empty glasses aside and places his hands on the bar. "I promise, I'm good."

Cordova glances at their reflection in the mirror behind the bar, then looks back down. "Remember when I said Hoffman would use the alley murder to try and create smoke?"

"Yeah."

"There's smoke, but not the kind we thought," he tells him. "We got DNA back for the blood found on Denise Morrow's clothing. It's a match for the woman we pulled from the dumpster on Eighty-Third, Mia Gomez. ME says the knife found at Morrow's apartment is a match for the knife that killed Gomez. He's sure."

Declan tries to wrap his head around this. "Denise Morrow killed Mia Gomez?"

"I didn't say that."

"How do they even connect?"

Cordova looks like he wants another shot, and Declan sure as shit does, but instead of signaling Maddie, Cordova retrieves a pen from the breast pocket of his jacket. He takes two napkins from the stack behind the bar, writes *David Morrow* at the top of one and *Mia Gomez* at the top of the other. Working from memory, he writes down what they know about each case—evidence, timelines, facts—turning the napkins into makeshift murder boards.

DAVID MORROW

- Murdered 11/10/2023 (Friday)
- Had arrived home at 4:40 p.m. (confirmed w/ doorman, video footage)
- Denise left for bookstore talk 7:15 p.m. (confirmed w/ doorman, video footage)
- TOD between 8:30 and 9:30 p.m. (confirmed by ME w/ body temp)
- Killed with 1-inch-wide, 5-inch-long serrated-edge blade (found hidden above Geller Hoffman's car)
- Denise Morrow home at 9:20 p.m. (confirmed w/ cab receipt, doorman, video footage)
- Denise Morrow called 911 at 9:31 p.m.

MIA GOMEZ

- Murdered 11/10/2023 (Friday)
- TOD 8:30 p.m. (approximate, based on time video showed her entering alley)
- Killed with a chef's knife (8 inches long, 2 inches wide, smooth edge), found in Morrow's apartment
- Blood from Gomez found on Denise Morrow's clothing

"The dumpster is less than two blocks from Morrow's apartment," Declan points out. "Right around the corner."

"Video puts Mia Gomez walking into that alley at eight thirty p.m.," Cordova tells him. "Denise Morrow was in the middle of her bookstore talk at eight thirty. Sign-in sheet has sixty people there as witnesses." He quickly rattles off the timeline, pointing at both napkins as he goes. "Her talk started at eight. Gomez walks into the alley and is killed around eight thirty. Morrow doesn't leave the bookstore until a few minutes after nine. Cab drops her at her building at nine twenty. She calls 911 at nine thirty-one. First responders arrive in under six minutes. There's zero chance she killed Mia Gomez, and, let's be honest, she couldn't have killed her husband either. If the blood on her clothes had been his, sure, but not if it belonged to Gomez. She didn't have a drop of the husband's blood on her. We would have found it. CSU processed her clothing multiple times and found no trace on her clothes or her person. Shower was dry as a bone. Nothing in the sinks. We even pulled the traps. You can't kill someone like that and vanish every sign in under eleven minutes. No way." Cordova goes silent for a moment, then looks Declan in the eye. "Have you considered she might be telling the truth? She found him dead, just like she said? Hell, maybe somebody else killed them both."

Declan's shaking his head. "You didn't see her face when I got there. She killed him. I have no doubt." He waves at the TV. "She knows I know, and that's why she's spinning all this bullshit."

"The facts don't get you there," Cordova states flatly. "No

way she killed him, and no way she could have killed Mia Gomez either."

Declan takes a sip of his beer. "So how did Gomez's blood get on her? How did Gomez's murder weapon get into the apartment? Security in that building is tight. Nobody else went up there. You confirmed that."

Cordova shakes his head. "I have no idea." Driving his point home, he repeats, "She couldn't have killed her husband, timeline doesn't support it. And she was across town when Mia Gomez was killed. Evidence makes no sense. The whole mess makes my head hurt."

Maddie fires up a blender, mixing some frozen concoction. Declan jumps at the sudden noise, then watches as she stops it, adds some fruit, a little tequila, and starts the blender again. An idea hits him, and he sways a little under the weight of its landing. "It's a fucking three-card monte," he says softly.

"Huh?"

Declan reaches for the napkins, tears them up, and shuffles the pieces around the bar top. "Morrow was somehow in on both murders and mixed up the evidence. On purpose. She confused everything so it wouldn't make sense."

"Not unless she was in two places at the same time," Cordova replies. "She couldn't have killed her husband—the window is too small to pull it off—and she couldn't have killed Gomez; she's got sixty witnesses placing her in the bookstore when that woman was killed."

It's clear what Cordova is thinking because it's impossible not to go there—Denise Morrow had an accomplice, and it might be Declan. Declan knows that's what Cordova is thinking because of the way his partner keeps looking at him while simultaneously trying not to look at him. He's thinking the knife that killed David Morrow came from Declan's kitchen. He's thinking about Declan's blood at the scene. He's thinking about Declan's whereabouts when both people were killed. Whether he wants to or not, he's trying to connect Declan to Denise Morrow. He's thinking all these things because he's a good cop and that's where the evidence points. Sometimes a frame-up isn't a frame-up—it's fact.

Declan finishes his beer and stands. "Where's the bookstore?"

"Tribeca. The Mysterious Bookshop."

"You know, I've been having trouble sleeping lately. I think I'll pick up a book, maybe try reading."

"LT said you're off the case, Dec. You wanna get suspended? Worse?"

"He said I was off the Morrow case. I'm working the Gomez murder. Try to keep up."

Cordova eyes him, attempts to read him, can't. Finally, he throws some cash on the bar and starts for the door. "Who needs a pension."

CHAPTER THIRTY-TWO

THE MYSTERIOUS BOOKSHOP is located just off Broadway on Warren Street in Tribeca. Declan rarely leaves central Manhattan, so it might as well have been a world away. Cordova drives, and they get there just as some kid is packing up a book display on the sidewalk, carrying things in for the night. When Declan shows him his badge, he gets that same worried look most kids get: *What have I done lately and where did I slip up?*

"We need to speak to your manager," Cordova tells him, glancing through the open door.

"You want Otto. He's the owner," the kid tells them. "Come on in, I'll get him."

They follow him inside and watch as he slips through a

brown door decorated in crime scene tape and fake blood-stains.

Bookstores remind Declan of the library, and that reminds him of school, and that makes him uncomfortable. Maybe it's that musty smell. Or maybe it's the quiet, as if all books hate sound. His mom was a big reader. Romances, mostly, but that stopped when asshole Pops died and she had to take a second job.

Cordova nudges Declan's shoulder and points up at a camera near the door. There's another mounted high on one of the shelves capturing the entire room and another at the back pointing forward.

"Took you gentlemen long enough. I figured you'd come by days ago."

They turn to find an older man standing behind them. He's balding with white hair and a neatly cropped beard, and he's wearing a dark blue button-down and black pants. He extends his hand. "I'm Otto Penzler."

"This is Detective Declan Shaw, and I'm Jarod Cordova."

"I recognize you from television. You're here to check on Denise's alibi, right?"

"What makes you say that?"

"I've been publishing and selling mysteries for nearly five decades. Whodunnits tend to have a pattern, a rhythm to them. You've got yourselves a whodunnit, and I'd be disappointed if you didn't look at Denise. Although I'm sure she had nothing to do with it. I've known her for years. She might be able to write about some nasty murders, but she's good people, she doesn't have it in her." Otto grins and gestures at the cameras. "Come down to my office, I saved the video for you."

He disappears through the brown door with the crime scene tape. Declan and Cordova exchange a glance and follow him. The door opens onto a staircase and they descend two flights into a basement office. Every wall is covered in books. There are stacks of books on tables. On the floor. Towers of titles and boxes everywhere. Crammed in the back corner is a large wooden desk, most of its surface also buried. There's barely enough room for a computer monitor and keyboard. The mouse is perched on a stack of Agatha Christie novels. Otto motions for them to come around so they can see the screen. "You already have the sign-in sheet, right? I sent that over last week."

Cordova nods. "Sixty people in attendance?"

"Sixty-three if you count me and my staff." Otto clicks Play. "Here's Denise when she got here, seven forty-three p.m."

Declan asks, "How accurate is your time stamp?"

Otto raises an eyebrow. "You mean can I change it if I want to?"

Declan shrugs.

"We replaced the entire system last year when we went to HD. This one pulls in the time from the internet automatically. I imagine there are ways to alter it, but I've never tried."

On-screen, Denise Morrow enters the store wearing her missing black coat. She talks to a couple of people near the entrance before the cashier comes around the counter and leads her through the same door Declan and Cordova just followed Otto through.

"That's Tom," Otto explains. "He works for me. Denise waited down here until it was time to start."

"Any cameras down here?" Cordova asks.

"Just upstairs." Otto fast-forwards until Denise Morrow

appears again. The crowd is settled in folding chairs and Otto goes to a podium at the front of the room and speaks for several moments. The crowd applauds, and Denise steps up beside him, takes her coat off. She drapes it over a chair, shakes Otto's hand, and addresses the crowd.

Otto taps the rolling time stamp. "Seven fifty-nine."

Denise Morrow is wearing the same white blouse and black slacks Declan found her in at her apartment. Pristine, recently pressed. No blood.

"There's Susan Reynolds." Cordova points. "Second row, third from the left."

"Susan's here a lot," Otto says. "She runs Denise's fan club. She got here early to set up."

They watch for about three minutes before Declan asks if there's a way to speed up the tape. Otto clicks a button a few times until they're watching at thirty-two times normal speed. He slows it back down as she finishes her talk about forty minutes in. Denise moves from the podium to a table and takes a seat as a line forms in front of her. "She signed books for about twenty minutes or so. Answered questions. Took selfies, but she never left. She—"

"Stop," Declan orders.

Otto freezes the image.

"Rewind a little bit."

He does.

Then Cordova sees it too. "Is that Geller Hoffman?"

Declan nods. "It sure as shit is. Play it again, normal speed."

On-screen, the attorney enters the bookstore behind the crowd. He stands there for a moment, then bypasses the line and hands Denise Morrow a brown shopping bag. They exchange a look, and she sets the bag under the table. Hoffman leans in and whispers something to her, a long something, takes him nearly a minute. From the look on Morrow's face, it's not anything she wants to hear. Then he steps to the side and watches as Denise goes back to addressing the line. The scowl on her face is replaced with a smile as she takes a picture with an older lady holding three of Morrow's titles.

Cordova reaches for the computer mouse. "May I?"

Otto steps back, holding both hands up.

Cordova speeds up the recording until Denise Morrow finishes with the line and stands. She retrieves the bag and her coat, then says something to one of the bookstore employees.

"Who is that again?"

"Tom," Otto says.

Tom leads Denise Morrow to the back of the store. When they enter a hall, Otto points at another camera icon on the screen. "You want that one. Double-click it."

This brings up the narrow hall. Tom ushers Denise Morrow into a room, flicks on the light, and closes the door.

"Bathroom," Otto tells them.

Tom leaves.

A few minutes tick by before Denise Morrow comes back out. When she does, she's wearing her black coat buttoned all the way to her neck. The brown paper bag is clutched tightly in her hands. She returns to the main room of the bookstore, locates Geller Hoffman in the thinning crowd, and hands the bag to him. He leaves without another word. She starts working her way toward the entrance too, saying her goodbyes, and is gone a few minutes later.

Cordova stops the recording.

"Fucking three-card monte," Declan mutters for the second time that night.

Cordova leans against the wall and looks up at the ceiling, putting all this together. "They're about the same size, right? Morrow and Hoffman?"

Declan nods. "She might have an inch on him, but they're close."

"Hoffman could have killed Mia Gomez wearing the same outfit, changed, and brought his bloody clothes to her. She changed into them and wore them home under her coat. Probably had the knife at that point too, right? Must have. She walked it all into her apartment. Then what? It still doesn't explain how she killed her husband without getting his blood on her."

"Maybe Hoffman did him too. While she was here."

Cordova shakes his head. "No sign of Hoffman on the building's security footage until he shows up later. After you. We confirmed that with the doorman too. He knows Hoffman, said he's there a lot. He wouldn't have missed him." He goes quiet, then looks down at the computer monitor. "We'll pull his schedule. Find out where he was leading up to all this. Maybe he knows some way in we don't."

Caught up in this new evidence, they both nearly forget that Otto is standing there. Declan says, "You can't mention a word of this to anyone—you understand that, right?"

Otto's hands are up, palms out, in a *Whatever you want* gesture. He turns and starts back up the steps. "I'll leave you gentlemen to it. Take all the time you need."

He leaves. Declan sits on a corner of the desk and absentmindedly scans the titles on the shelf as he thinks out loud. "The husband was a cheat, killing him lines up, but why kill . . ."

Declan doesn't know books. There are few he'd recognize. He can count the ones he's read cover to cover on one hand. So when his eyes land on a white spine with red print, a colorful image wrapped beneath the text, they lock on it. It's one of the few titles he knows intimately. One he wishes he'd never heard of. He steps over to the shelf on wobbly legs.

Cordova doesn't catch any of this; he's still working the case. Declan barely hears him say, "The husband was a cheater, right? Could he have been sleeping with Gomez?"

Declan pulls the book from the shelf, takes in the familiar cover, then tosses it on the desk. The bang gets Cordova's attention. The color melts from his partner's face as he reads the title: *Understanding Anatomy and Physiology.*

He glances at Declan, then flips open the cover, probably expecting to find the library card. It's not there. It's not the same book. It can't be. But they both know Denise Morrow left it for them because written on that page in carefree script are the words *What goes around…*

CHAPTER THIRTY-THREE

Excerpt from *The Taking of Maggie Marshall* by Denise Morrow

WHEN DOES A good cop go bad? I've asked myself that particular question often while writing this book. I like to believe none of us enter this world *bad*, that we're clean slates, empty chalkboards waiting to be filled with ideas, loves, wonders, and hopes until there is no more room to write. We erase our mistakes and replace them with lessons learned. Our sorrows become stepping stones. We grow. We hurt. We heal, the new skin thicker than the old.

The cards dealt to Declan Shaw were pulled from the

bottom of a stacked deck. No one would deny that. Declan's father was a bit of a cliché. Irish Catholic, more muscle than brain. Between bottles, he had jobs in construction, ironwork mostly. In 1989, if you happened to look skyward at the skeleton of a building going up in NYC, there was a good chance one of the men you'd spot walking those steel girders fifty stories up was Declan Shaw's father. I'm not going to mention his name here because, frankly, it's not important, not when it comes to Maggie's story. What you need to know is that some days he tried to provide for his family, other days he did not, and it's those other days that tend to shape the minds of children. Those are the days they remember. No arrest reports exist for Declan's father. During his forty-one years on this planet, he was never picked up for so much as jaywalking. On paper, I suppose, that makes him a good man. You track down any of his coworkers (I did) and they'll tell you he was a good man. You talk to any of his old friends (I did), they'll insist he was. But if you dig through some old file cabinets in the basement at Presbyterian General (I did that too) and happen to come across a very thick folder on a boy named Declan Shaw, you might think otherwise. Declan had his first broken bone at age three—his right index finger. He broke his left arm three different times over the next four years. During that time, he was also treated for a ruptured eardrum (right), a fractured cheekbone (also right), and numerous cuts, scrapes, and bruises. If you'd asked his mother, she would've told you he was a clumsy child. He stopped being a clumsy child in 1994, the year his father died. He was seven.

Declan's mother cleaned apartments for a living. When I spoke to her friends, that's what I was told. When I checked police records, I found four arrests for solicitation, two for possession, and one for child endangerment. Declan was twelve for that last one—his mother had gone to Atlantic City for two days and left her son back in the city with half a box of cereal, spoiled milk, and a television that received only two channels as a sitter. That's when Declan began his life in the system. He bounced from foster home to foster home until the age of fifteen, when he landed with a nice family in Brooklyn who simply wanted a child and couldn't have one of their own. They adopted Declan two years later. She was a waitress, he was a cop. They both died in a car accident three days after Declan's eighteenth birthday.

Like I said—many cards dealt in the life of Declan Shaw, all from the bottom of a stacked deck. I imagine he credits his stepfather for driving him toward a career in law enforcement, and that may very well be true. But under the uniform, beneath his skin, is a broken boy. You'll find he did his best to erase the worst of his story, replace it with something better, but those early words never quite went away. Although faded, they were still there, still legible, and still influenced all that was written later.

When does a good cop go bad?

The truth is it can happen anytime. Some cops, though, do start out that way. They're rotten at the core, and eventually that rot finds its way up to the skin.

When I first heard the name Declan Shaw, I wanted him to be good. For Maggie's sake, for the sake of justice, for the sake of the man Shaw put away for her death.

But that damn book.

I knew things would go sideways the moment I learned about that damn book.

CHAPTER THIRTY-FOUR

"FORGET THE BOOK," Cordova tells Declan as they pull up outside Mia Gomez's building off Washington. "What's done is done. There's nothing you can do about it. Just let it go."

"Fucking Harrison," Declan grumbles. "Had to be."

"Doesn't matter."

"Harrison fed her intel on an open investigation. Speculative intel; he doesn't even have proof." He turns to Cordova. "I didn't plant that book. You know that, right?"

The look Cordova gives him is quick, but it's enough. A brief flash of pity. His partner catches himself, twists toward the window, and resets before saying, "Look, she's trying to rattle you, Dec. Harrison too. *Don't let them.*" He nods up at the building. "We need to focus. Bring this case home. If David Morrow was sleeping with Mia Gomez, we've got motive on the wife. That means Denise Morrow will go away for a very long time. We prove Hoffman helped her, and we've got conspiracy. Tie him or both of them to the Gomez murder on top of the husband, and it's game over. They're both gone. Whatever she tries to tell people about you will be meaningless. She'll have zero credibility. Harrison won't hitch his wagon to that, no way. He'll drop it. He'd be an idiot not to."

"Nobody's saying Harrison's not an idiot." Declan looks down at his hands. "Some people will believe damn near anything. Even people who should know better."

He knows it's a dig, but he can't help it. If his own partner doesn't believe him, how the hell can he expect anyone else to?

Declan gets out, slams the car door, and stomps up the steps of the converted brownstone. He starts mashing buttons on the intercom until a woman's voice says, "Yes?"

"NYPD, ma'am. I need you to buzz me in." Declan pulls out his badge and holds it up to the small camera mounted above the door.

When nothing happens, he shakes the badge, holds it closer.

The magnetic lock disengages with a loud *click*. Declan tugs the door open and waits for Cordova to catch up. "What apartment?"

Cordova checks his notebook. "Three B."

There's no elevator, not in a building this size. While Declan makes quick work of the steps, Cordova is huffing by the time he reaches the top.

Apartment 3B isn't hard to find—they had uniforms seal off the door a week ago when Mia Gomez's body was found. A precaution, standard procedure. It wasn't considered a crime scene so nobody has been inside, but the yellow tape stands out like a sore thumb against the dark wood. "I don't suppose you brought her key?"

Cordova shakes his head. "It's with her purse back in evidence. I didn't know we were coming out here tonight."

It's likely someone is watching them. Probably the woman who buzzed them in, her eye pressed against the peephole of one of the other doors.

No matter.

Declan takes out his wallet and removes the lockpicks he keeps behind his driver's license. He has the dead bolt open in under a minute and uses the sharp edge of one of the picks to slice the tape.

When he opens the door, a foul odor wafts out. "Oh, man, I hope she didn't have a pet."

They step inside, close the door behind them, and take in the space. Maybe nine hundred square feet. Not small by New York standards, but not large either. There is a living room with a kitchenette off to the side and two bedrooms in the back, all decorated tastefully in neutral colors. Gomez used one bedroom as an office. In the other one, her bed is neatly made, covered in a white duvet. There's a bathroom sandwiched between. Prints are spaced evenly along the walls, most depicting famous locations — the Eiffel Tower, the Golden Gate Bridge, a few buildings from here in the city. On a table under the wall-mounted television, Declan finds several photos of Mia Gomez in happier times. She has an infectious smile and a carefree look about her. An attractive young woman living her best life in the city, until she wasn't.

"Found the source of the smell." Cordova is in the kitchen,

picking through some canvas shopping bags on the counter. "Looks like she went grocery shopping and didn't get the chance to put anything away. Got a receipt here, it's time-stamped seven forty-two p.m. On the night she was killed."

"How far are we from that alley?"

"Maybe a five-minute walk."

Declan considers that. "So she goes shopping, comes home, and something pulls her away before she gets the chance to unpack."

"Something or someone," Cordova says. "Keep an eye out for her cell phone. Maybe she left it here."

Declan steps into the office. With the exception of a pair of headphones and a few cords, her desk is bare. "Got a power adapter but no computer in here." Under the desk, there's a pedal plugged into a USB hub. "What did you say she did for a living?"

"Senior account exec at a company down on Eighty-First," Cordova calls from the other room. "Started in data entry and worked her way up."

Declan stretches his foot under the desk and taps the pedal. Maybe she was a gamer too.

The desk drawers are crammed with various office supplies, old bills, a few books, and menus for local takeout. Declan moves through it all so fast, he nearly misses the old Page Six column folded and jammed in the back of the center drawer. "I'll be damned," he says. "Hey, Cordova. Come here."

When Cordova steps in, he hands the paper to him. There's a photograph of Denise and David Morrow, clearly arguing, beneath the caption *Maybe Cinderella should have left the ball at eleven?* "It's the story Susan Reynolds mentioned, right?"

Cordova nods, skimming the text. "Yeah, says they were fighting on and off all night. Denise was drunk for her keynote speech. The piece doesn't pull any punches. It doesn't come right out and say David was hitting on other women, but it does say, 'The friendly husband wasn't shy about working the room while Denise Morrow was busy calming her nerves with liquid courage.'"

"Oh, shit, let me see that." Declan pulls the paper from Cordova's hands and smooths it out on the empty desk. He jabs his finger down on the photograph. "That's her, right? Mia Gomez?"

Cordova leans in closer.

She's in the back of the image, near the bathroom doors. Although she's turned at a slight angle, it's clearly her. She's watching the couple just like everyone else in the photo is.

"There's our smoking gun," Cordova mutters.

For the first time in a week, Declan feels they've caught a real break. What they find in the main bedroom is even more damning: Behind one of the nightstands is a discarded condom wrapper. Same brand as the condoms found on David Morrow's body.

CHAPTER THIRTY-FIVE

"THERE'S NO FUCKING WAY we're going after her again. Not with this circumstantial bullshit," Lieutenant Marcus Daniels tells them, shaking his head. "You got video of her attorney handing her a shopping bag. Good for you. A condom wrapper? Please." He blows out a harsh breath. "I don't know if you have time to catch the news between your various fuckups, but the press is all over you, and ain't none of it good. Hoffman is screaming dirty cop to anyone in the media willing to listen. The *Times* called twice today trying to get me to comment. That means they've got a story brewing too. I spent half of yesterday getting chewed out by the DA. When he was done with me, the mayor got on my ass. Apparently, Hoffman is a big donor, has the mayor on speed dial. Hoffman gave him a courtesy call to let him know he was prepping to sue the city on his client's behalf for false arrest. Plans to file Monday. Damage to her reputation, potential disruption in earnings—he's claiming her publisher threatened to hold publication of her latest book, and that's a seven-figure ding to her income by itself. If it happens and you're wrong about her, the city could be on the hook."

"I'm not wrong," Declan insists.

Daniels's face goes bright red. "You don't get to be wrong, and you don't get to be right! You're not on this case!" He stands and slaps the rumpled Page Six story spread out on his cluttered desk. "What part of *Stay away from her* are you having trouble understanding? Do I need to take your gun and badge? Lock your ass up? What?"

"Hoffman and Morrow killed the husband, then they lured Gomez into an alley and killed her too." Declan jabs his finger at Mia Gomez in the photo. "They left that woman's body in a dumpster. She was twenty-eight years old. You really want to stand in the way of taking them down? You gonna let the DA or the mayor tell you not to do your job?"

It's a low blow, but Declan doesn't have a choice.

Daniels looks like he might explode. He grips the edge of his desk and goes quiet for a very long time. Eventually, he asks, "Did you dust the condom wrapper for prints?"

Shit. Declan was really hoping he wouldn't ask that.

Cordova, who's been sitting quietly in a chair through all of this, says, "We pulled two latents—both from Mia Gomez."

"Not the husband."

"We found the box in her dresser drawer. CSU says perforation marks on one of the condoms found in David Morrow's pocket matches the marks on the last one in that box. That means the ones he had on him were torn from the condoms in Mia Gomez's possession. That's just as solid as a print. It puts him there. We've got CSU dusting every inch of her place right now. We'll find more."

That last part is a lie.

Cordova is buying time.

CSU finished with the apartment an hour ago, and none of the prints they found matched David Morrow.

Daniels drops back in his seat. "Look, if the husband was dipping his wick, I get why the writer would want him dead, and that woman too, but I see no reason for her attorney to go along with any of this. You don't take part in a double homicide because your client asks you nicely."

"Hoffman's not just her attorney. From what we're hearing, he's a friend . . . maybe more."

Daniels takes another look at the picture from Page Six. "Her and Hoffman?"

Cordova nods.

"Christ."

"This is why you have to let us stay on it," Declan says.

Daniels's face hardens again. "Cordova stays on it. You're taking the day off. I catch you anywhere near this case, and you're going to find yourself with a lot of free time."

"LT, I—"

Daniels starts angrily ticking off points on his fingers. "We got your blood at the crime scene. Morrow mentioned you by name on the 911 call—claims this is all you. The murder weapon came from your apartment, has your prints on it. You got some bullshit alibi—out walking in the park. You going to tell me where you really were?"

Declan goes quiet. He can't tell him. No way.

"Didn't think so." Daniels jerks his thumb toward Cordova. "This guy is the only reason you're not on leave right now. He's been vouching for you from the jump, but you know what? That only goes so far. When I look at all this, when I look at you, I see a mediocre cop with motive. I got Harrison in my ear telling me you're just covering your tracks. Something you're apparently damn good at. I got the *Times* trying to get me on the record about the dirty cop on my watch. If you think I'm gonna fall on my sword protecting you, you're more delusional than I thought. Harrison says he expects to finish his investigation by Monday. If he concludes you planted evidence on Lucero, I'm throwing your ass to the wolves. You're done."

"I didn't plant evidence, I didn't kill David Morrow," Declan says firmly. "This is all her."

Daniels's phone rings and he snatches it up. "What?"

As he listens, he drags his hand over his bald head, closes his eyes, and leans back in his chair. He hangs up the phone without so much as a goodbye. When he leans forward again, his eyes snap open and burn into Declan. "Hoffman sent a copy of the lawsuit to the mayor's office, the chief of detectives upstairs, and Harrison in IAU." He swallows, shakes his head in disbelief. "One hundred million dollars. That's what she's suing for."

Declan's heart cracks against his ribs with the violence of a gunshot. "That's crazy!"

For nearly a minute, Daniels stares at him. When he finally speaks, he manages only five words: "Get out of my office."

CHAPTER THIRTY-SIX

"THAT WENT WELL," Cordova mutters when they're back at their desks.

Declan is pacing in slow circles. He feels like the world is closing in on him. All of this bullshit is coming to a head. "She's engineering all this. You know she's behind it." He jabs a finger at Cordova's chest. "You *know* she is. *You know me.*"

"Dec, I—"

"I didn't plant that book. I didn't kill David Morrow. You might not be sure about that, and Daniels and the rest of the world might not believe me either, but *I* know I didn't do those things. That means it's her. Her and Hoffman. Nothing else makes sense. They're creating this elaborate smoke screen, and the rest of you are buying into it! Hanging me out to dry rather than seeing the truth!"

"You need to calm down."

Declan knows how crazy he sounds but doesn't care. "She knew we'd visit that bookstore. She knew we'd eventually end up in that basement office. She left that copy of the book there for no other reason than to spook us. How long ago do you think she did that? How long has she been planning all this?"

"Her prints weren't on the book, Dec," Cordova tells him. "I had CSU check when they dusted the condom wrapper. It could be some—"

"Come on, that's no coincidence." Declan groans. "It was her handwriting on that page."

"You some handwriting expert now? How do you know?"

"I know."

Cordova's lips form a thin line, then he says, "Look, Daniels is right. The video is circumstantial. We don't know what was in the bag Hoffman handed her, we don't know what she was wearing under her coat."

"Bullshit."

"We can't prove it," Cordova says. "We can't prove it any more than you can prove she left that book. There's zero proof. Just speculation. Circumstantial, that's all any of it is. The only hard evidence is—"

"Is on me, yeah." Declan waves that off. "Blood she somehow stole. A knife she *definitely* stole."

"No proof of that either."

Declan turns on him. "You seriously think I snuck into Morrow's apartment to kill her and killed the husband instead when he got in the way? All to keep some fabricated garbage about the Maggie Marshall case from coming out? Come on, man. Denise Morrow's event schedule is no secret. It's on her website. She's easy enough to find. If I'd really wanted to kill her, I'd have gone to the bookstore, not her apartment. Maybe got her at some other appearance. It would be stupid to try and take her out at home. You seriously think I'd kill the husband, panic, and leave my target alive? Leave a witness? I'm a homicide detective, I see this shit every day. You don't think I'd plan a little better than that? Hell, if I wanted her dead, I wouldn't use a knife. I'd go see Pooch over in Hunts Point and buy a gun, use that. Or I'd hire some random banger to take her out. Plenty of them around there. Why would I get my hands dirty?"

Hunts Point is arguably the worst neighborhood in the city. You walk in there, you've got a one-in-twenty-two chance of becoming the victim of anything from a mugging to sexual assault. Prostitutes and dealers litter the corners. Pooch runs the Southside Posse. He pays the smaller kids to squirm down into the storm drains and retrieve discarded guns, then he resells them. One of his many enterprises.

"This is three-card monte, remember? I'm just another card in the deck," Declan says. "We get in her head, we solve this."

Cordova presses his hands together and rests his chin on top of his fingers, thinking. Considering everything Declan just said. "Okay, let's...let's backtrack. We know Denise Morrow was researching the Maggie Marshall case from the start of it, right? Didn't you say there was something in the book about that?"

"She starts the book with the trial. She was there."

"And she specifically talks about you? Claims you were somehow guilty?"

I'd soon learn Detective Declan Shaw had a very good reason for feeling guilty. That, too, as much as everything else, was fact.

"Yeah. In the first line about me. But it's a book, right? Who knows what she knew and when. Whatever she got, she got from Harrison. We've got to pull Harrison's financials. You know he's on Denise Morrow's payroll. *Has to be.* We find one payment from her to him, and this all starts to make sense."

"It wouldn't change anything. You find payments between those two, all it proves is he was willing to share information for the right price; it doesn't take the spotlight off you."

"What if it was the other way around?"

"I don't follow."

"Maybe we're thinking about this backward," Declan says. "What if she pointed Harrison at me instead of the other way around? We don't know what put Harrison on this. Why not her?"

"That's still not a crime. How would she even come up with that?"

"You know how." Declan is thinking about what she wrote in that book: *What goes around . . .*

"Lucero?" Cordova says.

"She was probably talking to him early on, right? Maybe as far back as the trial. Maybe before that. She needs details for her story, and he gives her one. Tells her the cops set him up. Tells her how. She takes that to Harrison and he runs with it."

"Even if that's true, how does it help us here? Besides," Cordova says, "that doesn't track. Didn't you say she had Harrison's name and number written on a newspaper clipping that said IAU was looking at you? That means she got his contact info *after* the story broke."

Declan takes out his phone and scrolls back through his photos until he finds the ones he took down in the evidence locker. Cordova's right—the name and number are written in the margins of an article from the *Times* titled "Detective in the Maggie Marshall Case Under Internal Investigation."

Cordova squints and leans in closer. "Can I see that?"

Declan hands him the phone, and he pinches the image and zooms in on the handwriting. "Why is there a line through Harrison's name?"

"A what?" Declan never noticed a line, but now he sees it, faint, like the flick of a pen.

"Did you dial the number?"

Declan shakes his head.

Cordova keys the number in on his desk phone. It rings three times before a harsh male voice answers: "Daniels."

Cordova hangs up without a word.

CHAPTER THIRTY-SEVEN

OUTSIDE.

Declan drags hard on a cigarette he bummed off a patrol officer during his and Cordova's hasty exit from the Twentieth. He hasn't smoked in nearly four years, but he sure as hell needs one now. "Has the LT ever told you he spoke to Denise Morrow? Even once?"

Cordova is standing a few paces up the sidewalk, upwind. He hates the smell of cigarette smoke. If it gets in his suit, he's more likely to burn it than launder it, but he clearly understands why Declan needs one. "He and I have had our share of private conversations about this since it first started, and he's never said that. He took me to breakfast the morning of my deposition with IAU, and we covered every inch of the Maggie

Marshall case—every single thing you and I did—so there's been opportunity, but if they were talking, he kept it to himself."

Declan takes another hit of the cigarette. "I suppose you talked about me too, right?"

"What do you think?"

"So what do you think he told her?"

"This could mean nothing," Cordova says. "It might mean she tracked down Harrison's name from the article and got nowhere with him, then tracked down your supervisor and took a run at Daniels. It doesn't mean they actually spoke. Doesn't mean he told her anything."

Declan doesn't buy that. "That number didn't ring Daniels's desk line, and that wasn't his work cell either; I got that one memorized, I dial it so much. No, that was some other number. Some phone important enough he keeps it on him. Personal cell. Maybe a burner. Why would she have that number? Who would give it to her? Had to be Harrison, right?"

Cordova gives a dismissive shrug. "You ever know Daniels and Harrison to talk outside official channels? You ever see them say a word to each other at the Six?"

Declan considers that. The Six was seen as neutral ground for all members of the force; it was like Switzerland. For the most part, problems, conflicts, disagreements, and bad blood were left at the door. That meant you might find someone from IAU laughing it up with a homicide detective, or you might see a uniform putting away shots with someone from the DA's office. There was no rank inside the Six. But even there, Harrison was an outsider. Other members of his team might belly up to the bar next to someone they were investigating, but not

Harrison. He tended to occupy a booth in the back and hold court. As the alcohol flowed, some would wander over in hopes of gleaning some detail on an open investigation, while others might find themselves at his booth sharing something they'd bottled up, something they'd decided needed to come out. Declan has been going to the Six for years, but he can't recall a single instance of seeing Harrison and Daniels talking. Here's the thing, though: Guys like Daniels climbed the ranks because they understood information was currency. They also understood the importance of discretion.

Cordova takes a few steps down the sidewalk, turns, and comes back again. "He ever tell you he went up to Dannemora to talk to Lucero?"

Declan nearly chokes on the cigarette smoke. "What? When?"

"It was about a week before he had to give his deposition to IAU. A few days after I gave mine. Maybe a month after Lucero's trial. Remember when he had all the Lucero files brought to his office so he could rehash every aspect of the case? He re-created our whiteboards, reread every witness statement."

"Oh, you mean the first time he called me an ignorant bastard and tried to punch holes in our work?" Declan puffs. "You mean that time?"

Cordova nods. "Something triggered him, but he wouldn't say what. I asked him a couple times and he just clammed up."

"IAU was all over him, same as us. He was probably making sure we didn't miss anything, right?"

"He has forty-one officers under his command," Cordova says. "At any given time, he's got three to five open IAU investigations on his desk. He's not the sort to get rattled by that kind of thing. I doubt you last long on that job if you do. Something else spooked him."

"Before or after he drove up to Dannemora?"

"After," Cordova says. "He had everything brought to his office *after.*"

They both fall silent for several moments, then Declan stomps out the cigarette. "Denise Morrow contacts Roy Harrison. Roy Harrison points her to Daniels—"

"With a personal number."

"With a personal number," Declan repeats. "He takes a drive up to Dannemora and chats with Lucero, and Lucero tells him something that seriously twists his panties." Declan waits for Cordova to throw a wrench in that, because that's what Cordova does, but his partner remains silent. Finally, he nods.

Declan says, "We need to take a ride up to Dannemora."

"*I* need to take a ride up to Dannemora," Cordova replies. "You're going to do exactly what the LT said and take the day off."

"No way, I—"

"You can't give him or Harrison or anyone else an excuse to shut you down. Not until we know what this is about."

CHAPTER THIRTY-EIGHT

Excerpt from *The Taking of Maggie Marshall* by Denise Morrow

REMEMBER HOW I said Declan Shaw's father was a good man on paper? Well, on paper, Ruben Lloyd Lucero definitively was not. His rap sheet began with multiple arrests for statutory rape early in life and only got worse as he got older. He'd been dating those first two girls; the parents had pressed charges because he was over eighteen and their respective daughters were minors. While that is technically a crime in the good state of New York, I did speak to both girls (now women) and both confirmed the relationships were consensual.

I can understand that, and I'm willing to give him a pass for those.

Why?

Here's why.

When I was sixteen, I dated a guy who was in his second year at Columbia. He was twenty. If you'd asked me then, I would have told you I was madly in love with him and his feelings for me were so strong, it was like our souls were destined to spend eternity together. If you asked me now, I'd tell you the thrill and danger of dating a college boy when I was only a sophomore in high school was what sent my insides swooning, and he was most likely dating a half dozen co-eds in the days (sometimes weeks) we were apart. It wasn't romance; it was a cultivated experience. It certainly wasn't rape, not to me. And because my parents never found out and so never had the opportunity to press charges, it wasn't declared rape by the law either.

So, yeah, I can give Lucero a pass for those early relationships.

But Ruben Lucero didn't stop. After those two, there were no more underage girlfriends, no more parents pressing charges for statutory rape, but there were other girls, other charges. At twenty-two, just six weeks after completing probation, he was arrested for public indecency. He told police he was overtaken with the sudden urge to urinate while waiting for the subway and didn't feel he could make it to the bathroom before his business became the business of other people on the platform. The police found no urine on the pavement. What they did find were four teenage girls willing to testify they were standing five feet from Lucero when he decided to drop his pants and smile. That earned him thirty days behind bars, another year on probation, and an additional red mark on the sex offenders list. Two years after that, he was found in an alley with a fifteen-year-old female runaway from Ohio who had turned to prostitution rather than go back home to an abusive stepfather. Lucero pleaded no contest and agreed to enter a treatment program for sex offenders. His twenty-fifth birthday came and went. Post-treatment, Lucero reentered society as (hopefully) a cured man. On paper, anyway.

In order to secure the groundskeeping job at Central Park, he lied when asked if he had a criminal record. On his employment application, he reversed two digits on his Social Security number and gave his name as Lloyd R. Lucero rather than Ruben Lloyd Lucero. He told his interviewer everyone called him Lucky, and that stuck. That little bit of smoke and mirrors was enough to keep park personnel from discovering his past. They did fingerprint him, but apparently those prints were never processed, just placed in his file and forgotten. A former park administrator told me it was standard practice to hold processing during a new hire's probationary period due to high turnover and a small budget, but I never found proof to back that up. If it was true, it doesn't explain why nobody ran the prints when Lucero crossed the thirty-day mark.

Many would say Lucero kept his head down, managed to control his appetite for young girls, and stayed out of trouble. Again, on paper, that's how it looked. Following the death of Maggie Marshall, the police raided Ruben

Lucero's apartment and found a number of books that appeared to have been stolen from young girls, frequent visitors to the park. They were souvenirs; there is no denying that. He kept the books of girls who interested him and whom he fixated on. Along with stealing the books, he took photographs of many girls. Some of those photos were shot at a distance; others were taken by hidden cameras (attached to the undersides of brooms and rakes to capture up-skirt shots). A few appeared to have been taken with the subjects' consent: Girls in various stages of undress. Some pleasuring themselves. All underage.

Ruben Lucero was—is—a bad man.

He had a problem that didn't go away, only evolved. He simply got better at hiding it.

Here's the thing, though: The police didn't accuse Lucero of harming a single person other than Maggie Marshall. Not one.

They found all those books, those souvenirs, the photographs—damning evidence, for sure, but not a single victim. They did manage to track down three of the girls in those photographs, all of whom were alive and well. Two of them had no idea Lucero had stolen books from their bags, nor did they know he'd taken pictures of them. The third recognized Lucero from the park and said they'd spoken once or twice, but only in passing.

No other victims.

Not one.

Only Maggie Marshall.

Like I said, he got better at hiding. Maybe those skills extended to hiding bodies, but there is no proof of that.

There's only Maggie Marshall.

A girl found dead in the park. Strangled. Raped. With Lucero's footprints nearby, his lost watch, his cigarette butts.

During his initial interview, Lucero admitted to finding her body and telling no one. Given his past, do you blame him? He admitted to smoking a cigarette as he looked down on her. He said he prayed for her. He said there was nothing else he could do. He wanted to tell someone but couldn't. He feared what they would do to him.

I asked why he didn't phone it in anonymously. He said he was worried they'd find him.

I have spoken to Ruben Lucero multiple times. To the best of my knowledge, the man has never lied to me.

He told me the ugly stuff when nobody else would listen.

He also told me he didn't hurt Maggie Marshall.

And I believe him.

He claims he was framed.

And I believe that too.

Why?

When Detective Declan Shaw initially walked the Maggie Marshall crime scene, he made an audio recording. Without mentioning titles, he stated three textbooks were found in her backpack. Her backpack, currently sitting in the NYPD evidence locker, contains only two textbooks.

Detective Declan Shaw made a similar audio recording when he walked Lucero's apartment. He found Lucero's "souvenir" books and read off many of the titles. He made no mention of one called *Understanding Anatomy and Physiology*, a book police later said they found in Lucero's apart-

ment with the others. A book they claimed had belonged to
Maggie Marshall.

Why do I believe Lucero is innocent?

Maggie Marshall's prints are on that book.

Lucero's are not.

Only the police had access to Maggie's backpack when it
was found by her body.

Only Detective Declan Shaw.

CHAPTER THIRTY-NINE

THE DRIVE UPSTATE to Dannemora takes a little over five hours. By the time Cordova gets inside the correctional facility, it's after four.

Ruben Lucero looks rough.

Cordova hasn't seen him since the trial, and he appears to have aged a decade. His thinning hair, shaved close to his scalp, is gray at the temples. His former baby face is now impressed with deep lines. There's a cut on his right cheek, maybe a week or two old, repaired with sloppy black infirmary stitches. The skin surrounding his left eye is the deep yellow of a partially healed bruise. As a convicted sex offender, the murderer of a fourteen-year-old child, and a generally creepy asshole, Lucero, Cordova knows, spends much of his time in protective custody. Even in prison, there's a pecking order, a hierarchy of social classes, and sex offenders, particularly those with an eye for the young, are on the lowest rung, targeted by all the others.

Lucero is sitting behind one-inch-thick ballistic glass, stained and smeared with God knows what, his head tilted to the side, eyes nothing but slits. Cordova takes the seat opposite him, plucks the phone receiver from the wall on his left, and brings it close enough to his face to speak without letting it touch his skin. It smells like stale onions and sweat.

Lucero scoops up his receiver, balances it on his shoulder, says nothing. Letters spelling out *punk* cover four cracked knuckles on one hand. Typical prison tat, the kind made by carving letters into the flesh and applying heated ink from a ballpoint pen. Sometimes the word was still readable when the infection was over, sometimes not.

Cordova nods at the man's hand and breaks the silence. "New ink?"

Lucero glares through the glass. "What the fuck do you want?"

This particular visitation room has six booths. All of them are occupied. Most people speak in hushed tones, but a woman down at the far end is shouting into the phone, screaming at the inmate opposite her. Something about her son getting picked up for dealing. Their son, Cordova suspects, given the way the man is eyeing her. He's trying to look tough, but there's a quiver in his chin. Cordova doesn't have children. He was married once, but the job put an end to that. Back in the late

'90s, he'd come home from working a double to find an empty closet and a note on the refrigerator that said, simply, *Sorry, I can't anymore.*

Cordova loads a photo of Lieutenant Daniels on his phone and presses the screen against the glass. "Do you know this man?"

Lucero's eyes remain on Cordova for a few seconds, then shift to the small screen. He doesn't say whether or not he recognizes the man, just leans back in his seat and looks at Cordova. "What's it to you?"

Cordova returns the stare. He's not easily intimidated, and if being on the job for thirty years has taught him anything, it's how to read someone who doesn't want to be read. Lucero most certainly recognizes Daniels. He knows Cordova can review visitor logs, so why attempt to conceal it? He turns the phone back around, types in *Denise Morrow,* and finds a recent photo of her standing on the courthouse steps after being released on bail. "What about her?"

This time, Lucero hides nothing. "Yeah, she's been here. So what?"

"What do you talk about?"

"What do you think?"

"Has she been here recently?"

"Why do you care?"

This time, Cordova goes quiet, face dropping into his best *You know why* smirk. He eyes the other man until he breaks and starts talking.

"She's some reporter or some shit," Lucero finally says. "Come up here a few times. Said she's writing a book on all the ways you and your partner fucked me over. Gonna get me out." He lifts his arm. "This is still fucked from when your partner busted it. Can't raise it above my head half the time. I get out, you know I'll sue the shit out of you for the arm, false arrest, false imprisonment." He points at Cordova, then at himself. "You and me, we're gonna trade places. Your bitch-ass partner too."

Cordova notes that the man's arm seems to be working just fine. He swipes through the images on the phone and finds one of Geller Hoffman. He holds it up. "What about him?"

Lucero's eyes go wide, then narrow again as he leans forward to get a better look. A mix of emotions cross his face as he studies the image. When he drops back in his seat, there's nothing left but frustration. "Why you coming to me with this now? You didn't want to hear it back in the day. Why now?"

"What do you mean?"

The woman at the far end of the interview room slams her receiver down on the table, smacks it against the glass, then jumps up and points at the inmate she's been speaking to. "You ain't never been a father to that boy! He learned nothing from you but how to be some gangsta, and considering that got you here, he ain't no better off. He end up here, that's on you!"

With a harsh kick at her chair, she storms off. The corrections officer stationed in the room does nothing but open the door for her. Just another day.

Cordova tries not to let it all distract him. "What do you mean?" he asks Lucero again.

"What good's it gonna do me to tell you now? At least she's trying to get me out." His frustration shifts to agitation. "You actually think I belong here. You'll put in some kind of word for me? Reopen my case? Fuck no. You let this truth out, and your world comes crashing down. Think I don't know that?"

Whatever this is, it's got Lucero fired up. He shifts in his chair, eyes Cordova, the interior door, the corrections officer who likely brought him in here and who's still standing by that door.

Cordova tries to calm the man down. "Look, if we missed something on your case, good or bad, you can tell me. If a mistake was made, I'll do what I can to correct it."

Lucero lets out a soft laugh. "Ain't that some bullshit."

"Tell me."

Lucero scratches his chin, then tentatively brushes the black stitches in his cheek. "Show me that last pic again?"

Cordova raises the phone; the image of Geller Hoffman is still on the screen.

"I told you I was watching out for that girl that day in the park. I tell you the truth, and what do you do? You played that video. Told the jury I was following her. You never once showed them a video of the man I said was following her. Not once. That was on you."

"We searched all the footage and didn't see anyone but you. You know that."

"You didn't find him 'cause you didn't look hard enough. Easier for you to pin it on me."

"What exactly are you saying?"

"What I'm saying is that's the guy," Lucero says, tapping the glass between him and Cordova's phone. "That's the guy I saw following her."

"Geller Hoffman?"

"Think I thought to ask him his name? Think I'd be in here

if I had? Fuck no." He slouches back in his seat. "The first guy you showed me? I told him all this when he come up here. He didn't do a damn thing about it. Left me to rot. Fuckers. All of you."

Cordova swipes back to the photograph of Lieutenant Daniels. "You told this guy?"

Lucero nods. "Damn right I did."

CHAPTER FORTY

THE SUN IS down when Cordova steps back outside, and the air has taken on a definite chill. He's halfway to his car when his phone rings.

Lieutenant Daniels.

How the hell?

Does Daniels know he's here? Did some guard call and tip him?

He clears his throat and answers. "Lieutenant."

"Do you have eyes on your partner?"

Cordova glances around the prison parking lot. His first thought is maybe Declan followed him and Daniels tracked them both, then he realizes how paranoid that is. Declan knows better, and Cordova drove up in his personal car and he's on his personal phone—no tracking either of those without a warrant. "I haven't seen him since we left your office. I told him to do what you said and take the day off."

"And where are you?"

Cordova doesn't miss a beat. "Chasing a lead, but it didn't pan out." He reaches his car, climbs inside, and closes the door. "Something happen?"

There's a long pause. He waits for the LT to call him out or ask for more, but Daniels doesn't. Instead, he says something far worse. "A witness came forward. She says she was out walking her dog the night David Morrow was murdered and saw Declan enter the Beresford through the Eighty-Second Street entrance. She didn't think much of it until she saw him on the news, then she came down here to report it. She lives in the Beresford and knows everyone, so seeing him there was memorable."

"What time did she see him?"

"Quarter to nine."

Cordova swallows. The medical examiner put David Morrow's time of death between 8:30 and 9:30 p.m. Then he remembers something. "You can't get to the Morrows' apartment from Eighty-Second Street; you have to use the entrance off Central Park West. The building has some crazy design to help ensure privacy for its residents, so each lobby leads to only a few apartments. I went over all of this with the building's super and the head of security."

"I talked to the witness myself. She swears it was him. She picked Declan right out from that photo we have in the lobby too."

This just keeps getting worse. "Want me to get over there and check the cameras?"

"I had Lomax call the building's security chief," Daniels says. "The camera at that entrance has been down for about three weeks. Vandalized. There's no footage."

Both men go quiet for a very long time. Cordova knows where this conversation is heading—Declan's blood was found on scene, the murder weapon came from his apartment and had his prints on it, Denise Morrow named him in the 911 call and claimed he was in her apartment, the book she's writing about him gives him motive, and now there's an unrelated witness, which is possibly the most damning item because this woman has no skin in the game. Cordova runs his hand through what's left of his thinning hair. "What do you want me to do?"

"If you bring him in, we can do this quietly. Get him on the record with his union rep and ADA Saffi. Let Carmen decide if she wants to pursue charges."

"Can you keep Harrison out of it?"

Daniels doesn't reply.

"Look, Harrison gets wind of it, he'll leak it to the press. You know he will. The press gets this, and Declan's career is over. It won't matter how it plays out."

Daniels says, after a long moment, "Maybe it's time for that too."

"I'll call you back."

"I don't hear from you within an hour, I'm sending someone else to pick him up. I'm not risking any more blowback."

It will take him at least five hours to get to the city. "Understood."

The moment Daniels hangs up, Cordova dials Declan. He gets in his car, half expecting the call to roll to voicemail, but his partner picks up on the second ring. "You see Lucero?" he asks. "What did he tell you?"

Cordova exits the prison parking lot and gets on I-87. "Daniels has been holding back information. I'll fill you in when I see you. At the moment, we've got a much bigger problem, something we've got to deal with *right now.*" He tells Declan about the witness.

"She's wrong."

"That all you got to say?"

"What do you want me to say? Either she's mistaken or she's in on it. How well does she know Denise Morrow? Are they friends?"

"You need to cut the bullshit, Dec. This is too much. It's just too much. Take a step back and look at the evidence like a homicide detective, like it's all on someone else—you know we would have hauled them in by now."

"*It wasn't me. I wasn't anywhere near that building. I told you, I was in the park—*"

"Taking a walk. Right. Where the hell were you really? No more bullshit, Dec. They want me to bring you in and if I do, there's a good chance you're not leaving this time. Not on your own."

Seconds tick by. Then: "*I was at the Eighty-First Street subway station, the one under the museum. On the platform.*"

"That station's not even open that late," Cordova fires back. "Why would you..." Then it clicks. He gets it. Every cop on the force knows about that station and can rattle off a list of officers who ended their lives there.

End of watch. Nobody ever calls it *suicide.* It's *end of watch.*

Cordova's gut twists in a knot. He wants to pull off the highway, but he can't stop. He has to get back to the city. He flicks on his flashers and speeds up. "Christ, Declan. Why?"

Declan doesn't answer that. He doesn't say anything.

Cordova checks the dash clock. "I'm five hours out. I'll call the LT back and tell him I'm bringing you in myself. Tonight. The moment I get back to the city. This is what I want *you* to do: Go to my apartment. Stay there. Don't go to your place. Nothing public. We don't want to risk Harrison sending some-one for you or Hoffman trying to get a photo op of you on a perp walk. Go straight to my apartment and wait for me. Just keep your head down until I get back."

Declan still says nothing.

"You still there?"

"Do what you gotta do, Jarod."

When Declan hangs up, Cordova beats both fists on his steering wheel.

This kid *wants* to go down.

CHAPTER FORTY-ONE

DECLAN REMOVES THE BATTERY and SIM card from his phone. Satisfied it can no longer be traced, he slips the various pieces into his pocket.

He spent the day on a bench in Central Park with a clear view of the Beresford building across Central Park West. He watched the joggers and the mothers, fathers, and various nannies pushing strollers. He watched the groundskeepers come and go like little elves, trimming trees and flowers, mowing, edging, making bits of litter disappear. He wondered how many times Ruben "Lucky" Lucero had walked by this very bench. That fucker—he wasn't so lucky anymore. And he wondered how many times Maggie Marshall had walked past here, how many times she had safely crossed the park until that one day she didn't.

Daniels has been holding back information.

No shit.

Daniels.

And Roy Harrison.

And Cordova too, for that matter.

They're all holding pieces of the truth, but not one of them is willing to step up. Nope. They'd rather throw him under the bus.

Ain't that how it's always been, boy? You and me, we're nothing but garbage to them. Something to be left on the curb and forgotten.

"Fuck you, Pop," Declan mutters softly. "Don't you ever compare me to you."

You think we're different? We ain't no different. Work hard. Do what's right. Get shit on. Work harder. Get shit on again. It's all good if you keep your mouth shut and do what you're told, but the second you try to get up, a thousand boots are on your back putting you in your place. That Lucero fella was a twisted fuck; he got what he had coming. You saw him about to get off, you felt those boots on your back, you didn't let them hold you down. Nope. Not my boy. You shook them off. You put that dog down. You ask me, he got off easy. In my day we woulda tied him behind a car and dragged his ass around the neighborhood until all his nastiness was nothing but a stain on the pavement. But you got him your way—ain't nothing wrong with that. Maybe a little weak in execution, but you still got him. Good for you.

Declan looks down at his hands. His fists are clenched so tight, his nails are digging into his palms. Rather than release them, he squeezes tighter, hoping the pain will shut down his father's voice. It does not.

You ask me, the way you took me out showed more balls. Hell, to pull that off? At seven? Goddamn, boy. That's when I knew I raised you right. I raised you strong.

"You beat the hell out of me."

I made you a man! I was thirteen before I stood up to my old man. You were seven! Fifty pounds soaking wet. Maybe that's why I wasn't ready for it. Didn't see you coming. Another four or five years, hell yeah, I'd be watching, but not when you were seven. No way. I didn't figure it out until the moment I slipped off that girder. I was in the air, on my way to the pavement, and that's when it hit me. What was it you put in my coffee? Rat poison? Strychnine? No, that's not right. They would have caught that. What was it again?

"Benadryl."

Yeah, the same shit your mama slipped you when she couldn't get you to sleep. Benadryl. I felt nothing. Not a damn thing. Not at first. Up on that building. Walking around. Doing what needed doing. I was maybe an hour into my shift, two-thirds through that thermos of coffee, when the Benadryl kicked in. Not in a bad way; more a warm-blanket kinda way, like slipping-into-a-nice-tub-of-water kinda way. I shoulda known something was wrong, but that's the beauty of a drug like that. It dulls all the senses, numbs you. There's no anxiety, worry, or fear — all the things that'd kept me alive on those girders day after god-awful day slowly dimmed. Dimmed so slow, I didn't notice them go. And with them went my coordination, my balance... when I took that last step, when I realized my foot had missed the edge of the girder and I tumbled, even then, there was no fear. I suppose that ain't what you want to hear, is it, boy? I'm guessing you want to believe I went out in a bad way, but it just wasn't like that. You know what my last thought was? What went through my head when I realized what you'd done? It was pride. It was pride in my boy. I knew in those last few seconds you'd get through the shit of this world just fine. I knew I'd put that in you. My boy, who don't let nobody push him around. Not even me.

Declan unclenches his fists, studies the red marks on his palms, then squeezes them again. Tighter. As tight as he can. He wants the pain. He needs it. All those broken bones. The cuts. The bruises. He needs to remember every ounce of pain his father inflicted on him.

Without me, think you could do the things you do? Think you'd have it in you? Not a chance. I made you.

"Yeah, well, Pop, you're gonna love what comes next."

Declan stands, stretches, feels the blood course through every inch of his body. He exits the park and crosses the street, heading for the Beresford building, the night thick all around him. He's never felt so alive.

CHAPTER FORTY-TWO

DECLAN REMEMBERS THE dog walker. He caught only a glimpse of her, an older woman bundled in a thick coat tugging some little kick-me dog of indeterminate breed. He knew it was probably some expensive purebred that cost more than some cars, but Declan didn't know dogs. She'd come around the corner and stood in front of the Beresford. He noticed her but didn't think she noticed him; clearly, he'd been wrong about that. Not that it matters. None of it will matter much longer.

He stops at the edge of Central Park West, glances up at the Beresford, and takes it all in. Twenty-two stories with separate entrances for what's basically three buildings pressed together. Declan knows of no other building like it in New York. Or anywhere, actually.

To access the Morrows' apartment, you have to go through the entrance on Central Park West, then take the elevator up to the tower. There's no other way to reach it.

It's a beautiful design.

Designed for privacy.

Designed for the elite.

From where he stands, Declan can see the Central Park West entrance, but when he starts walking, he doesn't go that way. He passes right by the spot the woman with the dog had been; he half expects to see her again but does not. He goes into the building through the service entrance on Eighty-Second and immediately looks at the camera. When he disabled it a few weeks back, he didn't just disconnect the wire—he clipped the wire at the base of the camera and again at the spot where it vanished in the wall. This wasn't something that could be repaired; it needs to be replaced, and that still hasn't happened. There's no doorman at this entrance, another plus for those owners so concerned about their personal security and privacy that they choose to have no one watching their regular comings and goings. And a bonus for Declan, who also values privacy, who also doesn't want to be watched.

He takes the service elevator to the fourth floor. The doors open on a dingy hallway lit by bare bulbs hanging from the ceiling. The narrow space is filled with cobwebs and discarded furniture from an era long gone, all thick with dust. This hall is one of many in the bowels of the Beresford that don't appear on the blueprints filed with the New York City building inspector. They were added after permits were issued and were originally meant for servants and household staff to use so they could navigate the building unseen. Cross from section to section unseen. In a building designed for the elite, designed for privacy, the last thing residents wanted to see in the gilded halls they traveled was a maid hauling groceries or a butler carrying a bundle of laundered shirts. That was all best left to the dark.

Declan stops at a door about two-thirds of the way down the narrow hall. On this side, the door is clearly marked—EXIT painted in faded red letters. Declan presses the weighted latch and steps through, and on that side, there's no sign; the door vanishes in the intricate woodwork of the tenant foyer of the fourth floor. Like the lobby, this space is deserted. There's only one apartment off the foyer, and it's quiet. Declan steps over to the tenant elevator opposite the hidden door and presses the button. When the elevator arrives, he enters and hits the button that will take him to the Morrows' tower apartment.

To Denise Morrow's apartment.

The last time he was here, the vestibule off the elevator was filled with half of New York's Finest, but now the space is empty and silent. The ding of the elevator closing sounds like a trumpet blast to him.

The lock on the Morrow door has been replaced with a beefier model, but Declan makes quick work of it. He grew up picking far harder locks. He slips inside the dark apartment and eases the door shut at his back. The LED on the alarm panel is green. Disarmed.

Declan takes out his gun.

He's halfway down the entry hall when he feels eyes on him. He turns and spots Denise Morrow's cat hovering in the shadows a few paces behind him, his bright green eyes shimmering in the dark. What is his name? Quincy? Quinton? Quimby. That's it.

The cat rockets past him, a blur of fur and a jingle of tags, and stops at the place where David Morrow's body was. The cat pads back several more steps, then looks up at Declan like he's showing it all to him. The body is long gone; the tiles have been scrubbed. No sign of what happened. Yet Declan still feels the dead man in the air. Feels like he is stepping over a body when he walks past that spot. He goes through the kitchen to the main bedroom.

The door is open, and Denise Morrow is barely visible in the faint moonlight. She's lying atop the large bed, naked save for a white satin sheet that doesn't cover her legs; looks like she kicked it aside to feel the chilled air on her skin.

Declan's grip tightens on his gun as he steps closer to the bed.

The floor creaks.

Denise Morrow's eyes flutter open, and she lets out a soft gasp at the sight of him. She sits up, clutching the sheet against her chest. "You shouldn't be here," she whispers.

"You shouldn't have gone off script," he tells her, setting his gun on the nightstand.

He sits on the edge of the bed, brushes the hair from her eyes. Declan strokes Denise Morrow's cheek with his thumb and presses his lips to hers.

CHAPTER FORTY-THREE

EVEN WITH THE FLASHERS and siren, it's after eleven by the time Cordova gets back to the city. He doesn't find Declan at his apartment; he doesn't find him at his own apartment either. He probably dialed him two dozen times, and every call went straight to voicemail. Aside from a few of the late-shift cops, the station is deserted. None of the cops there have seen Declan.

Cordova grabs a cup of tar-thick coffee from the machine, drops in front of his computer, and checks the carpool logs. Nothing registered to Declan. He doesn't have a car of his own and hasn't taken out a PD vehicle in more than three weeks. Cordova minimizes that window, opens another, and logs into

Fog Reveal, their mobile phone-tracking software. He keys in Declan's cell number, waits as the machine chugs away, then swears softly when it comes back with *Device offline*.

The coffee tastes like shit, but he needs it. Needs the caffeine. He forces it down and looks up at the crime board.

David Morrow and Mia Gomez silently stare at him. So do Denise Morrow and a handful of others. There are photos of the bodies. Of the various murder weapons. Of the blood smear on the Morrows' door frame.

Declan's blood.

Declan is a hothead, always has been, but a murderer?

Cordova just doesn't see it.

So why is the kid hiding?

Cordova picks up a pencil, taps it on the edge of the desk a few times, then reaches for his phone and dials IT. Despite the late hour, someone answers.

"Barksdale."

"Hey, it's Jarod Cordova from Twenty. I need you to do something for me."

"What's up?"

"Can you pull the CCTV footage for the Eighty-First Street subway station for the night of Friday the tenth between eight and nine?"

"The station under the museum?" Barksdale goes quiet for a moment. "I didn't see anything in the papers. Did we lose another—"

Everyone in the department knows that station.

"No, not this time. I think someone might have been scoping it out, though. Can you call me back with what you find?"

"Yeah. Sure." A slight quiver in his voice.

"Just keep it to yourself, all right? No need to start any rumors."

"You got it."

Cordova didn't want to go there; he knows word will get out now. The blue grapevine is like that. A lot of *You didn't hear it from me, but*...He has no choice, though. Declan is in deep, and proof of him in that station when both David Morrow and Mia Gomez were killed will keep the bracelets off his wrists. If Declan is in the wind, Cordova can use that footage to stall Daniels until his partner turns up.

If he turns up.

Christ. What if Declan is on the platform at the Eighty-First Street station right now? What if he went there earlier? What if that's why he isn't picking up?

He dials the Central Park Precinct and asks when they last patrolled the station.

An hour ago, they say.

Nobody was there, dead or otherwise.

At least there's that, Cordova thinks.

He swallows the rest of the coffee, has to squeeze his eyes shut to do it, then looks back up at the board.

Denise Morrow couldn't have killed either victim, not from across town.

Geller Hoffman had time to kill Mia Gomez.

It's very possible Denise Morrow put him up to it.

Lucero fingered Hoffman for the Maggie Marshall murder. Maybe he also told Denise Morrow about that. Maybe she found proof and used that as leverage on Hoffman: *You kill my husband's lover for me, and this never gets out.*

Could Hoffman have killed David Morrow too?

How far would Geller Hoffman go to keep a secret like that?

Damn far. If it's true and it gets out, his life is over.

If it's true.

So why give his bloody clothes to Denise Morrow and make her wear them?

Three-card monte.

Shuffle the evidence.

Muddy the case.

Declan might just be right about that.

Maybe Declan is right about all of it.

Across the bullpen, Lieutenant Daniels's office is dark. The door's closed.

If Lucero told Daniels about Hoffman, why didn't Daniels tell him or Declan? Lucero was their case.

Investigating the investigation is Harrison's case. IAU's case.

Cordova grabs a sheet of paper and scribbles out a possible timeline:

Lucero tells Denise Morrow about Geller Hoffman.

Denise Morrow tells Harrison.

Harrison tells her to call Daniels, gives her the lieutenant's personal cell number.

Daniels drives up to Dannemora to talk to Lucero himself.

He returns and has every file related to the Lucero investigation brought to his office.

Those files aren't there anymore.

Cordova is in the LT's office all the time. They're gone.

That means either he didn't find anything worth pursuing and he put it all back—or he found something worth pursuing, something so damning that he had everything moved to someplace more private.

Private like IAU.

Cordova and Daniels go back nearly sixteen years. If Daniels found something, he'd tell him, right?

Right?

Maybe not if it implicated Declan. IAU wouldn't let him. But how would a tip on Geller Hoffman be tied to Declan?

Then it clicks, and the second it does, Cordova wants the thought out of his head. Wants it gone. But it digs in its claws. *What if Declan heard about Hoffman too? What if he uncovered something that proved it was true after they put away Lucero? What if Declan buried it? What if he learned they'd put away the wrong man?*

That might explain why his partner was standing on that subway platform.

Guilt.

It would explain why Daniels has gone quiet, why he's working with IAU. As LT, he ran point on that case. He was just as responsible for putting away Lucero as Cordova and Declan.

Cordova scratches his temple. Could Geller Hoffman have killed Maggie Marshall?

Cordova can't picture it. Not the man he knew from court, from the press.

But Hoffman has the bloody clothes. The murder weapon. All evidence points at him for Gomez and more.

Cordova looks at the photo of Mia Gomez after they pulled her from the dumpster, her body ravaged by stab wounds. If Geller Hoffman killed her... *if he did that...*

Could the man who did *that* kill Maggie Marshall?

Yes.

Cordova needs to talk to Hoffman. Tonight. Now.

Because there's another angle to this. If Daniels put the pieces together with IAU, there's a very good chance he and Harrison have teamed up to put it all on Declan.

Declan keeps insisting he's being framed.

Maybe he's right about that too.

CHAPTER FORTY-FOUR

IT'S A LITTLE after midnight when Cordova steps through the automatic doors of Central Park Tower. Two security guards are on duty. He shows them his badge, tells them he's there to see Geller Hoffman, and adds that if either calls up to warn the attorney, he'll bring them up on interference charges. Then he feels like an ass because when he gets to the elevator, he has to ask them to give him access to the eightieth floor because he doesn't have a key card and the damn thing won't move without one. Cordova tips an imaginary hat when the elevator doors finally close between them with a soft *swoosh*.

The lobby is all glass, marble, modern furniture, and strategic up-lighting, and the eightieth floor is no different. There's a small sitting area off the elevator, mirrors on the walls, and a striking view of the city through the floor-to-ceiling windows.

Defending the city's worst criminals clearly pays well.

Hoffman's apartment is at the end of the hall, flanked by two others. The crime scene tape placed there the day they found the knife above Hoffman's car in the garage is long gone. ADA Saffi never did get a special master appointed. When the prints and knife came back as Declan's, when the shit hit the fan and the case fell apart, she dropped it, no doubt on orders from higher up.

The last time Cordova was here, he got no farther than this hallway.

This time he knocks on Hoffman's door.

He knocks loud.

When that brings nobody to the door, he presses the doorbell a few times.

When that doesn't work, he tries the knob and finds it unlocked.

He gives it a twist and pushes the door open slightly. An alarm panel on the left issues a soft chirp but doesn't sound. The alarm isn't activated.

"NYPD!" Cordova calls out. "Geller Hoffman, this is Detective Jarod Cordova. Are you home?" As far as he knows, Hoffman is unmarried and lives alone.

Cordova opens the door a little wider and steps into the foyer. "Geller Hoffman? NYPD."

There is no response.

No doubt this is a safe building, but it seems odd for anyone in New York to leave their door unlocked overnight.

Cordova spots a set of keys in a silver bowl on a narrow side table. The BMW key fob is there too. An uneasy feeling comes over him at the sight of those. He has no real frame of reference, having never stepped foot in this apartment before, and at a glance, nothing appears out of place or disturbed, yet something feels off.

Cordova quietly takes the gun on his hip out of its holster. "Geller Hoffman! This is Jarod Cordova with NYPD. Are you home? I'm coming in!"

His voice echoes off the marble and fades.

No response comes.

Cordova walks farther into the apartment, realizing he didn't tell a soul he was heading here. If Hoffman barrels out of a back room and unloads on him, nobody will come to his rescue. They'll find his body in a dumpster before the night is over, no different than Mia Gomez. He tries to shake that thought off but manages only to tamp it down.

The living room is dark save for the city lights filtering in through the wall of windows. They create an eerie glow on Hoffman's white furniture, on the artwork on the walls, a series of abstracts that might have cost a million each or might be the pictures that came with the frames—Cordova has no idea.

"Geller Hoffman!" he calls again, and again receives no response.

The living room is open to the kitchen, separated only by a giant island of white marble surrounded by barstools. A cutting board, a loaf of bread, a jar of mayonnaise, and bits of lunch meat litter the countertop. Not the kinds of things you leave out unless you're nearby.

A prickle runs across the back of Cordova's neck, goes down his spine.

Something is very wrong here.

Cordova wants to believe the man made himself a sandwich, took an Ambien, and is passed out somewhere in the apartment, but his decades on the job tell him otherwise. There is a stillness to the apartment you don't find when someone is there.

Beyond the kitchen and expansive living room is a wide hall. Gun raised, finger on the trigger guard, Cordova goes down the hall, passing a luxuriously appointed office with floor-to-ceiling dark wood bookcases on two walls and an oversize window behind the desk offering sprawling views of the city. An open briefcase rests on the desk next to a MacBook, the screen alive with images of fish swimming lazily in blue water. Opposite the office, on the other side of the hall, is a guest room and a bath. The main bedroom is at the end of the hall, its double doors open. The faint glow of a flickering candle dances across the wall.

"Hoffman! This is NYPD! Show yourself!" Cordova calls, knowing it will do no good.

The king-size bed is unmade, the sheets a rumpled mess at the foot of it. The candle burns in a glass jar on one of the nightstands, about half gone.

Cordova finds Geller Hoffman in the spacious walk-in closet off a bathroom large enough to be a basketball team's locker room.

Hoffman is on the floor, his pants and underwear around his ankles, one hand around his erect penis. Dead. A leather belt is looped around his neck and secured to a clothing rod above his head. Hoffman's open eyes, lined with the deep red of burst vessels, are bulging so far out of his skull, they look like they might explode. His skin is bluish purple from oxygen deprivation — asphyxiation.

Autoerotic asphyxiation.

That's the official term.

Cordova saw it once before, about twelve years ago, a junkie they'd pulled out from behind a dry cleaner on Eightieth. Lack of oxygen at the moment of ejaculation was supposed to heighten the experience. Downtown, they called it gasping. Declan had once joked it was all good until it killed you.

Cordova gently pinches the sleeve above Hoffman's free hand, raises it a few inches, and lets it drop. Rigor mortis has only just begun to set in, meaning Hoffman has been dead less than two hours. The ME will be able to narrow that window further. Cordova holsters his gun and kneels to get a better look.

Scattered around Geller Hoffman's lifeless body are pictures of young girls. Some were torn from the pages of magazines; others came from a photo printer. Still others are Polaroids. Polaroids similar, if not identical, to the ones they found in Ruben Lucero's apartment years back. Candid shots, some taken at a distance, others from up close. Others from too close — these girls, these children, clearly aware they were being photographed in ways they shouldn't be. There's a shoebox off to the side filled with more of the same. Probably twice the number of pictures they found at Lucero's.

That is a problem.

That is a *big* problem.

Cordova takes out his phone; his fingers hover over the keypad. He needs to call Daniels, but what the hell will he tell him?

This long night just got longer.

CHAPTER FORTY-FIVE

DECLAN WAKES TO the warmth of morning sunlight stream-ing through the large windows of Denise Morrow's bedroom. He rolls to his side, reaches for her, and finds she's no longer in bed. The sheets are still warm, though. She hasn't been gone long.

Denise's cat, Quimby, is sitting on her pillow, licking a paw and eyeing him curiously.

"Where'd your mama go?" Declan mutters. "Bathroom?"

The cat tilts his head, seems to consider that, then goes back to licking his paw. His collar jingles with tags, trinkets, and who knows what else with every movement.

Declan gives Denise a few minutes, and when she doesn't come back, he climbs out of bed and heads for the bathroom, scooping his underwear off the floor on the way. He does his business, uses her toothbrush, splashes some water on his face and through his hair, then combs his hair back with his fingers. When satisfied, he wanders through the large apartment. He finds Denise in the kitchen.

Her back is turned, so she doesn't see him at first. She's wearing nothing but his blue oxford shirt and looks so incredibly sexy, it takes every ounce of willpower he has not to walk up behind her, wrap his arms around her, and take her right there on the countertop. He can't, though. They have too much to discuss, and the clock is ticking.

"It was only supposed to be your husband and Mia Gomez," he says, his voice low.

Denise doesn't turn around. She's frying bacon in a pan with one hand while stirring shredded cheese into scrambled eggs with the other. All of it sizzles, pops, and smells delicious. "No such thing as two-card monte," she tells him. "You taught me that."

Declan steps past her to the coffee machine, kissing the back of her neck as he goes. She has this automated doohickey, the kind of machine you find in a high-end restaurant. He retrieves a mug from a hook under the counter, sets it on the machine's tray, then scrolls through the options on the touch screen. He selects cappuccino and presses the brew button. A moment later, frothy milk steams out, followed by vanilla-scented coffee from freshly ground beans.

"When we go to Belize, I don't mind leaving everything else behind, but not this coffee maker. The coffee maker is coming with us. The rest doesn't matter as long as we have freedom, palm trees, and this coffee maker." He slides the mug off the silver tray, brings it to his lips.

"It's a coffee maker, Declan. We'll order a new one."

"This exact model."

She rolls her eyes. "If you must. That complicated thing was David's." She pushes the bacon around the pan, lowers the flame. "All I need is a burr grinder, a French press, and Quimby."

The cat comes jingling into the kitchen at the sound of his name. She abandons the range, scoops him up, and kisses the top of his head. "I could never leave you, my boy. Never ever."

Declan sips the cappuccino. "You sure you can bring cats to foreign countries? There are probably strict entry requirements. Papers to be filed. Doesn't that seem unnecessarily messy?"

Denise gives him a calm, dark look. "I have it handled. I'm not going anywhere Quimby can't go. I could be convinced to leave you behind, though."

There is a flash of time during which Declan thinks she might be serious, that this whole thing might be closer to the edge than he realizes. That storm in her gaze. Her cool, level tone. It's gone just as soon as it comes, and she laughs.

"Oh my God, your face. Lighten up, Declan. I would never leave either of my boys behind. Here, eat some breakfast."

He shakes his head and changes the subject. "Did Hoffman put up much of a fight?"

Her shoulders bounce in a dismissive shrug. "Not really. No more than I expected."

She takes two plates from the cabinet above her head and

divides the food between them, then slides one of the plates with a fork across the counter to Declan.

"Can you do that again?"

"Do what?"

"Reach for something high up while wearing my shirt. You might be the most beautiful creature I've ever seen."

Denise grins playfully and drags her finger from Declan's chest to the waistband of his underwear. "Down, boy."

"That's not helping."

Standing on her toes, she kisses him. A long, lingering kiss, deep and full. Declan doesn't want it to end. It sets something off in him even stronger than their first kiss all those months ago, back when she cornered him about the Maggie Marshall case. She'd been sly about it; she didn't approach him directly. Instead, she phoned in a tip on another case he'd been working and arranged to meet him at a restaurant downtown, a fancy-schmancy place he'd never go to on his own. A place his coworkers would never go to. She'd told him the tip was bogus. *Would you have come otherwise?* she said. He'd nearly gotten up to leave, but she put her hand on his and said the words that bound him to that chair: *I know Lucero didn't do it. And I know exactly what you did. So how about we chat for a bit?*

It was a veiled threat, and Declan respected that. He respected the fact that she'd come to him rather than taking it to someone else, so he heard her out. What she said scared the piss out of him because he knew it would unravel his life, but he couldn't walk away from her. He'd never been one to believe in fate, destiny, or any of that bullshit, but he knew when he was falling for someone, and in the weeks that followed, he fell for Denise Morrow hard. Telling himself not to only made him want her more. It started with talk of Maggie Marshall, what she had learned. That evolved into talk about him, his past, his upbringing, his father. It wasn't until she opened up to him about her marital problems that he knew she was falling for him too. She was a strong, proud woman—the fact that her husband was cheating on her was not something she shared lightly. As far as Declan knew, she hadn't told anyone else. Except Geller Hoffman. She'd told him only because Hoffman handled her finances and she needed his legal advice. She'd had no idea Hoffman had feelings for her, not at first. Hoffman made that clear later when he jokingly told her that even with the prenup, the only way for her to make a clean break from David was to kill him. It was a joke until it wasn't. When Denise told Declan what the attorney had proposed, what he was willing to do for her, Declan knew that was their chance to be together. *Let him*, Declan told Denise. *Let him do it and we'll use it. Here's how...*

And Declan explained it to her.

Three-card monte.

One of the few good things his piece-of-shit father had taught him.

He knew it would end his career, but that was over anyway. Once IAU got wind of what he'd done, they wouldn't let up. Not Harrison, no way. Didn't matter what Declan did or didn't do after that or what he told them. So they used that too. All of it. *I'll help you build a case against the city if you give me half*, he told her one night after they made love. *I don't need the money*, she replied, nuzzling against him. *You can have all of it.* Oh, man, and then the smile on her face when she finally said, *This could work.*

And it is working.

One hundred million dollars.

They'll be in Belize long before anyone figures it out. If anyone ever figures it out, and Declan doubts anyone will. Hell, when the truth comes out in that book of hers, *the real truth*, there's a good chance he'll be able to file a lawsuit of his own. Double down and come back like some fallen hero.

When the kiss ends, Declan brushes the tip of Denise's nose with his. "I would have done it for you. You know that, right?"

She slips onto a chair at the counter, crosses her slender legs, and nibbles on a piece of bacon. "Cook breakfast?"

"Hoffman."

Denise shrugs. "Too many eyes on you. This was better."

Maybe it was. Maybe it wasn't. A building like Hoffman's probably had more cameras than an episode of *Survivor*. No way Declan could have gone in and out unseen. Denise, though—she was Hoffman's friend, a client. Anyone questions her, and it will be easy enough to explain why she stopped by. They'll deal with that when they need to. There's a more pressing issue now. "If he's dead, what happens with the lawsuit?"

"They'll settle. They always settle. One of Geller's associates will take over and work out the details. I'm not worried." She grabs a towel from the counter and dabs the corner of her mouth. The words *I fell asleep beside the kitchen sink. I feel completely drained now* are printed on the fabric. Denise loves her puns.

Declan can't exactly walk into Hoffman's offices and demand an update; he'll have to take her word on that. He trusts her. Besides, he can fuck her six ways to Sunday if she tries to double-cross him. No reason to believe she would. Like she said, she doesn't need the money.

Declan picks up his fork and spears some eggs. They're delicious. "Cordova drove up to Dannemora yesterday to see Lucero."

She takes a sip of his coffee. "I know. Lucero called me after. Can't beat the timing. I bet your partner's head is about to explode. Do you think he confronted your lieutenant yet?"

Declan isn't sure, and with his phone in pieces, Cordova can't call and tell him. Before he can respond, there is a loud knock on Denise's door, followed by a voice they both recognize.

"NYPD!"

It's Cordova.

CHAPTER FORTY-SIX

DENISE'S WIDE EYES lock with Declan's for the briefest of seconds, then she grabs his breakfast, dumps his food on top of her own, and stashes his plate and fork in the dishwasher. "Get in the bedroom. Go out on the terrace if you have to."

"NYPD, Mrs. Morrow! We know you're home. Open the door!"

Declan scrambles through the apartment to the bedroom, closes the door, then opens it again. Cordova's sharp; he'll expect Denise to be here alone. If Declan closes that door, his partner will pick up on it, because why close the door if you're alone? He's about to open the terrace door when he sees the alarm sensor in the upper left corner. He knows the alarm isn't on, but if he opens that door, it will chirp. Cordova might pick up on that too. Looking around, he realizes there's no place to go. If they're executing some kind of search warrant, he's screwed. He and Denise both are.

At the opposite end of the apartment, the alarm chirps as Denise opens the front door. Did it do that when he came in last night? He can't remember. Declan presses his back against the wall and doesn't make a sound.

"Detective," Denise says in a voice so calm, Declan wonders if she's on some medication he doesn't know about, because who can do that? His heart is pounding so loud, it feels like it's rattling the pictures on the walls. How the hell can she stay calm? He loves it, though. Every second.

"You remember Carmen Saffi from the ADA's office," Cordova says. "May we come in?"

Denise hesitates, but only for a moment. "I'm not sure that's a good idea," she tells them. "Maybe I should call Geller."

Oh, that's good, Declan thinks. *She's good. Make them say it. As far as you know, Hoffman is still alive.*

"That's why we're here," Saffi says. "Geller Hoffman is dead."

Bingo.

Declan hears a soft gasp and can picture the look on Denise's face, a mix of surprise and horror. Maybe her hand is over her mouth. Maybe she'll work in a swoon. Nah, she won't oversell it. She'll give them just enough.

"Oh my God," she finally says with a hitch in her voice. "Yes, come in. Come in." Then: "Do you mind if I put on some clothes?"

"Please, by all means," Saffi tells her.

Declan hears the front door close, then Denise's fast-approaching footsteps. In the bedroom, she partially closes the door and calls out to them, "What happened?"

That's good too, because Police 101 says if suspects don't ask how someone died, they already know.

Although Denise is only a few feet from Declan, she does nothing to acknowledge his presence as she strips out of his shirt and slips into a pair of jeans and a sweater she finds on a chair in the corner of the room. Declan realizes his clothes are still piled on the floor. Denise sees them too and with a swift kick sends them under the bed. She's back out in the living room a moment later. Saffi says, "He committed suicide."

"Suicide?" Denise repeats, her voice edged with shock.

"*Accidental* suicide," Cordova adds.

Then they tell her.

Cordova explains how he found him. In the closet. Pants down. Belt around his neck.

He doesn't hold anything back; he tells her everything, even the parts Declan wouldn't have shared had their roles been reversed. The fact that Cordova mentions the photographs means they don't suspect her, and why would they? How could she possibly be responsible? Hoffman was a small guy, but Denise is small too. No way she could force someone to do something like that, right? Honestly, Declan has no idea how she did it, and he can't wait to hear. He wishes she'd filmed it. He would have loved to watch that pretentious prick go out like that.

When Cordova and Saffi finish, Denise is crying. The tears turn into sobs. She manages to get out, "It's finally over. Finally..." Then she's crying again.

"Maybe you should sit down," Saffi says.

Declan doesn't have to see her to know that she does. When he closes his eyes, he can picture the entire scene: Denise dropping into a chair, Cordova standing there looking for a way out—he hates it when women cry. Saffi has her hand on Denise's shoulder or maybe she's even hugging her. Saffi is tough as nails, but she can turn on the empathy. Dangerous waters, because she also knows how to use it. More than once, she got a perp to confess simply by switching from Lawyer Saffi to Friend Saffi. Hell, she's better at it than half the detectives Declan knows. All part of the game. When Saffi says, "Finally over? How do you mean?" Declan feels every muscle in his body tense. He has to remind himself Denise is good too. Denise is better.

Denise sniffles. "Geller Hoffman was blackmailing me."

CHAPTER FORTY-SEVEN

"BLACKMAILING YOU HOW?" Cordova's voice sounds raw. Declan doubts he got much sleep, if any, last night, but he's never known that to slow his partner down or cloud his judgment. Like Saffi, Cordova is a machine.

Denise is good, he tells himself again. *Denise is better.*

Better than both of them.

Denise speaks in a thin, quiet voice that reminds Declan of a wounded animal. "You know I'm writing a book about Maggie Marshall, right?" she begins. "Early on in the process, I visited Ruben Lucero in prison. I went several times." She sniffles again. "It was important to me to get his side of things. With a book like this, it's best to have all sides so readers can make their own decisions. From our first meeting, he insisted he was innocent. I didn't believe him. Who would, right? Then he told me the police fabricated the case against him." She pauses for a second. "He said your partner planted evidence." Declan can picture her looking right at Cordova. "Lucero said Detective Shaw took a book from Maggie Marshall's backpack in evidence and placed it in his apartment. He admitted to having all the other books you found, all those souvenirs, but not that one. He swore it was planted."

"What about the pictures?" Saffi asks.

Several seconds pass. Declan wishes he could see her, playing them as effortlessly as Giancarlo Stanton sends a baseball over the fence at Yankee Stadium.

"He told me the pictures weren't his either. He didn't know where they came from. Lucero insisted he saw another man following Maggie that day in the park. Every time I spoke to him, he drove that point home. 'Why aren't the police looking for him? They've got to have DNA, right? Did they check all the cameras? He couldn't have dodged all of them. You gotta believe me, I didn't touch that girl! It was him.'"

"The other guy," Saffi says in a quiet voice.

"I didn't believe him either," Denise admits. "My first thought was somebody like him would say anything to save his own skin. Nobody locked up at Dannemora is really guilty, right? Then..." Her voice trails off.

Saffi prompts her. "Then what?"

Denise says, "I was on my fifth visit to Dannemora, maybe ten minutes into a conversation with Lucero, when Geller called me." She pauses. "My marriage with David was on life support. I suspected David might be having an affair, and I'd confided in Geller. He'd had David followed and confirmed it.

He said her name was Mia. He offered to show me pictures, said he'd caught them...you know. I told him I didn't want to see them. Geller insisted I keep my phone close in case he learned more and needed to reach me. Anyway, that's why I had my phone on while I was talking to Lucero at the prison. When it rang, Geller's photo came up on the screen. Lucero saw it and jumped out of his chair, started shouting, pointing—the guards had to restrain him. When he finally settled down, he told me that was the man he'd seen following Maggie. That was the man who killed her. He didn't know Geller's name, but based on his reaction, I believed him."

Declan expects Cordova or Saffi to push back on that, and when they don't, he realizes why—they already know. Maybe something they found at Hoffman's place. Maybe something Lucero told Cordova at Dannemora.

Cordova says, "Why didn't you take that to us? To the police?"

Denise doesn't miss a beat. Her voice is so low, Declan has to strain to hear her. "Because I think Geller would have killed me. And frankly, after what Lucero told me about planted evidence, how could I trust you? You and your partner seemed just as dirty as Geller."

Saffi asks, "Did Geller Hoffman know that you knew?"

"A few weeks ago, I came home and found Geller in my office, going through my notes. He had pages for the book I was writing all over the desk. He'd logged into my computer, and everything I'd put together with Lucero was there. Geller was just sitting in the dark. He told me it wasn't true, but I could tell it was, I could see it in his eyes."

"How did he get in?"

"He had a key. Whenever David and I went away, he checked on the apartment for us. Fed my cat, that sort of thing."

"He had a key," Cordova repeats. No doubt thinking about the faked forced entry the night David was killed. A key made perfect sense; the bogus lock jimmying did not.

"That night, when I found him there in my office, I was sure he meant to kill me. I panicked. I swore I wouldn't say anything. I told him we went too far back, I'd never do that to him. I told him anything I could to get him to trust me. I—" Her voice breaks. "I told him Lucero was obviously some kind of pedophile and prison was the best place for him. That he'd say anything to get out of there and I wasn't about to stir things up based on the word of some convict. Geller had my book right there, I knew he'd read it. I think that's why he spared me. It didn't contain a word about him. The only damning evidence was against your partner."

"Evidence you got from Harrison?"

"And Lieutenant Daniels. They all know what Declan did—they just can't prove it."

"Did Hoffman believe you?"

"I thought he did. He didn't say another word for weeks. Then he came to the bookstore in Tribeca with...with that bag. He told me...he said he'd killed David's lover and that he had someone in my apartment ready to kill David too, unless I did exactly what he said. If I didn't, he'd make it look like I killed them both in a jealous rage. He forced me to put on his bloody clothes and wear them home under my coat. He said if I did that, we'd both have blood on our hands and he'd know he could trust me." Her voice rises, pleading. "You've got to understand. I knew he was a killer, so he had nothing to lose. On top of Maggie Marshall and God knows how many others, he confessed to killing that woman, Mia Gomez. He didn't seem rattled by it at all. I had no doubt he'd kill David and hurt me and maybe others unless I did exactly what he told me. So I did. *What choice did I have?* If I wanted to stay alive, I had to do what he asked." She starts to sob but reins it in. "When I got home, I found David's body. Geller had him killed anyway. When Geller got there, he told me his partner did it, and they would pin it on me in a heartbeat if I crossed him. He switched the knives, and who knows what other evidence he manipulated. I knew he was the only one who could keep me out of jail."

"The bloody clothes," Saffi says, "they were identical to yours. How did Hoffman know what you would wear to the bookstore?"

Denise gives her the perfect answer. "I have no idea."

Let them prove her wrong.

Silence falls over the three. Cordova finally breaks it. "How do you know Mia Gomez?"

Denise goes quiet for a moment. When she replies, she sounds confused. "Me? I didn't. I only learned her name through Geller."

"Page Six had a photo of her standing near you at the Academy of Art Tribeca Ball."

"At the..." Again, Denise goes quiet. Then she says, "There were a lot of people at that event. Maybe I met her, but I certainly didn't know her. I didn't even know her full name until I saw her on the news when her body was found, *after* what Geller told me at the bookstore, and I connected the dots. By then it was too late for me to do anything. I kept quiet, I had to, to... to stay alive." She sucks in a breath. "Was she at the ball to see David? My God, was she *with* David? How long was the affair going on? I wonder if Geller knew. Maybe he knew the whole time and was just waiting for the right moment to use it. He collected dirt on everyone. How do you think he settled half his cases?"

Saffi says in a low tone, "You should have taken all this to the police."

"You still don't get it," Denise says flatly. "How could I go to the police? Geller's partner was the police."

"Who?"

It comes out on a breath. "Who do you think?"

"Declan Shaw?"

"Your partner didn't frame Lucero to guarantee a conviction. Geller paid him to do it."

Still pressed against the wall in the main bedroom, Declan listens to all of this. It hurts to hear it, but he doesn't move. She's telling the story exactly like they discussed.

Three-card monte.

If the evidence isn't clear, no way you win at trial, and this case is a muddy mess. The evidence is so convoluted, there's zero chance of prosecution. There's something else, something he's sure Cordova or Saffi will realize in the car on the way back to the precinct. They didn't Mirandize her. Not for one second of that.

In the hands of the right attorney—and he has no doubt Hoffman's successor will be the best available—none of what Denise said will be admissible.

CHAPTER FORTY-EIGHT

Excerpt from *The Taking of Maggie Marshall* by Denise Morrow

THE EVIDENCE LOCKUP for the NYPD's Twentieth Precinct is located in the basement of 120 West Eighty-Second Street. It's accessible by a single elevator and emergency stairs. It's a quiet dungeon in the bowels of the castle. As a civilian, I normally wouldn't be permitted to visit the place, and I'm not going to lie to you — I had to grease a few palms to get down there. Considering the part police corruption played in Maggie's story, I suppose it was wrong of me to capitalize on it. But this wasn't a "When in Rome" scenario. I didn't take it lightly. I had to get down there if I wanted to learn the truth, and sometimes the commission of a minor infraction is necessary for the greater good.

The evidence cage is manned by a single officer. He or she is stationed behind a cinder-block wall next to a wire-mesh window with a pass-through. The space can be entered only via a magnetically sealed steel door that wouldn't look out of place in a nuclear bunker. The evidence locker screams *secure*—until you get a little closer. I didn't see a single camera inside or out (and yes, I did get inside). You would think that when an officer needs to see evidence, the person in the cage would retrieve it and maybe bring it to a secure space where the officer could view it under the constant watch of a camera. At least, that's how I would set things up. Nobody asked me, though, and whoever was asked came up with a process more appropriate for managing toys at a day care than handling life-changing evidence at a police facility. This is how it works:

A police officer who wishes to review evidence is given a clipboard on which to provide the case number, his or her badge number, his or her signature, and the date. The attending officer locates the box housing the evidence in the inventory database and enters that information on the clipboard next to the requesting officer's information; the location is usually something like *box 16, shelf 2, row 4.* But rather than that officer fetching the box, the requesting officer is granted access to the room and permitted to locate and review the box on his or her own. With zero supervision. On any given day, a dozen officers may visit that room. Once they sign that clipboard and enter the "secure" space, there is no way to know what they actually do.

Declan Shaw's signature and badge number appeared on a clipboard sixteen times from the date Lucero was arrested through the conclusion of his trial. The box (number 6 with that case number) containing Maggie Marshall's backpack sits two shelves down from the box containing the books found in Lucero's apartment (number 2 with the same case number). An object could be moved from one to the other in seconds and nobody would be the wiser. Declan Shaw could have done that, but he didn't. The book appears in photographs of Lucero's apartment. That means it was retrieved from the box and brought to Lucero's place before the CSU techs arrived to document the scene.

Here's where things become problematic.

There's no record of Declan Shaw visiting the evidence lockup during that time frame. There is one signature during that window, and that signature belongs to Declan Shaw's supervisor, Lieutenant Marcus Daniels. Lieutenant Daniels was questioned by IAU but quickly dismissed—the signature in the log did not match his actual signature. It was a clear forgery. The officer on duty the day of this particular visit made a sworn statement to IAU (of which I have a copy) stating he had no recollection of the lieutenant coming to the evidence lockup (something that he did only rarely), but he did recall seeing Detective Shaw. When pressed on how he could be sure, he said Shaw's shirt was torn and when he asked him what happened, Shaw said he'd ripped it chasing a suspect across rooftops.

The only known rooftop chase involving Detective Declan Shaw was the apprehension of Ruben Lucero. That would mean he retrieved the book at some point between Lucero's arrest and when Lucero was brought to the precinct for questioning. Ruben Lucero's arm was broken during that arrest. He was transported to Memorial for treatment and brought to the precinct three hours later. This window offers Declan Shaw ample time, and there is no record of his whereabouts during that period.

Can I prove he took a side trip to evidence before admitting CSU into Lucero's apartment for processing?

No.

No more than IAU can.

Does that mean it didn't happen?

CHAPTER FORTY-NINE

WHEN DECLAN STEPS out of the elevator and into the precinct bullpen, a silence falls over the room. Eyes follow him all the way to his desk.

No sign of Cordova.

He's probably still with ADA Saffi, maybe at her office. After Saffi and Cordova spoke to Denise, they asked her to come in and provide an official statement. She said she would, but only after obtaining new counsel to replace Geller Hoffman. Maybe later today.

Maybe never.

They can't force her, not without charging her, and he seriously doubts Saffi would do that. Denise played it perfectly. Damaged goods. It was all on Hoffman.

And him.

But that is about to change.

When Declan put the battery back in his phone and powered it on, he had nine missed calls from his partner. Three more from the lieutenant. A few others he didn't recognize. An insane number of texts. And he was fairly certain someone was watching Fog Reveal to get his location. The moment his phone pinged the first tower, they knew where he was. That's why he didn't insert the batteries until he was standing on the sidewalk outside his building. He stood there for about a minute, then walked to the precinct.

"Declan." Lieutenant Daniels's voice cuts through the quiet like nails on a chalkboard.

Declan turns to find him standing in the elevator holding the door open, ADA Saffi at his side. No sign of Cordova.

"Lieutenant. I heard you were looking for me."

The expression on his supervisor's face clearly says *No shit*, but he bites his tongue. Instead of chewing Declan out, he nods his head to the left. "Conference room. Right now."

"Should I call my union rep?"

"I already did."

Ten minutes later, they're all sitting around the large conference table, Daniels and Saffi on one side, Declan and his rep on the other. Declan is pretty sure his union rep is wearing the same shirt and tie as last time. The man looks so disheveled that if someone told Declan he'd been sleeping on a bench out in the park, Declan would believe it. Roy Harrison also came down for the party, and in an effort to appear as intimidating as possible, he has opted to stand in front of the door, one hand resting on his service weapon. *What a tool.*

Daniels looks to Saffi, then back to Declan. "Where have you been, Detective? And if you tell me you were out on another walk, I'll cuff you myself."

"I was with a friend."

"That 'friend' will vouch for you if asked?"

"I'm sure she will."

"Why'd you turn your phone off?"

"People kept calling for the wrong reasons. You'd shut yours off too."

Declan's rep slides him a note. In a nearly illegible scrawl are the words *Geller Hoffman is dead.*

Declan does his best to look surprised, then turns to Daniels. "What happened to Hoffman?"

Daniels tells him.

Slumping back in his seat, Declan can only shake his head.

ADA Saffi places her briefcase on the table, clicks it open, raises the lid, and narrows her eyes at Declan. "I'm going to ask you this one time, Detective. Did you kill David Morrow?"

There is no hesitation. "No."

She removes a stack of pages from her briefcase and sets them in front of Declan's union rep. The man flips through and actually surprises Declan when he's able to identify what they are. "These are the results of Detective Shaw's blood test?"

"They are," Saffi says. "Detective Shaw's DNA matches the blood found on the door frame at the Morrow apartment."

Declan says nothing to that. Nothing to say. He knew it would match.

Saffi reaches back into her briefcase. This time she removes a witness statement from a woman named Beverly Marchant. The dog walker.

Saffi taps it with the tip of her manicured finger. "This woman places you at the Beresford building at quarter to nine the night David Morrow was killed."

"She's wrong."

Harrison coughs into his hand. "Bullshit."

Tool. "She's wrong," Declan repeats. "I was nearby, but she's off on the time." He looks to his union rep. "Did you bring it? That thing I sent you?"

His rep fishes around in his battered messenger bag and takes out an equally battered laptop old enough to be part of the Y2K issue. He logs in, locates a video file, and clicks Play, then turns the screen so everyone can watch as the hard drive hums with the strain.

Declan says, "Cordova told me about Mrs. Marchant yesterday, so I spent some time at a few of the area businesses. This footage comes from a Starbucks across the street from the Beresford with a direct line of sight to the building's corner, near the entrance frequented by Mrs. Marchant, according to your statement." He leans closer to the screen. "And, wait for it . . ." A woman comes around the building, tugging the leash of a small white dog. Declan freezes the video. "That is your witness." He presses Play again and freezes it ten seconds later. "And there's me." When he presses Play, the on-screen Declan goes around the corner the woman had just come from and disappears from view.

"That doesn't prove anything." Harrison points at the laptop. "She says you went inside. You can't even see the door on this."

"Unfortunately, that's the only camera facing that way. The door is right there around the corner. I didn't go in. I went around the side of the building and kept going."

"Out on your famous walk, right?" Harrison mutters. "This is meaningless. The time's not even correct. That says six thirty-two."

"The time's right," Declan tells them. "When you visit the Starbucks, ask for Zach, the manager. He'll give you access to their security system. He cleared things with his corporate office while I was there. You'll find they use a top-of-the-line system from a company called Lorex. It pulls the time directly from the internet to ensure it's always accurate. There's no way to change it. I called Lorex to confirm." He points at the screen. "ME has TOD for David Morrow between eight thirty and nine thirty p.m. Your witness saw me at six thirty-two p.m. Two hours too early. When you visit Starbucks, review the next few hours. You'll find she doesn't come back out again until nearly ten p.m. for one final dog walk, and there is no other footage of me near there again, period. She's mistaken on her time. Your witness statement is worthless."

Daniels and Harrison exchange a glance. Saffi's eyes remain locked on Declan. "Where exactly were you between eight thirty and nine thirty that night?"

Declan looks to his union rep, who nods.

He tells them exactly where he was, and they have the same reaction Cordova did when he told him. It's all over their faces.

The museum closes at five thirty. That subway station is a ghost town. Why would you . . . oh.

Isn't that the station where Murphy jumped? Nunez? That fire-fighter last year and the EMT a few months back?

Suicide Station. That's what they call it down at the DA's office. It isn't just the police who know about it.

Saffi's eyes go glossy; the woman actually tears up. Declan shouldn't feel good about that, but he does. It's nice to know somebody gives a shit.

Saffi says, "You could have talked to me. If things are that bad…if you…" Her face twists with concern. "Declan, why?"

He'd told her once about his father. Not about the Benadryl, not what he'd done. He'd told her how his father used to beat him and his mother. How his dad would come home drunk and angry and take out the world's problems on them. How his mother had vanished. The hell of foster care. He told her about everything but the Benadryl. He imagines all of that is flying through her head now; he can see it in her eyes. Declan forces a weak but disarming smile. "You know. Sometimes it's just…it's just too much, but I'm okay."

The room goes quiet for a very long time, the implications hanging over all of them.

Declan finally looks at Daniels and Harrison and says, "I told Cordova where I was. I didn't want word to get out. I'd appreciate it if you didn't say anything."

Daniels swallows. "I can't unring that bell, Detective. At the very least, I'll need to put you on leave and go through the proper channels with an evaluation."

Declan nods solemnly. "Okay."

Harrison's gaze drills into him. He's not buying any of it. "Your word's not enough. Your word isn't shit."

Remaining calm, Declan says, "Cordova pulled the camera

footage from the subway platform. You can too. You'll find I got there a few minutes after eight and I didn't leave until Cordova called me and told me to get to the Beresford."

There's a knock at the door. A uniformed officer sticks his head in, studies the group, and locates Lieutenant Daniels. "Cordova is on six for you. He says it's important."

CHAPTER FIFTY

DANIELS SLIDES THE LANDLINE to the center of the conference table and mashes down the button for line six. "Jarod, I'm here with Harrison, Saffi, Declan, and his rep. You're on speaker."

Cordova shuffles the phone, then says, *"Are you sure you want to do this with..."*

Daniels's eyes shift to Roy Harrison, who raises both palms but says nothing.

Daniels looks at Declan, then at the phone. "No secrets, Detective. I want it all out on the table. Roy Harrison backed a new search warrant with the judge when Saffi submitted it. He's one of the reasons we were able to have a special master assigned so quickly and get into Geller Hoffman's office. He deserves to hear this too."

"*Understood*," Cordova says.

Declan didn't expect that. Why would Harrison help? What did he hope they'd find in Geller Hoffman's office?

"*The special master is going through Hoffman's files marking what we can look at and what we can't*," Cordova says. "*The way she explained it, anything specific to Denise Morrow's defense is off-limits, although I've got a feeling she may no longer need a defense. Declan either, for that matter. We started with Hoffman's safe. This guy's been playing all of us.*"

"Explain."

Cordova says, "*Well, for starters, he's got an opened unit of blood in here. There's no name on the bag, just an ID number, but I bet it will tie back to Declan. It came from Mercy, where Declan said he made regular donations. I'll have the lab run it, but if it's a match to Declan, it will explain how his blood got on the Morrows' door.*"

Declan can feel Harrison's eyes burning into him, but he doesn't look up; his gaze remains fixed on the phone as Cordova continues.

"*He has a file on Declan as thick as my arm. Bank statements. Credit cards. Residential history. Juvenile records, foster care. His full NYPD jacket is here—someone will need to explain how he got that—with every reprimand, psych eval, and note from the time he was a rookie until about six months ago.*"

Declan doesn't look away from the phone, but from the corner of his eye he spots Saffi frowning at both Daniels and Harrison; either of them could have slipped his file to Hoffman.

"*Declan, what size shoe do you wear?*" Cordova asks.

"Eleven."

"You missing any shoes?"

Declan thinks on that for a few seconds. All his shoes are in a pile at the bottom of the closet near his apartment's front door. When he doesn't answer, Cordova goes on.

"Got a pair of men's size eleven Merrell Moab black tennis shoes here in a large zip-lock bag. I don't think he was trying to keep them fresh by wrapping them up. They look like yours."

Harrison smirks. "You know your partner's footwear, Detective?"

"I spend a lot of time with the guy, and I'm paid to notice things; comes with the job. If you can't close your eyes right now and rattle off what the people in that room are wearing, you should take a refresher at cop camp, Roy."

Daniels glances at Harrison, then looks back at the phone. "What else is in there?"

"We got a bag with hair. An empty prescription bottle with Declan's name on it—cholesterol meds. A beer bottle in another bag. If I had to guess, he paid someone to raid Declan's apartment or trash and take anything that could be used as identification at some point."

"That's a leap," Harrison mutters.

"If you have another reason for this man to have these items in his possession, I'm all ears," Cordova replies. *"We also found Mia Gomez's missing cell phone and a burner. Mia's battery is dead, but when we fired up the burner, it contained a single text message sent to Gomez's number. It said 'Meet me,' followed by an address near the alley where she was killed. Time stamp on that was eight oh two p.m., which ties in."*

"Holy hell," Saffi says in a low voice. When she looks at Declan, her eyes are wide. "I'm sorry. I should have believed you when you said someone was setting you up."

The conference-room door slams with a loud bang, and Harrison is gone.

Declan's heart is racing. He knew he'd be vindicated, but it still feels good to finally be there, hear it all out loud. Now it's time to pound in the next nail. He tells Saffi and his union rep, "I want to know how that man got my file. If the two of you can't figure that out, I'll be hiring outside counsel to represent me. You can expect a lawsuit. Nobody deserves to go through what I have."

Daniels raises both hands defensively. "Now, wait a minute—"

"Someone sold my personal information to that asshole. I've been wrecked in the press and here internally. All this bullshit around Lucero and IAU, you can bet Hoffman was behind that too. I'm done being everyone's punching bag."

Saffi leans back in her seat. "Denise Morrow said you were working with Hoffman. Hoffman told her that. He said you were his partner."

Declan snickers. "I'm no lawyer, but that's hearsay, right? Unless you got Hoffman on record with that bullshit, it's meaningless. I've been screaming *setup* from the start of all this, and Cordova just proved it." He jerks a finger toward the door. "My gut says he got my file from Harrison. Here's hoping it wasn't one of you."

On the phone, Cordova clears his throat. *"There's something else."*

Daniels is ready to jump across the table; he's fuming, but he says nothing. Neither does Saffi. Selling an officer's file is career-ending. It could lead to criminal charges.

"You still there?" Cordova asks.

Finally, Daniels says, "Go ahead, Detective."

"*Hoffman also has detailed blueprints for the Beresford. Old. I don't think they came from the Department of Buildings. They might be originals. They're far more detailed than the ones we pulled. Saffi, can you meet me down there?*"

"I'm going too," Declan says. He stares at Daniels defiantly. "*I'm going too.*"

Daniels does not object.

"*Use the Eighty-Second Street entrance,*" Cordova tells them. "*Not the one that takes you to the Morrow apartment—go to the service entrance.*"

CHAPTER FIFTY-ONE

TWENTY MINUTES LATER, Declan and ADA Saffi cross Central Park West toward the Beresford, and he's still fuming. Talking it out with Saffi after they left the precinct just made Declan angrier. All those things in Hoffman's safe were damning, *but his employee file*? He knows that's the kicker, and he plays it up. It's his ticket to making a bunch of problems disappear. He laces his voice with anger as he tells her, "Come on, you know it was either Harrison or Daniels. Who else had access?"

Walking faster, Saffi starts to tick off people on her fingers. "Your lieutenant's boss, your lieutenant's boss's boss, whoever is above them, their assistants, the department shrinks, file clerks, secretaries, janitor with a screwdriver . . . come on, Dec, if you wanted to walk a file out of there, you know you could. Anyone could have pulled it."

"It wasn't just anybody. It was Harrison or Daniels."

"We'll follow the money," Saffi states flatly. "Cordova found more than enough to get Hoffman's financials. Nobody gave him that file out of the goodness of their heart—they got paid. We'll figure it out."

They won't find any money to follow, Declan is sure of that. "I doubt he cut a personal check. Hoffman was many things, but an idiot wasn't one of them."

They stop at the corner, waiting for the light. Both are quiet for a moment, then Declan asks, "What do you think this means for the IAU investigation?"

Saffi is silent for a beat, then kicks at the edge of the sidewalk. "You want my honest opinion?"

Declan nods.

"This is so far off the record that if you repeat it to anyone, I will have you killed. You get me? You don't tell a soul what I'm about to tell you. Not even Cordova."

"It stays between us. I swear."

"If I were you, I'd use this as leverage. If IAU continues to come at you, you file a suit against the department on the stolen employee file. They drop it, you drop it. It's called mutually assured destruction. Both sides have a finger on the nuke button but nobody presses because nobody wants to deal with the consequences. You'll have your shield back untainted, and there's zero chance they'll hold you down in the coming years on rank. Just the opposite—they'll promote you to keep you happy. You've got the department by the short-and-curlies,

Declan. Hell, if this happened to me, I'd be running the DA's office inside of two years or on a beach somewhere."

This is exactly what Denise said would happen.

Declan tries not to smile.

When the light changes, they cross with the crowd, and Saffi says, "I need to prep for the blowback on Hoffman. The way they found him, *what* they found with him. When the press gets wind of all that, my office will get bombarded."

"Do you think Lucero walks on all this?"

Saffi blows out a breath. "Honestly, I don't know. His attorney will file an appeal for sure. Odds are he'll get a new trial, but the evidence against him is still damning. Geller Hoffman gives the defense another suspect, that's reasonable doubt, but it doesn't mean a jury will buy it. It's too early to guess how all this will play out."

When they reach the Beresford's service entrance, Declan opens the door for her and they step inside.

In one corner, a technician is on a ladder repairing the broken security camera. Cordova is sitting in a chair on the far side of the room, a banker's box resting on his lap. His eyes are heavy from lack of sleep but he perks up at the sight of them and motions them over. He sets the box on a small table and removes the lid. "This is everything we pulled from Hoffman's safe."

Both Saffi and Declan know better than to touch anything, but they lean over and study the contents. Declan lets out a soft whistle. "That motherfucker."

Cordova produces a latex glove from his pocket, slips it on his right hand, and removes a large plastic bag containing the shoes he mentioned. He holds them up. "Look familiar?"

Declan's eyes go wide. He lifts his leg and points at the shoe on his foot—it's identical. "We spend so much time on our feet, I burn through shoes. I usually buy a few pairs of these whenever they're on sale. I probably have two or three boxes on the shelf in my closet. He must have snagged them from there." The blood from Mercy is in the box. And his file. Beer bottle in another zip-lock. The bag of hair. A wad of it, like he plucked whatever was on Declan's hairbrush in his bathroom. "What do you think he planned to do with that?"

Cordova shakes his head. "Who knows."

The box also contains one of Declan's shopping lists. The last time he saw it, it was stuck on his fridge with a magnet. "He plan to buy my groceries?"

"I'm thinking he wanted a handwriting sample," Cordova says.

"Jesus."

Saffi takes it all in. She's obviously reeling. "I'm still trying to wrap my head around the fact that Geller Hoffman is a murderer, and not just of Mia Gomez but possibly of young girls. What if Maggie Marshall wasn't the start of all this? What are we going to find when we run Hoffman's DNA against other open cases? Cold cases?" She shakes her head. "As a defense attorney, he knew exactly how the system worked. This box isn't something a first-timer puts together—this is practiced behavior."

Cordova meets her eyes. "I think we've got him for David Morrow too."

Saffi tries not to look at Declan when she replies, but she can't help herself. "He told Denise he had a partner. Are you saying he didn't?"

"He wanted her to think he had someone in her apartment when he made her put on those clothes, but that seems unlikely," Cordova says. "I think he killed Mia Gomez, killed David Morrow right after, then cleaned up, changed, and went to the bookstore. There was no partner. Certainly not a cop." He puts everything back in the box.

"There's zero sign of him on security footage," Saffi points out. "First visual on Hoffman is long after the murder, when the rest of you are already on scene."

"If he came through the Central Park West entrance, correct."

"You said there was no other way to get to the Morrows' apartment."

Cordova calls over to the maintenance man on the ladder. "Hey, how do we get to tower number two from here?"

The man has a new camera in one hand and a wire nut in the other. Without turning, he says, "You can't get there from here. Go back out and around to the Central Park West entrance. No other way to get there."

"You're sure?"

"I've worked here for eleven years. I'm sure."

Cordova thanks him and reaches back into the box. He removes blueprints so old, they look hand-drawn. A path has been marked with a yellow highlighter. "You're gonna love this," he tells Declan and Saffi, then he closes the box, picks it up, puts the blueprints on top, and starts for the service elevator at the far end of the room.

CHAPTER FIFTY-TWO

IN THE SERVICE ELEVATOR, Cordova hands the banker's box to Declan. "Hold this." Then he presses the button for the fourth floor.

When the doors open on the dingy hallway, Saffi looks out at abandoned furniture, bare bulbs hanging from the ceiling, cobwebs and blankets of dust, and promptly sneezes three times.

Declan pretends he's never seen the space before. "What the hell is this?"

He starts to exit the elevator, but Cordova puts his arm out. "There's something I need to show you first." He holds back the elevator door, kneels down, and, using the flashlight on his phone, lights up the floor. There are several footprints in the dust, trails leading to and from the elevator. He reaches a hand back to Declan. "Let me see the shoes."

Declan takes the shoes out of the banker's box and hands them to him.

Cordova flips them upside down so they can all see the tread pattern. "Your shoes are a match for the tracks. I imagine Hoffman figured we'd eventually find this and wanted to be sure it tied back to you, not him."

Saffi leans over Cordova's shoulder to get a better look. "The little bastard must have stuffed something inside to get them to stay on his feet."

Declan thinks of the shoes on his feet now—they're a match too. Cordova and Saffi are looking at the tracks he made last night when he came to visit Denise. But since he told Cordova that he has multiple pairs of the same shoes, he's covered. Another one of Denise's ideas. Making that statement in front of a representative of the court drives it home. If Saffi is questioned, she'll have no choice but to back him. He puts the shoes back in the box and points to a different set of tracks beside the first, even fresher. "Are those you?"

Cordova nods. "It will be difficult to preserve this, so I filmed everything before you got here. Let's try and stay on my tracks, though. Walk single file. Hoffman's dead, but we'll still want CSU to document what they can."

They exit the elevator with their phone flashlights on, the beams playing over the old walls. There is writing everywhere:

DALE WAS HERE, 1935.

SHAKE A LEG!

THE ONLY GOOD RODINGTON IS A DEAD RODINGTON!

HENRY, CLASS OF '41!

Dozens of names and lots of comments, some pleasant, some not. Hundred-year-old graffiti.

Saffi studies an intricate ink drawing of a woman penned on the bare plaster between disintegrating strips of wallpaper before playing her flashlight beam up and down the narrow hallway. "What is all this?"

Cordova holds up the blueprints. "Servants' tunnel. The original building was riddled with them. Far as I can tell, most were absorbed into the apartments—they took a wall down, found the extra space, and incorporated it into the room. Some, though, are still intact. Like this one." He holds a finger up. "Do you feel a breeze?"

Saffi looks around, then nods. "Not much, but yeah."

"These tunnels also serve as ventilation. Heat rises, so it enters the tunnels through vents on each floor and escapes the building through the roof. Maintenance used to close the rooftop vents during the colder months to help retain the heat, but I think that process has been forgotten over the years, and now they're open year-round. The residents all have their own HVAC, so nobody notices. If you listen carefully, you can hear the air move."

Declan has been in these tunnels a dozen times and didn't know that. Where the hell did Cordova learn about it? He's right, though. They all go quiet, and there's a faint whistling sound around them. They're standing in a giant air duct.

Cordova bends down and shines his flashlight beam on the tracks. "See how they're fading? Even with the limited airflow, these tracks will be gone soon. Another week and we wouldn't have found them at all." He straightens. "Try to stick to the right and follow me. We're not going far."

He leads them down the narrow hall to the door with EXIT painted on it in faded red letters. He presses the weighted latch; the door opens, and they enter the fourth-floor foyer. Cordova closes the door behind them, and it vanishes into the millwork with a soft click. Not one single seam or visible hinge. Saffi is in awe. "This is right out of a movie."

Declan tries to brush the dust from his shirt and jeans, a look of disgust on his face. "Yeah, Norman Bates would love it." He looks around the small lobby. "Where exactly are we?"

"Still on the fourth floor of the Beresford but in a different section." He presses the elevator button. "Something everybody has been telling us is impossible to do without leaving the building." The elevator arrives, and he presses the button for the tower. "Hoffman intricately planned out every second of this."

A moment later, they're standing in the tower apartment's foyer. "No camera up here," Cordova reminds them. "With the camera disabled in the Eighty-Second Street entrance and his knowledge of the building's design, he was able to come and go as he pleased without anyone noticing. He gets up here and knocks—"

Saffi completes the thought for him. "David Morrow lets him right in. No reason not to. They were friends, right? By the time Hoffman has the knife out, it's too late."

Declan sets the box down on the floor and leans against the wall, building on all of this, even though he knows it's utter bullshit. "He kills Mia Gomez first, right? He had to because he left the knife he used up here next to David's body. So he kills her, probably changes out of the bloody clothes and bags them in that hidden hallway, comes up here, and kills David. Then he stages the scene with my blood, jimmies the lock a bit so it looks like a break-in, and leaves. He cleans himself up somewhere, then heads to the bookstore to confront Denise Morrow with his ultimatum. Maybe he changed clothes a second time to ensure he didn't have any trace on himself. If he did that, he could have dumped everything anywhere between here and Tribeca. He had plenty of time for all that."

"That fits," Saffi says. "Covers all evidentiary bases."

Cordova is nodding slowly. "No crime is perfect, but that's damn near close."

Declan looks at the Morrows' door. "So do we tell her?"

Saffi considers that, then shakes her head. "I need to talk to my boss. Maybe the mayor. We still have her lawsuit to contend with. She's more concerned with her reputation than the money, so maybe we can issue a formal public apology, and that would make it all go away. It's best we keep everything under wraps for now, at least until we figure out how to approach it." She glances at the clock on her phone and winces. "I need to go. Can the two of you get Daniels up to speed?"

Declan rubs his scruffy chin and pats his filthy shirt and jeans. "Can we stop at my apartment before heading back to the precinct? I need to shave and shower, change my clothes."

"Romeo here didn't go home last night," Saffi says flatly.

Cordova glances at Declan, then looks down at his own rumpled suit. "Maybe we should hit my place too. We'll call Daniels from the car."

CHAPTER FIFTY-THREE

Excerpt from *The Taking of Maggie Marshall* by Denise Morrow

LIFE IN PRISON for Ruben Lucero is difficult. It is difficult for anyone, but particularly for Lucero. As a convicted sex offender with a fixation on teenage girls—*children* in the eyes of most—he is considered the lowest of low. The guards torment him. He was beaten within hours of entering the general population and suffered a gash in his lower abdomen when someone attacked him in the showers with a weapon fashioned from a toothbrush. While in the prison infirmary, he was attacked again. Someone sodomized him in the middle of the night with what is believed to be a mop handle while two other inmates held him down. A month after arriving at Dannemora, he had chalked up three stays in the infirmary and a combined seven days in solitary, isolation being the only place the guards could guarantee his safety.

I'm not telling you this so you'll feel sorry for Ruben Lucero; I only want you to understand what life in prison is like for him. Something as simple as showering or eating a meal can easily turn deadly. And while most prisoners find safety with one of the groups or gangs, no group or gang is willing to accept Lucero, not even when offered payment. Nobody is willing to protect him.

When Ruben Lucero was sentenced, he wasn't a strong man. I mean that in both the literal and figurative sense. According to his intake form, he weighed only one hundred and thirty-two pounds. His job as a groundskeeper kept him reasonably fit but did nothing to add bulk to his almost girl-like frame. He was timid, had been picked on his entire life. He had no friends. He lived life in a bubble, and that did nothing to improve his social skills. Had the folks in Vegas taken bets on Lucero's survival, the odds would not have been good. How he made it through those initial months, I don't know, and when I asked him, he refused to talk about it.

Although I followed Lucero's trial closely, the first time I met him, the first time we spoke, Lucero was three years into his sentence and no longer resembled the man I'd seen in the courtroom and the press. He'd put on at least forty pounds, all muscle. His long hair had been shaved away, and several tattoos covered his scalp as well as his arms and hands. His wide, childlike eyes had receded deep into his skull. And he was covered in scars, too many to count. Looking at him was painful and sent a single thought through my head: *Prison made this.*

Then he proceeded to tell me the truth.

He was guarded at first, rightfully so. But he was also clear, concise. He laid out the evidence against him and dispensed with each item systematically, not as a man who would say anything to gain freedom but almost as an impartial observer. Someone who was familiar with all aspects of the case and whose only goal was to set things right.

I didn't want to believe him, but I did. Because his truth, *the* truth, made far more sense than the case laid out by the prosecutor had. When I asked him why he hadn't testified in his own defense, he told me his court-appointed public defender advised him not to. When I asked why that same public defender hadn't raised these issues in court, he only shrugged, shook his head, and said, "I met with her twice before the trial and we covered everything I just told you. I told her I had a fondness for young girls, I admitted to that, but I also told her I never touched Maggie Marshall. I described the man I saw following her. I told her to run prints on the evidence found in my apartment because I knew she wouldn't find mine, but she did none of that. On the final day of my trial, her last day to present my defense, I asked her why not, and she only stared at me. I realized she had already made up her mind about me and decided I needed to be in here, not out there."

Ruben Lucero's public defender was a woman named Carolyn Douglas. She was two years out of law school and had a caseload on her desk tall enough to tickle the ceiling. She also had one foot out the door, ready to move into private practice. Lucero firmly believed Carolyn Douglas had been asked to throw his case by her new boss, one of New York's preeminent criminal defense attorneys.

A man named Geller Hoffman.

CHAPTER FIFTY-FOUR

"DO YOU HAVE any coffee in this kitchen?" Cordova calls to Declan. Cordova uses the term *kitchen* loosely because the small space doesn't function as a kitchen. The refrigerator is bare, most of the drawers are either empty or stuffed with random junk, and only one cabinet actually houses dishware; the others are full of everything from old magazines to car parts, which Cordova finds odd, since Declan doesn't own a car. He does find a box of protein bars buried under some laundry on the counter. Unfortunately, they expired six months ago. Cordova takes one anyway and tries to ignore the fact that it contains dairy, which he tries to avoid, and is far more crunchy than it probably should be. "Dec? Do you have coffee?" he calls again, louder.

"Sorry! I meant to do some shopping, but..." Declan's voice trails off, muffled by the running water of the shower in the other room.

The only bare spot on Declan's kitchen counter is the place his knife block, now in evidence, once occupied. Cordova sees dirty dishes sitting in putrid water in the sink, and his stomach lurches. He has no idea how the kid can live like this. He has no idea how anyone could live like this. He tosses the rest of the protein bar in the overflowing trash and steps back into the living room. The door of the closet nearest the entrance is still open from the search, and half its contents are on the floor. Cordova counts five shoeboxes, and that's without moving the coats and other items that are most likely covering more. All the shoes are the same brand and design as the ones he found in Hoffman's safe: Merrell Moab, size eleven. Black. Declan can't be bothered to buy a loaf of bread, but shoes? Shoes he's got.

In the bathroom, the shower cuts off. A moment later, Declan opens the door. He's wrapped in a towel, and white humid steam lofts out of the confined space and into the living room. He wipes the mirror with a balled fist and lathers shaving cream on his face. "Mind if I ask you a question?"

"Shoot," Cordova says. *As long as you're not going to ask me to help clean this shithole.*

Declan says, "I need you to be completely honest."

"Always am."

"Did you seriously think I killed David Morrow?"

It's been so long since Cordova got any sleep, he isn't sure about much of anything. His brain is reeling from the events of the past twenty-four hours alone, and he hasn't had time to try and make sense of it all. When Declan got in the shower, he tossed his shirt on the floor outside the bathroom door, and Cordova finds himself staring at it. He's not sure why. Something about it knocks around in the back of his tired mind, but the thought is so greasy, he can't grip it.

"If you did," Declan says, "I forgive you. I'll be the first to admit, things got a little sketchy."

Cordova is still staring at the shirt.

"I've decided not to give a shit about Denise Morrow and her tell-all book," Declan goes on. "Let her release it. With what you found on Geller Hoffman, if she puts that bullshit out there, I'll sue her for slander, defamation, and whatever else I can come up with. Hell, pain and suffering, mental anguish...I'll find a lawyer who makes Hoffman look like a saint, a bottom-feeder who has no problem getting dirty. It's not like they're in short supply around here. Maybe I'll use the money to get a better place. Maybe I'll get out of the city altogether. Who knows."

"Who knows..." Cordova mutters.

When he finally turns away from the shirt, his right foot is tapping incessantly. This nervous tic that comes on whenever his mind is working a problem. He puts an end to the tapping and returns to the only other thought rolling around in his head. "I'm not sure I buy that Lucero is innocent in all this."

"That scumbag is hardly innocent."

When Cordova found Geller Hoffman in that closet, he felt like everything was coming together. The items in the attorney's safe clinched it. If Cordova were the star of some weekly television detective drama, those things would have happened at the fifty-three-minute mark. The case would be tied up with a nice little bow, and he'd be at a bar joking with his costars, setting things up for next week's episode. Outro music would be cued up. But this is no television drama, and real life is anything but convenient. In all his years on the force, Cordova can recall only a single case that wrapped up as tight as this one. Cases are usually sloppy. There are usually unanswered questions. There are usually doubts—not enough to tip the scales, but doubts nonetheless. When you put somebody away, you make your peace with that. This is different. He's missed something. You *don't* make your peace with that.

"Geller Hoffman kills Maggie Marshall. Ruben Lucero sees him all those years ago, then fingers him for the murder to Denise Morrow?" Cordova wonders aloud. "Think about that. If she doesn't go up to Dannemora to interview him for her book, if her phone doesn't ring at that exact second, none of that comes together."

"What, you don't believe in kismet?"

"Do you?"

"I think Ruben Lucero was found guilty by a jury of his peers. Saffi said he might get a new trial after what you pulled out of Hoffman's place, so we let that happen. You saw Lucero's apartment—that monster was tying girls to a mattress on the floor. Making them shit in a bucket. He had all those books, souvenirs. A cell at Dannemora is too good for him." He glances at Cordova in the mirror. "Daniels told me about the pictures you found with Hoffman. You worried about those?"

"Shouldn't we be?"

"Hoffman tried to frame me, so it's not a stretch to see him frame Lucero," Declan replies. "Lucero said he saw Hoffman in the park that day. If that's true, odds are good Hoffman saw Lucero too. Pedos like them, they got this sort of radar, they home in on each other. Hoffman was sharp. He saw an opportunity to clean up a mess and he took it. Might even explain how that book got in Lucero's apartment. Hoffman would know exactly who to grease to pull something from evidence. If he already knew what was in Maggie's bag, it makes even more sense. You said Lucero mentioned Lieutenant Daniels. You ever stop and think maybe *he* really did it? It was his name in the log, right? Maybe he used the wrong hand to throw the handwriting. What better way to cover your own tracks? I sure as shit didn't do it. Makes sense Daniels might've. Maybe that's how he paid for that cozy cabin of his out at Riverhead. You want to make yourself feel better about it all, why don't we run the Polaroids we found at Lucero's place for prints, see if Hoffman's are on them? They are, and you got your answer."

Cordova hasn't considered that, and he should have. He blames it on his lack of sleep. He makes a mental note to send those Polaroids to the lab when they get back to the precinct.

Declan finishes shaving, washes the remaining foam from his face, and begins popping pills from the slew of supplements in his medicine cabinet. Cordova remembers the prescription bottle he found in Hoffman's safe. "You know, if you stopped living off takeout and learned to cook a real meal, you probably wouldn't need that prescription. You're too young to have high cholesterol."

"Yeah, yeah, yeah. Like you're the picture of health." Declan dries his face and steps into the living room. He kicks through a pile of clothes on the floor, grabs a pair of jeans, tugs them on under his towel, and starts picking through shirts. "Look, I want to be sure we—"

Declan coughs.

A puzzled look crosses his face.

"Dec, what—"

Declan coughs again. His hand goes to his throat, and his eyes go wide. He starts to gasp.

Is he choking on the pills?

Declan gasps again, a harsh rush of air.

He stumbles back into the bathroom and yanks open the medicine cabinet. Searches. Starts slapping the pill bottles off the shelves, looking for something that apparently isn't there.

When Cordova gets to Declan, he's clasping his throat with swollen fingers.

He's not choking—he's having an allergic reaction.

"Where's your EpiPen?" Cordova shouts.

Declan doesn't answer. Can't.

He pushes by Cordova, goes to his nightstand, and yanks the drawer open. His eyes are so large, they look like they might pop out of his head. He rifles through the drawer, but his movements are growing thick and sluggish.

Cordova jerks the drawer all the way out, tips it over, and spreads out the contents. There's no EpiPen; there's nothing but junk.

Declan makes a horrible noise—it sounds like he's trying to suck through a clogged straw. His body jerks, spasms, and he drops onto his back.

Cordova gets his phone out, dials 911 on speaker. "This is

Detective Jarod Cordova. I've got an officer down! I need an ambulance at —"

Silence.

Declan is no longer moving.

He's not breathing.

He's looking up at Cordova with vacant eyes from a face so swollen, it's unrecognizable.

CHAPTER FIFTY-FIVE

TWENTY MINUTES LATER, Cordova is sitting on the floor, his back pressed against the wall, every inch of his body still trembling.

The paramedics arrived in under four minutes, record time in this part of the city, but it wasn't fast enough. Although they got a breathing tube down Declan's throat, started CPR, and administered a series of medications—epinephrine and others Cordova didn't recognize—they did so with practiced robotic movements that suggested they were going down a checklist but knew it would do no good. At one point, the female paramedic called out that she'd gotten a pulse, but her partner checked Declan's neck and slowly shook his head. Eventually, they sat back on their heels, panting, and after a brief phone conversation with the ER physician, the male paramedic said the words still echoing through Cordova's head: *Time of death, 11:43 a.m.*

He closed Declan's eyes, and Cordova is thankful for that, because he had never seen anyone look so afraid.

"Detective, would you like me to call someone for you?"

It's the female paramedic. He didn't notice her approach. Her large brown eyes are moist; her face is filled with the empathy and understanding of someone who sees far too many people in their final moments.

"I'll call our lieutenant," he manages, his voice gravelly.

"What about family?"

Cordova only shakes his head.

"Okay," she says softly. "Okay."

Her partner is busy packing up their gear and making notes on a tablet. "Any idea what he ate? What he was allergic to?" she asks.

"He's...he's allergic to peanuts," Cordova tells her. "But he didn't eat anything—"

"Looks like he ate *something*," the male paramedic says in a dismissive tone, tapping away on his tablet.

"The ME will confirm, but this looks like anaphylaxis," the woman explains as she picks up discarded wrappers and needles around Declan's body. Her eyes land on the overturned drawer near the bed.

Cordova says, "He tried to find his..."

Although he doesn't finish the sentence, she understands.

"We've seen it before. EpiPens never seem to be around when you really need them."

It all happened so fast. Cordova tries to piece it together. Declan hadn't eaten anything. He'd showered, shaved, and was—

He scrambles to his feet and pushes past both of them to the bathroom. Half the contents of Declan's medicine cabinet are on the floor; some bottles are in the sink. A handful of supplements and—

His eyes land on a prescription bottle with Declan's name on it. A bottle of Livestor, used to reduce cholesterol. A bottle identical to the one he found in Geller Hoffman's safe. He removes the top and sniffs. The scent is faint, but it's there—peanuts.

Cordova turns and says, "I need a plastic bag."

The male paramedic eyes him and then the pills on the floor. "Cheaper supplements sometimes use ground peanuts as filler, it could be—"

"Bag. Now," Cordova tells him.

The woman finds a bag in her pack and hands it to him. "If that's what he ingested, we'll need to take it with us. The ME will want it."

"Not a chance—it's evidence." Cordova carefully places the bottle in the bag and slips it in his pocket, then takes out his phone and dials Lieutenant Daniels. When he gets voicemail, he leaves a quick message. He nearly trips over Declan's shirt on the floor exiting the bathroom, and it clicks—

Denise Morrow was wearing that same shirt when he and Saffi confronted her earlier.

Declan was sleeping with Denise Morrow.

The thought hits him like a punch in the gut.

He picks up the shirt. There's something in the breast pocket—a USB drive. Cordova knows exactly what's on it because CSU didn't find it when they tossed Declan's apartment. It's the copy of Denise Morrow's book. Declan had it on him this entire time.

CHAPTER FIFTY-SIX

CORDOVA STEPS INTO the bullpen at the precinct house in a daze, his heart heavy with an overwhelming mix of disbelief and anguish. It's midafternoon, and nearly everyone is out in the field. Daniels's office is empty and the handful of people there don't know where he is. News of Declan's death hasn't spread yet, and Cordova doesn't tell anyone. On some level, he feels like it's not real and it won't be real unless he talks about it. So he won't; he just won't.

He can't.

Because this isn't done yet.

Not even close.

Rubbing the back of his neck, he drops into his chair and

stares at Declan's cluttered desk. Every muscle in his body is twisted into a tangled knot and growing tighter.

Declan was sleeping with Denise Morrow.

He tries to wrap his head around that and can't.

Denise Morrow was out to destroy Declan. She trashed him on television. Her book systematically dismantled his career, attacked his character. Hell, Declan was ready to kill himself over the IAU investigation and she'd done nothing but throw gasoline on their roaring fire. How the hell did he end up sleeping with her?

Cordova glances up at the whiteboards detailing the murders of David Morrow and Mia Gomez and grows more confused, because none of it is right. It can't be. Not when you factor in Declan's affair and Geller Hoffman. *Especially* Geller Hoffman. Not when you consider what Cordova found in the man's apartment and at his office. Not when you add in what Lucero told him. What Lucero had apparently told Daniels, and Daniels never shared . . .

Cordova picks up the landline and dials his lieutenant again. Again, he gets voicemail. He slams the receiver back in the cradle and is about to dial one more time when it rings. "What?"

"Jarod?" It's Oscar Martinez from the ME's office.

"Sorry, Oscar. It's been . . . a day." He doesn't tell him about Declan; he can't.

"Did you get my email?"

"Your . . ." Cordova hasn't checked his email. "Hold on a second." He scans the various messages, finds one from Martinez, and opens it. Attached is a picture of a man's bare chest. "What exactly am I looking at?"

"That's Geller Hoffman. COD is certainly asphyxiation, but I can't explain that mark on his chest. I don't know what it is. There's nothing in the database. I can't pin it down."

"What mar—" Then Cordova sees it. A small, round bruise about the size of a dime in the center of Hoffman's chest, between the attorney's flabby pecs.

"I believe it's a compression bruise," Martinez says.

"From something pressing down?"

"Yeah. Or it could be nothing. Might be completely unrelated. I've got no reason to connect it, it just seems...off. You know?"

Cordova does know. Everything about this damn case is off.

"I wanted you to see it," Martinez says. "If you find something that's round and about three-eighths of an inch wide, I might be able to match it up."

Cordova thanks him and hangs up. He prints out the picture, tacks it up on the evidence board under the photograph of Hoffman, then steps back to take it all in.

He thinks of the napkins back at the Six, how he and Declan had written everything out and how Declan tore them apart and mixed up the pieces.

Three-card monte.

Was that Declan being a cop and sharing an actual realization, or was that Declan being Denise Morrow's lover, her pawn, and telling Cordova what she wanted him to hear?

How long had they been sleeping together?

Was she pulling the strings?

Had to be.

Nothing else fit.

This woman has been three steps ahead of them from the

jump. That means she was playing him, and Declan too—maybe even Geller Hoffman—and nothing on the evidence board is really what it appears to be.

Things get worse when Cordova glances up at the television they keep in the office and sees ADA Saffi and her boss standing on the courthouse steps, hands at their sides, heads hanging, a picture of contrition and self-loathing. The words *Famed author Denise Morrow cleared of all charges* scroll across the bottom of the screen. A photograph of Morrow is superimposed over the top corner.

He fumbles with the remote and turns up the sound as Saffi speaks.

"While we're still working diligently to uncover all the facts, it is the opinion of our office that local defense attorney Geller Hoffman was responsible for the deaths of Mrs. Morrow's husband, a woman named Mia Gomez, and possibly others. Any involvement by Mrs. Morrow appears to be the result of a detailed blackmail scheme hatched by Hoffman. She was acting under duress. We would like to extend our deepest apologies to Mrs. Morrow for any inconvenience our office put her through as a result of the misdirection perpetrated by Mr. Hoffman. His duplicity was far-reaching and skillfully deployed. If not for the untiring efforts of the NYPD, it might not have been uncovered."

"In other words, 'Please drop your lawsuit, Mrs. Morrow,'" Cordova mutters. "'We'll give you the key to the city if you do. Don't make us write that check.'"

From somewhere in the swarm of media people, a male voice shouts, "What about Detective Declan Shaw?"

Rather than addressing the reporter, Saffi looks directly into the camera. "Detective Shaw is as much a victim in all this as Mrs. Morrow. Hoffman painted a target on his back, and he was relentless in his efforts to discredit a fine officer. More on that will follow in the coming days." She looks out over the large group for a moment, then adds, "Thank you all for coming out. There will be a formal written statement later today detailing—"

Another voice interrupts her. "Can you comment on the death of Ruben Lucero?"

The words come and go so quickly, Cordova isn't sure he heard them correctly, but the text at the bottom of the screen changes from the message about Denise Morrow to *Convicted killer Ruben Lucero found dead in his prison cell.*

Saffi turns to the DA at her side; he gives her a slight nod. She clears her throat and continues. "We learned of this only moments before coming out here, but apparently someone gained access to Lucero's cell and beat him with a sock containing several cans of soup pilfered from the kitchen. When Lucero was discovered, a doctor was summoned from the infirmary and rushed to his cell. He informed the duty officer and the warden that Lucero had been dead for at least an hour, possibly longer, and had suffered multiple blunt-force traumas. The improvised weapon was left behind and is currently being processed. I expect the warden will release additional information as it becomes available."

Cordova quickly keys Lucero's name into Google, and his computer screen fills with stories about the convict's death. More speculation than fact. An inside job? Did someone open his cell, or did they get to him through the bars? Where were the guards? New evidence suggests he might have been innocent; was this some sort of retaliation?

On the television, the text at the bottom of the screen shifts again, replaced with a scrolling message:

STATEMENT JUST RELEASED BY DENISE MORROW: I WOULD PERSONALLY LIKE TO THANK THOSE WHO WORKED TIRELESSLY TO CLEAR MY NAME. THIS HAS BEEN A TRY-ING TIME FOR ALL INVOLVED AND I'M GLAD IT IS BEHIND US SO I CAN FINALLY MOURN THE LOSS OF MY HUSBAND, MY PARTNER IN LIFE, MY GREATEST LOVE, DAVID. I HAVE NOTHING BUT THE DEEPEST RESPECT FOR THOSE IN LAW ENFORCEMENT AND ALL THEY DO, THE CHALLENGES THEY FACE, AND THE HURDLES THEY OVERCOME IN THE PURSUIT OF TRUTH. I HOLD NO ILL WILL AGAINST THOSE WHO INITIALLY THOUGHT ME GUILTY; I TAKE SOLACE IN KNOWING THAT THE MAN RESPONSIBLE CAN NO LONGER HARM OTHERS. I WOULD ALSO LIKE TO EXTEND MY HEARTFELT SYMPATHY TO THE FAMILY OF RUBEN LUCERO. HE WAS A HORRIBLY MISUNDERSTOOD MAN, AND WHILE HE WAS DEEPLY FLAWED, I BELIEVE THE WORLD WILL SOON LEARN HE WAS NOT THE MAN HE WAS PAINTED TO BE.

By the time Cordova finishes reading the message, the live shot of ADA Saffi is over and has been replaced with a still image of Lucero in a suit and tie being led into the courthouse. Cordova remembers that day well, the start of Lucero's trial. When the broadcast returns to the studio, Denise Morrow's photo is once more in the top corner of the screen, and the anchor begins reading Denise Morrow's statement, her face filled with sympathy.

Cordova's vision goes red. He sees nothing but Declan lying dead on the floor, that damn shirt inches away from his swollen hand.

The anchor drones on; he can't hear her anymore.

It's bullshit. Every bit of it. Well-orchestrated bullshit.

He turns off the TV and throws the remote across the room. It cracks against the far wall and showers the floor with pieces.

The single word starts in Cordova's chest and barrels up his throat. It escapes with a violent shout that burns his vocal cords: *"Fuck!"*

It's the first time he's cursed aloud in maybe a decade, and it feels damn good. He clambers to his feet, comes around his desk, and knocks over both whiteboards, and that feels even better.

Several people in the bullpen glance over at him, then go back to whatever they were doing. Just another day. Nobody says a word when he rakes everything off his desk with one arm, then does the same with the mess on Declan's. Papers, pens, binders, books, computer, crusty coffee mugs—it all crashes to the floor. He doesn't stop until it's all on the ground, then he drops down with it, breathing heavily.

"Better?" a cop across the room asks.

Exhausted, Cordova waves a hand at him dismissively.

He sits there for maybe five minutes before his eyes fall on a page from Denise Morrow's book; Declan must have printed it out from the file he pilfered from evidence. It's a transcript from their initial interview with Lucero.

Because it was introduced as evidence, it's currently in the public record, accessible by anyone. Authors regularly use transcripts when writing about crimes. That isn't the part that jumps out at him. Cordova is staring at the bottom of the page, trying to make sense of what he's found:

[*End of recording.*]

/MG/GTS

CHAPTER FIFTY-SEVEN

Transcript: Dateline interview with Denise Morrow

Present: Daphne Brown

Denise Morrow

[Daphne Brown] I truly appreciate you taking the
time to sit down with us tonight on such
short notice. I can't imagine it's easy for you
to talk about all this so soon. I'm so, so sorry
about your husband.

[Denise Morrow] Thank you for that. And thank
you for having me. These last few weeks
have been difficult, to say the least.

[Brown] There is so much speculation floating
       around out there . . .

[Morrow] We live in a time where the desire for rat-
       ings will sometimes trump the truth. People
       will say anything.

[Brown] Your husband wasn't just murdered. You
       were blackmailed.

[Morrow] [*Nods.*]

[Brown] By your own attorney, a man named Geller
       Hoffman. Someone you considered a family
       friend.

[Morrow] I did.

[Brown] This man — Geller Hoffman — killed your
       husband, killed an . . . associate, and —

[Morrow] She was my husband's mistress. It's
       okay — you can say it.

[Brown] Hoffman did all this, hurt these people,
       because you were writing a book that could
       potentially expose him as a serial killer. He
       wanted to stop you.

[Morrow] Yes.

[Brown] [*Shakes head.*] I can't imagine.

[Morrow] When I . . . I first suspected David was
       having an affair, I confided in him, in
       Geller. He used his resources to confirm it
       was true.

[Brown] Hoffman found the other woman. Showed
       you pictures. Proof.

[Morrow] I was devastated. The person I gave my life

to... When you're all in and you suddenly find that he's not, it's heavy, you know?

[Brown] You wanted to fix things. Most women would be angry.

[Morrow] Oh, I was angry, but...

[Brown] But you loved him.

[Morrow] [*Nods.*] David was my soulmate. I didn't want to lose him. When you've been with someone as long as we were together, when you've worked through some of the worst this world can throw at you *together*, then you get through it, same as any other crisis. I wanted to save us. We were bigger than this.

[Brown] Geller Hoffman, he knew all that. He was your attorney, and you confided in him.

[Morrow] David and I knew Geller for years. He sometimes vacationed with us. We regularly shared meals. We were all very close. At first, I thought he wanted to help. Who knows, maybe in the beginning he did, but that all changed...

[Brown] It changed when Geller Hoffman learned you were writing a book about a teenage girl who had been brutally assaulted and murdered in Central Park in 2018.

[Morrow] Maggie Marshall.

[Brown] Did you know he had a connection to that case?

[Morrow] [*Shakes head.*] No. He never mentioned her name.

[Brown] You had no suspicions?

[Morrow] Suspicions? No. Why would I? Things
with Geller weren't like that. David and I
saw a side of him most people didn't—he
was funny. Sarcastic, but funny. He was an
early reader of my books. He helped me get
the legal aspects correct. He'd always been
there for me. Me *and* David. I had no reason
to suspect he was involved in Maggie's case.

[Brown] Not at first.

[Morrow] Not until I started speaking to the man
convicted of her murder.

[Brown] Ruben Lucero.

[Morrow] Yes.

[Brown] What did Lucero tell you?

[Morrow] In one of our early interviews, he said his
public defender had accepted a job in the
private sector and he felt she had one foot
out the door and didn't provide the defense
he deserved. Ruben felt betrayed by the
system.

[Brown] Rightfully so. The woman's focus was no
longer on her caseload; she was looking at
her cushy new job. But that's not the worst
of it, right?

[Morrow] No. During my research, I learned her
new employer was my attorney.

[Brown] Geller Hoffman.

[Morrow] Correct. Now keep in mind, Lucero's
trial, Hoffman hiring Lucero's attorney, that

all happened four years ago. I had no clue
back then. I only learned of that connection
recently.

[Brown] When you started researching your book.
When you first interviewed Lucero...

[Morrow] Yes.

[Brown] We now know Geller Hoffman killed your
husband. He killed your husband's mistress.
Evidence now suggests he may have killed
others.

[Morrow] Yes.

[Brown] As an observer of all this, putting the
pieces together, I think it's safe to say Hoffman hired Lucero's attorney away from the
public defender's office in an attempt to
insinuate himself into Lucero's defense.

[Morrow] Or lack of. Geller wanted, *needed,* Ruben
Lucero to go to prison for Maggie Marshall's
murder.

[Brown] And why was that?

[Morrow] [*Long pause.*] From my first meeting
with Lucero, he swore he was innocent. He
consistently told me the same story — how
he witnessed another man following Maggie
Marshall in the park shortly before she was
killed.

[Brown] He told the police too, right? And they did
nothing?

[Morrow] If they investigated that angle, I never
found evidence of it.

[Brown] And he was able to identify the man he saw?

[Morrow] He did.

[Brown] Who was it?

[Morrow] My attorney.

[Brown] He identified Geller Hoffman.

[Morrow] From a photograph.

[Brown] Wow.

[Morrow] Yeah.

[Brown] Did you take this information to the police?

[Morrow] I should have. I know that now, looking back on it, but at the time, I just wanted to make sense of it all.

[Brown] So you wrote it down.

[Morrow] I wrote it down. I needed to do that. That's how my brain works. That's how I process. I'd already been working on Maggie's story, so I began plugging in this new information. Researching Geller's background, looking for overlap not only with Maggie Marshall but with other victims possibly associated with Ruben Lucero.

[Brown] And you found that overlap . . .

[Morrow] It was like finding missing puzzle pieces. It all fit. *He* fit. I realized Lucero was innocent. He'd been telling me the truth the entire time. Telling *everyone*, and nobody listened.

[Brown] Then, after that realization, did you finally take everything to the police?

[Morrow] [*Long pause.*] I never got the opportunity.

I came home one night to find Geller in
my office reading my notes, the draft of the
book, everything. He knew that I knew.

[Brown] And that's when the blackmail started, the
intimidation...

[Morrow] He made it very clear that if I said a word,
I was done.

[Brown] He controlled you. Kept you under his
thumb. That wasn't enough for him, though.
He felt he needed something he could hold
over you. Something to ensure you'd stay in
line. That's when he did the unspeakable.

[Morrow] [*Wipes her eyes but says nothing.*]

[Brown] Take your time.

[Morrow] I was at a bookstore appearance in Tribeca. He came in and handed me a bag.
He told me he'd just killed my husband's
mistress. He told me he had an associate at
my apartment and if I didn't change into the
clothing in that bag, his associate would kill
David. He started to explain how he mixed
up the evidence, how he could pin it all on
me or make it all go away, how once he had
this over my head, he knew he would be
able to trust me... he started in on all that,
but honestly, I barely heard him. My only
thoughts were of saving my husband, so I
did what he asked.

[Brown] He lied. We know that now. Your husband
was already dead.

[Morrow] [*Soft sob. A nod.*] I found him when I got
home. He'd been stabbed. I called 911, but
he...he was already gone.

[Brown] You were in shock when the authorities
arrived.

[Morrow] [*Nods.*] I still can't believe David's gone.

[Brown] [*After a long silence.*] We all know what
happened next. You were arrested, but
the charges were quickly dropped when it
became clear you had nothing to do with
either murder.

[Morrow] [*Looks to the floor, then back at Daphne.*] I
don't blame the police for initially thinking
I did it. My attorney painted this picture for
them; he put the guilt on me, then shifted it
away, just as he'd said he would. It was his
idea to file a suit against the city when their
case came apart. I think he saw it as a way to
profit from it all. I had to go along. He made
that very clear.

[Brown] This man controlled you.

[Morrow] I'm not proud to say it, but yes, he had
complete control over me. [*She goes silent
for a moment.*] I woke once and found him
standing over me, just watching me sleep. I
don't know how he got in—I imagine the
same way he did when he killed David. He
didn't say anything. When he knew I'd seen
him, he smiled and left. The implication was
clear. He'd made his point. He could get to

me at any time, and he would if I somehow
crossed him. I can't begin to explain how
terrified I was.

[Brown] When he died, you must have been so
relieved.

[Morrow] [*A deep sigh followed by a soft smile.*] You
have no idea. I was finally able to tell the
police everything. When they searched
his home and office, they realized the true
extent of his manipulation, and it was finally
over. At least, I thought it was...

[Brown] [*Long pause.*] Ruben Lucero died in prison.
Murdered in his cell. Do you think your
attorney somehow orchestrated his death as
a last-ditch effort to protect himself?

[Morrow] I really can't speculate on that. I only
hope Ruben Lucero has finally found peace.

[*End of recording.*]

/DB/GTS

CHAPTER FIFTY-EIGHT

DENISE MORROW'S AGENT, Kirby Neilson, raises her cosmo and beams. "To QuimbyCam!"

"To QuimbyCam!" the guests at the crowded table echo, then sip their cocktails. Gordon Brennon, Denise's film-rights manager, lets out one of his infectious laughs, and it's heard in all corners of the quaint Italian restaurant.

Denise's editor, Jennifer Henke, is there too. She brought Jada Reed, Denise's publicist, the latest in a long line of them. It's the first time Denise has met her.

They seem to get younger with each book, Denise thinks when she sees her. *This one barely looks old enough to drive, let alone drink.*

Jennifer once told her that the publishers would pluck them

right out of high school if they could. Who better to run a social media campaign than someone who regularly posts Tik-Tok videos detailing every aspect of her existence? Most adults couldn't name four social media platforms. It's a young person's world.

An overflowing box of Denise Morrow's books pokes up from the only empty chair. Promotional copies she promised to sign for Kirby.

"Okay, so you gotta tell us," Gordon says, then pauses to wipe some lint from his shirt. "You're updating the new book with everything that's happened, right?"

Denise tilts her head and starts to drop the bombshell she's held back all night. "To tell the truth, I'm not sure I'll release this book."

The entire table goes quiet. She knows this isn't what they expected. Tonight was meant to be a celebration. All of them — herself included — stand to make a lot of money if she publishes the Maggie Marshall book, particularly with everything that's happened, but that doesn't mean it's the right call. If she releases the book, all this nonsense will be in the public eye for years. Gordon will surely sell the film rights, which means a movie or maybe a television show or a docuseries. There's no telling what direction it will go. The only thing that's certain is that it won't go away, and Denise wants it to go away.

"That's a joke, right?" Jennifer says, giving Kirby a harsh glance. "You said we had a deal. I went to bat with my boss for you. It's the most lucrative offer I've ever put out there."

Kirby sends Jennifer a comforting smile. "I'm sure Denise is kidding." She looks back to Denise. "You are kidding, right?"

Denise Morrow studies the faces around the table. They're all turned to her.

She wipes her finger through beads of condensation on a water glass. "I'm just a little overwhelmed right now. Before I came down here, I was getting ready in the bathroom, and I saw David's toothbrush and razor over on his vanity. I…I haven't moved any of his things. There's a water glass on his nightstand. His laundry in the dryer. He loves…loved to eat pickles. There's a big jar in the refrigerator. I hate pickles…"

"Geller Hoffman was a fucking animal," Kirby says in a quiet, flat tone. "He had no right to take David from you."

Denise swallows. "He had no right to hurt anybody."

"That's what I meant."

This wasn't the first time the two women had talked about this. Denise called Kirby yesterday and they were on the phone for nearly an hour. She told her she would have forgiven David for all of it, every single indiscretion. If there was a void in their marriage, a door left open wide enough for another woman to step through, Denise felt that was as much her fault as it was David's. Kirby told Denise she might be experiencing survivor's guilt. Suggested that she should talk to someone. A *professional* someone. And Denise said she would, and she sounded serious.

Page Six snapping a photo of her walking into a therapist's office? *Yes, please.*

And Kirby Neilson hanging up, quickly calling a dozen of her closest friends, and telling them that Denise Morrow was grief-stricken over the loss of her husband, coming apart at the seams, how sad that this once strong woman was broken now? *Yes to that too, please.*

Denise makes no mention of her affair with the detective. Of course not. Instead, she paints a picture, she spins a story, she lays out the narrative she wants others to follow. As any good writer would do.

Oh, how she hoped the young and gullible publicist Jada Reed would excuse herself to the bathroom so she could fire off the series of messages no doubt brewing in her thoughts. Maybe she'll even snap a couple of clandestine photographs.

"Look," Denise says with a forced smile. "I just need a little time."

Kirby pounces on that. She reaches over and gently pats Denise's hand. "Of course you do. You're not going to get any pressure from anyone sitting at this table. You decide what's best for you when you're ready to decide it, and know that we're all here for you regardless. If you want to take a match to that book, that is fine by me."

"Yeah. Take your time," Gordon mutters. He picks up his glass, realizes it's empty, and holds it in the air until their waiter spots him.

A few moments later, the waiter sets Gordon's scotch down on the table and places a drink in front of Denise.

When she speaks, she has trouble getting the words out. "I . . . I didn't order that."

The drink was bright green.

In a martini glass.

A grasshopper.

The waiter says, "It's from the gentleman at the bar."

Denise turns, but there is no gentleman at the bar, only two older couples deep in conversation. "What did he look like?"

The waiter follows her gaze, then looks back at her. "I'm sorry, ma'am, I didn't see him. He placed the order through the bartender and I was told to bring it here, since this is my table."

Denise is about to go talk to the bartender when her phone rings.

The caller ID reads *Declan Shaw.*

CHAPTER FIFTY-NINE

DECLAN SHAW.

On the table, Denise's phone rings a second time.

A third.

"Denise?" Kirby says softly. "Your phone. Are you going to get that?"

Denise realizes she's been staring at it. At the name blinking up at her. Everyone at the table is watching her. Her eyes drift to the grasshopper, then back to her phone.

Fourth ring.

She picks it up, thumbs Accept, presses the phone to her ear. She says nothing as the call connects. At first, there is only soft breathing, then—

"Declan Shaw wasn't just my partner—he was my friend."

Not Declan.

It's the other one.

Jarod Cordova.

"Declan's in a drawer right now down at the medical examiner's office. A goddamn drawer. I suppose that's better than being in the dirt like your husband, David. Or did you have him cremated? That seems like something you'd do. I imagine you learned that particular lesson when you wrote *Bones Tell a Tale*, the one about Simon Ross, the guy who was murdered in the seventies. Thirty years later, they exhumed his body and were able to match marks on a rib bone to a knife found in his stepsister's home. She would never have been convicted had Ross's body been cremated. You're a quick study; I can't imagine you making a mistake like that."

Denise doesn't realize she's shaking until she looks down at her hand.

In the seat to her left, Jennifer Henke notices too and mouths, *Everything okay?*

Denise draws in a breath to settle her nerves, wills it to reach every inch of her body, then raises the same hand, no longer shaking, and mimes a jabbering mouth. She follows that with an eye roll and mouths, *Accountant.*

Her editor nods and turns to the young publicist at her side, and the two of them are quickly lost in a hushed conversation of their own. Across the table, Kirby is busy blotting Gordon Brennon's spilled water from the tablecloth. Apparently, he knocked the glass over, but Denise had missed that entirely.

Cordova's hushed voice drifts from her phone; the eerie calmness of it causes the back of her neck to prickle.

"Mia Gomez's mother flew in a few hours ago to claim her daughter's body. She's taking her back to Iowa so she can be buried in the family plot. You ever see the look on a mother's face when she's thinking about how to put her dead child to rest? No one should ever be in that position. She desperately wanted to be stoic — she seemed like a strong woman — but she fell apart before she made it through the door at the ME's office. Simply collapsed. They brought her over to Mercy, your husband's old hospital. Had to sedate her. I rode over with them in the ambulance, held her hand, tried to calm her down. Once they got her settled, I figured I'd take the opportunity to talk to some of your husband's coworkers." He pauses for a second, then: "Hey, how are you holding up? You look a little flustered."

Denise's head jerks up, more a reflex than a conscious thought. Nobody at her table notices; they're all wrapped in their own conversations. She looks through the large plate-glass window at the front of the restaurant, expecting to find Cordova standing outside, staring in, but there's no sign of the older detective. She doesn't see him inside either. Louie's isn't a large place, no more than twenty tables with a hundred people on a good night. Maybe two-thirds of the tables are full now, but she doesn't see Cordova among the diners. He did order the drink, though. That had to be him. So where —

She almost misses the Harlan coat.

A long trench identical to hers.

Identical to the one Geller Hoffman had.

It's draped over the back of a chair at an empty table on the opposite side of the restaurant, a black leather glove sticking out of one of the pockets.

She knows it's not Geller's coat; he burned that one. And it couldn't be hers. NYPD returned her coat when they dropped the charges, and she promptly shoved it in a trash receptacle on Eighty-Sixth after ensuring nobody was following or watching her.

She hadn't been followed or watched, right?

No, she was careful. And even if someone did see her, there was nothing incriminating on that coat. And there certainly wasn't anything illegal about throwing it away.

"I wish you could see yourself, the look on your face," Cordova says. "You couldn't be more pale if David walked through the door and ordered the fettuccine."

Denise twists around in her chair and softly says, "What do you want, Detective? This is borderline harassment. Do your friends in the DA's office know you're contacting me? I imagine they'd be upset. I'd hate to see you get in trouble."

The door leading to the kitchen at the back of the dining area swings open for a moment and Denise catches a glimpse of one of the chefs standing there. He's sharpening a knife. And although it's difficult to be sure from this distance, it looks a lot like the knife that killed David, the one they found in the garage above Geller Hoffman's car. Five inches long, one inch wide, a serrated blade with a black handle. She's still staring at it when the kitchen door swings shut.

"Jeffery Varano had a lot of interesting things to say," Cordova says.

That snaps her back. Jeffery Varano was David's best friend. He runs Mercy's cardiology department. "How is Jeff?"

"They decided to leave David's seat at the weekly poker game empty. Some symbolic gesture. I thought that was kinda nice."

Is that man watching her? The one in the navy sports jacket

four tables over? He's eating with another man. There's a phone in his hand, but he's holding it up slightly on the table, angled toward her. It looks like the camera is on, reversed. Is he watching her? Taping her? Photographing her? Denise can't tell for certain, but it sure as hell looks like it, and—

That woman at the bar—she's definitely watching. When did she sit down? She wasn't there a minute ago. Why does she keep touching her ear? Is she wearing an earbud? She looks away when Denise meets her eyes.

"Jeff said he and your husband go back all the way to college. Shared an apartment for a while. Known each other for most of their adult lives. Same thing with the other guys at that weekly game. All lifelong friends. Jeff said there were no secrets in that group. You'd be surprised what a bunch of guys will discuss when you put them in a room with cards, cigars, and alcohol. The good, the bad; they talked about it all. They talked about you a lot."

CHAPTER SIXTY

DENISE TWISTS IN her seat and shields her mouth with her free hand to keep the others at the table from hearing her. "Detective, I have zero interest in the gossip of middle-aged men."

"Really? Because I found it rather interesting. Certainly not what I expected."

"I'm hanging up, Detective."

"Your husband wasn't sleeping with Mia Gomez. He wasn't sleeping with you either."

The woman at the bar is watching her again. This time when Denise glares at her, she doesn't look away.

"Do you want me to give her one of these signed books?" This comes from her editor, Jennifer Henke.

"What?" Denise snaps.

"The fan at the bar." Jennifer gestures in the woman's direction. "She's been looking over here with that *When is a good time to interrupt her?* face. Maybe if I give her one, she'll back off."

Denise bobs her head and waves Jennifer away. She barely registers her words. Cordova is talking again.

"How long have you known about David and Jeff?"

"David and . . . you can't be serious."

Cordova says nothing. There's only his soft breathing.

"Jeff is happily married with two children."

"That was part of the problem, right?" Cordova says. "Jeff wasn't willing to leave his wife and kids. Unlike David, who—"

"Where are you right now?" Denise spots at least four other people watching her. No, five. They're spread out around the restaurant. Strategically placed, she realizes. Near the kitchen, the hostess station, all the exits. "If you've got half a ball, maybe you should step out of whatever closet *you're* hiding in."

"I imagine that frustrated you, the idea of David leaving you not for another woman but for a man. How would that play out in the press? It being the twenty-first century, I suppose it would make some headlines but nothing like it would have a few decades back. The betrayal, though. I'm guessing that's the part that stings. You put David through medical school, right, supported him all those years? Then you learn he's in love with his former college roommate? Wow. The way Jeff tells it, this has been going on the whole time, even when you were struggling to make ends meet and pay his tuition. Back when you were working two jobs and writing at night, trying to keep the lights on—David and Jeff were off doing what David and Jeff did. David called you 'the Checkbook.' Did you know that? That has to hurt. Do you think he ever loved you, even a little bit? Or did he play you the entire time?"

The woman at the bar shifted seats, moved two closer. Her back is now to Denise, but that doesn't mean she's no longer watching.

"Denise, are you okay?"

Kirby. Her agent is crouching next to her, a worried look on her face. Denise didn't notice her get up. She realizes Gordon Brennon is no longer at the table and finds him halfway to the restroom, a rough stagger to his gait.

"Maybe you should keep an eye on Gordon," Denise tells her in the calmest voice she can summon. "I'm not sure he'll get to where he's going without help. We don't want . . . an incident."

Kirby nods and starts after him, no doubt thinking about tomorrow's headlines on Page Six if there is some kind of scene. She's predictable like that. The kitchen door opens again. The chef is no longer there, but Denise catches a glimpse of a man who looks a lot like Declan. Same height. Same build. Same — when a waitress carrying a large serving tray pushes through, the door opens wider, and she realizes it's not Declan. She doesn't know who it is. He doesn't look like he works here, though.

She needs to pull it together.

"You seem agitated, Ms. Morrow," says Cordova. "Why don't you try the grasshopper? Declan did. Said it helped calm his nerves. Maybe it will help yours."

Denise ignores that and tells Jennifer, "I'm going to finish this call outside. I'm having trouble hearing in here."

She doesn't wait for her editor to reply. What she does do is watch everyone in the restaurant as she rises from her table and starts for the door, her phone still pressed to her ear. She expects a few people to get up with her, follow her, possibly attempt to take her into custody, but none of them do. Not a single person comes after her. They don't stop watching, though. She can feel their eyes burning into the back of her neck as she steps onto the sidewalk in the chilled night air. She tells herself they're only fans. They recognize her from television. Nothing more. And this Cordova asshole is only fishing. "You have this all wrong, Detective. Jeff might have had a thing for David, but it wasn't reciprocated. If he's telling you otherwise, it's a lie. David and I were very much in love, and I don't appreciate you harassing me like this."

Denise looks up and down the sidewalk, but there's no sign of Cordova. In New York, that means nothing. He could be in any one of the surrounding buildings watching her from a window. NYPD has surveillance cameras everywhere; maybe he's tapped into one of those. None of that matters. If he had anything on her, anything at all, he'd arrest her. A taxi flies by, and Denise realizes she's far too close to the curb and takes a step back.

"Is the fresh air helping?" Cordova says. "Declan was big on getting outside when he needed to work out a problem. The guy loved to walk. Constantly wore out his shoes. But you knew that, right? You've seen his closet. Always bought the same kind—Merrell Moab, size eleven. Same kind we found in Geller Hoffman's safe. Same shoes that made the tracks leading up to your apartment." He pauses. "Are you a walker too, Ms. Morrow? Like Declan?"

More people are watching her out here on the street. There's a guy dressed like a bicycle messenger. Two women standing at the corner who didn't cross when the light changed. A man at the newsstand who doesn't appear to be buying anything, only idly browsing the magazines. All of them keep glancing at her. Stealing looks. Quick. Barely noticeable. But she notices. She notices everything.

Denise is not much of a walker.

But she starts walking now.

Without so much as a glance back at her table in Louie's, Denise Morrow spins to her left and starts down the sidewalk. Her apartment is only four blocks away, and she'll be damned if she'll let this man torment her in the street.

CHAPTER SIXTY-ONE

"YOUR HUSBAND WASN'T sleeping with you," Cordova says. "According to Jeff, he wasn't sleeping with Mia Gomez either. I'd be willing to bet they didn't even know each other. What do you think, Ms. Morrow, as an author, as an accomplished investigator of true crime? What does your gut tell you? Did the husband have a mistress or is that just another deal of three-card monte?"

Three-card monte? Christ, what did Declan tell him? Denise picks up her pace. She should hang up, she knows that, but she can't. She's not so worried about what the man has said so far—she can spin all that. She's more concerned about what he hasn't said. What hasn't he told her? Every story comes down to narrative, a simple string of words. Put them in one order, they mean one thing; put the same words in another order, and they mean something else entirely. This is *her* story, *her* narrative, not his. She won't let him hijack it. "I'd follow the evidence, Detective. And the evidence says David was sleeping with that woman Mia Gomez. I read your report. You found condoms in my husband's pocket that are the same brand as a condom wrapper found in her apartment. David was a well-documented flirt. Not with men, *women*. You have photographic evidence tying him to her. As an investigator of true crime, I figure if it quacks like a duck, that makes it a duck. There's no evidence suggesting David was gay, and Jeff isn't going to blow up his life to put something like that out there. Even if he did, it wouldn't make the evidence linking my husband to Mia Gomez go away. You can spin whatever tale you want, but I'm successful because I stick to the facts no matter where they lead."

"Like learning Geller Hoffman, not Ruben Lucero, killed Maggie Marshall?"

"Exactly like that."

Denise goes around a pothole and stops with the crowd at the corner of Seventy-Seventh and Central Park West, the Museum of Natural History on her left. When she looks back over her shoulder, she thinks she sees the woman from the bar at Louie's, but she can't be sure. Across the street, near one of the entrances to Central Park, a tall Black man is staring in her direction. He looks familiar too, and it takes her a moment to place him, then she does—he's that police lieutenant, Declan and Cordova's boss. Davids—no, *Daniels*, that's it. Then the woman clicks too. It's the assistant district attorney who tried to prosecute her—Saffi, Carmen Saffi. She's wearing a wig;

that's why Denise didn't recognize her. Her hair is tucked up in a damn wig. Denise wants to look back over her shoulder again, but doesn't dare. Instead, she stares across the street with everyone else, waiting for the signal to change. When it finally does, she moves with the crowd. The Beresford is only one long block up, just past the museum. She's nearly home.

On the phone, Cordova clears his throat. "How long have you been writing? Ten, fifteen years, right? How many books in all that time? You've got *Why Corrine Had to Die*, *Bones Tell a Tale*, *Wyatt Loved His Mama*, *The Bronx Ripper*, *The Devil of Hell's Kitchen*, this latest one about Maggie . . . a bunch more. And not just the books—you've got movies, television shows, speaking engagements. Is it true you get upwards of twenty thousand dollars for a one-hour appearance? Christ, I'm lucky if someone buys me pizza for showing up somewhere. Twenty thousand dollars? Good for you. You've built yourself quite the little empire. It's the writing, though, that really ropes people in. You've got this relatable voice. I've read a couple of your books over the past few weeks, and honestly, it's like sitting at a campfire listening to someone spin a tale. Like eating popcorn, it's hard to stop. But you know what really got me? Not only as a reader, but as a cop? It's the way you lay out the facts. You dig so damn deep into these cases. You pull facts and piece together theories that completely slipped by the investigating officers. Like in *The Cornerstone of Marriage*. The couple in that one were married for, what, forty-seven years? Then the husband dies of a severe allergic reaction at a steak house in Poughkeepsie. He was allergic to shellfish, and the medical examiner blamed it on cross-contamination in the restaurant's kitchen. Then you go and find some old transcripts from when the CSU techs were poking around in their house. They listed the items they found in the wife's medicine cabinet, and the name of a popular herbal supplement jumps out at you. Hell, I take it for my joints. Works great. Who would know it's sometimes made with fish oil? In your book, you pointed out that only three of the ninety pills were missing even though the bottle was over a year old. You, not the police, found the purchase in the wife's Amazon history. You floated your theory to the local cops, and when they brought the wife in, she cracked, confessed to slipping her husband a mickey at dinner. Said she hadn't loved him in years and just wanted out. You pieced that together — not the police, you. Maybe you should have been a cop."

"The pay is shit. No, thank you." Denise can see the Beresford just ahead.

Across the street, Daniels is making no attempt to hide. He's matching her stride for stride. She can feel the woman somewhere behind her but doesn't turn. She doesn't pick up her pace either, as much as she wants to.

"The fish allergy. Is that how you came up with the idea to kill Declan? Did he tell you he was allergic to peanuts, or did you figure that one out on your own?"

Denise has had enough. "Goodbye, Detective. Don't call me again." She mashes the disconnect button and slips her phone into her pocket.

The Beresford doorman spots her coming up the sidewalk and opens the door for her. "Lovely evening, Mrs. Morrow." He must see something in her face, because his grin disappears and he says, sounding worried, "Everything okay?"

She's lost track of Daniels and the Saffi woman but she knows they're both out there. "I've got a lot of work to do tonight, Teddy. Nobody comes up, okay? If anyone shows up looking for me, send them away. I don't want to see anybody."

He nods. This isn't the first time she's given these instructions, and Teddy is better than most bouncers at the trendiest midtown clubs when it comes to enforcement. He reaches into the breast pocket of his uniform jacket and produces a business card. "You did have a guest earlier. He left this, but I can give it to you tomorrow if you'd rather not be bothered now."

The NYPD logo is partly visible between his chubby fingers. Denise takes the card from him, expecting it to be Cordova's, but it's not. It was left by Roy Harrison with Internal Affairs.

"Did he say anything? What did he want?"

"He said cops like to play cards too."

CHAPTER SIXTY-TWO

TEDDY'S FROWN DEEPENS. "Are you sure you're okay, Mrs. Morrow? You're sweating and you look pale. Maybe you should rest down here for a minute so you're not—"

Alone. That's what he was going to say, but he stops himself and gestures over his shoulder. "You're welcome to use my office as long as you like."

"I don't think my dinner agreed with me. Shellfish never does." She has no idea why she said that; she had a steak, but there's no point in walking it back. "I'll be fine."

Before Teddy can push the issue, she's in the elevator heading up. She doesn't realize she's been holding her breath until it slips out in one long exhale like a deflating balloon. She wipes the clammy sweat from her palms on the hem of her skirt, tears Harrison's card in two, and balls up the pieces in her fist. She's done with him. He didn't give her anything useful. She should have cut ties with him a long time ago.

I'm done with all of it, she tells herself.

The second she gets inside her apartment, she'll delete the Maggie Marshall book and burn what's left of her notes, the fallout from that be damned. It is time to move on.

When the doors open, Denise screams—

A man is standing at the threshold facing her.

He stumbles back, his eyes wide, hands raised defensively. "Whoa, Denise, it's just me."

It takes a second for her to recognize him. Russell Bookholz, one of her neighbors. He and his wife travel most of the year; she hasn't seen either of them in months. "I didn't...I didn't realize you were home," she says.

"Got in from Switzerland a few hours ago." His hair is a little longer than she remembers, and his leathery skin is pink with the kind of windburn you find only in avid skiers. "Liz and I are exhausted. I'm running out for a few supplies, then I plan to sleep for a day so I can get myself back on New York time." He tilts his head to the side. "I just stopped by to say we heard about David in Zermatt, and I can't begin to tell you how sorry we are. If there is anything we can do, anything at all, don't hesitate to ask, okay?"

Denise nods because there's nothing else she can do. Her heart is beating like a jackhammer. All she can think about is the Valium in her bathroom and the bottle of Château Mouton Rothschild on her kitchen counter. "I'm glad you're back," she manages. "It's been too quiet around here."

He smiles warmly and steps into the elevator. "Anything at all, you knock," he says as the doors close with a soft *whoosh*.

Denise is at her door in an instant. Her hands are shaking again; it takes a moment for her to get the key in the lock and the door open. She scrambles inside, slams the door behind her, locks it, and twists both dead bolts (she added a second after Declan snuck in). She keys in half her alarm code before realizing she didn't arm the system when she left.

Her phone rings. It's Kirby.

Denise answers and says before the woman can get a word in, "I'm sorry, something came up and I had to run home."

Her agent does a poor job of masking her frustration. "Are you coming back?"

"Tell everyone I had a wonderful evening. It was good to see all of you."

"Denise, call me tomorrow. We need to discuss—"

Denise hangs up.

She can't. Not now.

Quimby appears from nowhere, weaves around her ankles with a loud purr, and heads to the kitchen, a not-so-subtle attempt to point out that dinnertime came and went an hour ago.

Denise drops her keys in the bowl by the door and navigates the foyer and hallway without turning on any lights. In the living room, she tosses her phone onto the couch. It bounces softly and settles near the far end.

Feed cat. Valium. Wine. Bath.

In that order.

Tomorrow she'll hire a new attorney and file restraining

orders against all of them—Cordova, that lieutenant, the whole lot. Maybe she'll revive her lawsuit. She doesn't need the money, but she does need to send a message.

A loud message.

In the shadows just beyond the kitchen, someone clears his throat and says in a gravelly voice, "I'm curious, Ms. Morrow—as a writer, what's the one question you get asked most?"

Denise gasps and turns to see a vague outline stamped in the darkness. The can lights above the kitchen island come to life when Detective Cordova brushes the switch near the back hall with a gloved hand; with his other hand, he's holding a revolver that's pointed at her.

CHAPTER SIXTY-THREE

ALTHOUGH DENISE MORROW appears startled at the sight
of him, she recovers quickly. She makes no attempt to move.
She says, her words sharp, cold, "How did you get in here?"

Cordova can't help admiring her strength, her resilience.
Her mind is clearly dancing, weighing every possible option,
moves and countermoves. She's probably thinking about the
.22 she has hidden in her pantry five feet to his left. "Answer
me," he says in a soft, even tone, the gun steady in his hand.

"What question am I asked the most?"

"Yeah."

A long silence ticks by. Beyond her floor-to-ceiling windows,
the city breathes and moves, a living thing of harsh lights and
rumble of traffic, distant sirens and horns. All of it seems a

world away. Inside the apartment, the air is still, growing thick.

Denise Morrow's left hand twitches; she presses her thumb and forefinger together and gently rolls them in a slow circular motion. He's seen her do this before, in court. Saffi told him autistic people sometimes do it to center themselves, to force their brains to focus on the now. Her cold gaze locks with his and stays there. "They ask where I get my ideas."

The words hang between them for a moment, suspended.

"Have you ever answered honestly? Just once?" Cordova shakes his head before she can reply. "Never mind; we both know you haven't. Probably not even to yourself." A wry smile crosses his lips. "Does your agent know the truth? What about David? Did he know? I can't imagine you've gone all these years without telling anyone."

The expression on her face turns to steel, and when she speaks, her voice is eerily calm. "Breaking and entering. Holding me at gunpoint. I hope you understand you're living your final moments outside of a cell, Detective," she says flatly. She looks around her apartment. "I saw your friends outside. Are you alone?"

Cordova shifts his weight to his left foot. "I sent them home. It's just us. I think it's been a long time coming."

Morrow's cat darts across the room, eyes his empty bowl on the floor, then hops up onto a stool by the kitchen island, does an elegant spin, and settles down on it, watching them both.

Denise Morrow's eyes narrow. "I have no interest in talking to you."

Cordova thumbs back the hammer of his .38. He's not ready to shoot her, not yet, but he wants her to know he will if he has to. "Mia Gomez worked for GTS. I wrote that down when we found her body, and I blame myself for not digging deeper. Her death initially looked like a mugging, then things tied to Geller Hoffman. Her employment didn't seem important, but as you've pointed out in your books, sometimes everything hangs on the little details. Those three letters completely slipped my mind until I saw them again this morning. GTS—that stands for Gerhardt Transcription Services. Of course you already know that, right?"

She says nothing, only stares at him.

"GTS is an NYPD subcontractor. I've seen those initials on a million reports over the years," Cordova continues. "Court transcripts, crime scene dictations, interviews, depositions. Private material. *Privileged material.* That got me thinking. What if a person somehow gained access to those transcriptions? Not just the public material, but all of it? What if that person found a way to get copies of whatever they wanted? Impossible, right? A company like GTS, they keep sensitive data like that behind a firewall as thick as a concrete bunker. They've got safeguards to prevent access. They'd have to, right? Top-of-the-line encryption. Hacker-proof." Cordova shifts his weight back to his other foot. "I'm not a big tech guy, but over the years, something about all that high-tech wizardry has jumped out at me. All that security is no different than the lock on the front door of a house—it can be the best, most impenetrable lock on the planet, but it does no good if the wrong person has a key." He smirks. "You of all people get that, right? You said Geller Hoffman broke in here while you were sleeping. But didn't he have a key?"

"Nobody gave *you* one. You're trespassing," she tells him.

"And I want you to leave. My neighbors are back from Switzerland. If I scream, they'll hear me."

Cordova waves the .38 in the air. "I imagine they'll hear the gunshot too. Neither of those things will change the outcome."

Denise Morrow says nothing to that.

Cordova lets the silence linger for a second, then goes on. "Mia Gomez started in data entry and worked her way up. Her coworkers tell me she practically ran the shop. They all trusted her. She was the fastest transcriptionist they'd ever had. She was promoted to account exec, but she'd still help out when the transcriptionists fell behind. They'd give her their usernames and passwords and she'd catch them right up." Cordova reaches into his pocket and takes out a folded sheet of paper. "I found this in her apartment. She had log-in credentials for more than half the employees, including three of her bosses. I don't think there was a single file on GTS servers she couldn't access. Imagine that. Information like that"—he whistles softly—"that kind of information is gold. Particularly if you know how to peddle it. *If you know who needs it.* Imagine if you were a criminal defense attorney who had the means to view that kind of information without having to go through the discovery process. You'd see the prosecution's case laid bare, and you could completely undermine it. Or," Cordova continues, "what if you were an author who wanted details for your books, details nobody else could possibly have?"

A flicker of fear passes across Denise Morrow's face, but it's gone as quickly as it appeared. "Authors spend a lot of time playing the what-if game, Detective. That doesn't make any of it true. Truth is only what you can prove."

Cordova nods. She's not wrong about that. "Did you know Mia Gomez owned a boat?"

She says nothing.

"A thirty-five-foot Sea Ray Sundancer. She docked it at Dyckman Marina out on the Hudson. Slip twenty-eight B. Bought it nine months ago for two hundred thirty-two thousand six hundred dollars. Paid cash. Named it *Play on Words*. Gotta love that. I drove up and took a look. Nothing but teak and smooth lines. The kind of thing that screams *money*. I could never afford something like that on a cop's salary, so I pulled Mia Gomez's financials. I'm not sure how she could afford it either. She made a hundred and three thousand dollars last year at GTS, and that's her best year in the four I looked at."

"Maybe she came into an inheritance."

"Yeah." Cordova licks his lips. "That must be it. Wonder who left it to her."

Cordova steps over to the bookcase and, without lowering the gun, runs his finger along the spines of her books. "I called Mia Gomez's boss at GTS and read off your titles, told her what cases they were about. I asked her if Mia Gomez had access to transcriptions from any of those cases. I heard her click away on her computer, and you know what she said?"

Denise Morrow remains quiet.

"She didn't say anything. Then I read off the names of several of Geller Hoffman's high-profile cases. I heard her click away again, and then she said she wouldn't be able to answer my questions without a warrant. Not exactly a 'Yes, Ms. Gomez had access,' but she certainly sounded nervous." Cordova lowers his voice and says, "I'm sure if I pull your finances or Hoffman's, I won't find the payments to Mia Gomez. I imagine they're buried so deep, even you can't find them, but we both know they're there. You've been paying Mia Gomez for years." He nods at the books. "Probably for every one of these. So what happened? She got greedy, right? They always do. Left you and Hoffman no choice but to take her off the board."

Morrow says nothing, and although she looked rattled when she first saw him, the fear is gone now. It's like she feeds on it. Like it makes her stronger. Cordova is still pointing the gun at her, but she crosses the room to him. She closes the distance until they're less than a foot apart. She reaches up with tentative fingers and begins unbuttoning his shirt.

CHAPTER SIXTY-FOUR

"I'M NOT WEARING a wire," Cordova tells her, but she doesn't stop.

When his belly is exposed, she pats him down with the thoroughness of a practiced prison guard, starting with his arms, then moving on to his shoulders, torso, and legs. She turns him around and untucks his shirt in the back and doesn't hesitate to check between his legs. Although he's holding the gun, she doesn't make a grab for it. She finds his phone in his back pocket, powers it off, and tosses it on the couch near hers. Then she steps back. "What exactly do you want from me?"

"An exchange of information. A chat. That's all," he tells her. "I want to understand why Declan had to die."

"He was a dirty cop."

"No, he wasn't."

This seems to frustrate her. She frowns and begins ticking off points on her fingers. "He broke Lucero's arm taking him into custody. He browbeat him trying to get a confession. When the evidence wasn't there for a conviction, he signed into police lockup as your lieutenant, pulled that book from Maggie's possessions, and planted it in—"

Her voice cuts off with the sharpness of a whip and for several seconds she looks at the floor, her mouth moving silently as she processes the thought that just entered her head. She looks back at Cordova, and her words come out slowly as she absorbs the truth: "It wasn't Declan, was it? *It was you.*"

Cordova sighs. He's never told anyone. He's never spoken the words aloud. Not until now. "That monster would have walked."

"So you planted evidence."

"I rewrote the narrative."

"Lucero died in prison. You put him there with false evidence. If this gets out, you'll be charged with homicide." For the first time, she looks confused. "Why are you admitting this?"

"Because I want you to understand I'm not here to arrest you. I'm done playing cat and mouse. You win. I can't touch you," he says. "You know something about me; I know something about you. I'm retiring soon and I just want to fill in the blanks so I can put this to bed."

She doesn't believe him and he doesn't expect her to. Most likely she believes he's recording this or has someone listening. He doesn't, though. He only wants answers. He scratches the side of his chin. "I know you and Declan were sleeping together. I know he thought the two of you were going to run off somewhere. That man hasn't left the five boroughs in his entire life, and last month he got a passport. He must have been in love to torch his career, even if he knew he'd be exonerated in the end. What did you promise him? Where were you planning to go?" When she doesn't answer, he waves his hand dismissively. "It doesn't really matter. We both know it was bullshit. You used him, and when you were done, you made him go away. Damn peanut allergy." He shakes his head. "You know, I didn't find a single EpiPen in his apartment. What'd you do? Fuck him and then round them all up while he was sleeping it off? Must have killed you to slink around that filthy place picking through drawers and cabinets. You keep your apartment immaculate."

Denise smiles smugly. "You dusted his apartment for prints, right? How many of those prints were mine?"

Cordova holds up his hand and presses his thumb and pointer finger together. "Zero."

"Exactly."

Cordova runs his hand through his thinning hair. "You know, when I figured out the two of you were sleeping together, I honestly thought Declan killed David. Then I pulled the subway footage from across the street, and that drove it home—I was positive he did it. On the video recording, he comes rushing in, obviously distraught, and shoves something in a trash can. Then he gets up on the platform and spends the next two hours thinking about jumping. He sure as hell looked like a man who'd just committed murder. I'm certain he entered this building that night at six thirty, just like that eyewitness said, but when he got to your apartment, I think he found your husband already dead."

"Geller Hoffman killed my husband hours later."

"Drop the bullshit. We both know he didn't."

"What we know," Denise says, "is the medical examiner said my husband was murdered between eight thirty and nine thirty p.m. He couldn't have been dead at six thirty p.m. You know as well as I do that with current techniques, MEs can be fairly precise about time of death."

Cordova nods. "Yep. From what I've been told, if someone has been dead for less than five hours, MEs can use body temperature to narrow time of death to a window of forty-five minutes, sometimes less. In your husband's case, the ME is very confident on TOD. Between eight thirty and nine thirty p.m. That means Declan couldn't have killed him. He's on video from six forty-seven p.m. until I called him to the scene just before ten. He didn't leave the camera frame once. He's even on there taking my call. It's like he knew to stand exactly there. You were at that bookstore, also on video, with dozens of people watching you. But the thing is, even Geller Hoffman is off the hook if David died before eight thirty p.m. Hoffman had appointments until eight, and then he had to go kill Mia Gomez for you. I timed the ride from that alley to the bookstore in Tribeca. Works out perfectly if he left right after killing Mia, but it falls to shit if he came up here to kill David too.

There's no way he could have killed them both. He only did Mia Gomez."

Denise walks back across the living room and leans on the couch. "So if it wasn't Declan and it wasn't Geller, who killed David?"

"You did."

CHAPTER SIXTY-FIVE

DENISE MORROW ISN'T FAZED. "You just said I couldn't have killed David."

"No, I said you couldn't have killed him while you were at the bookstore between seven fifteen and nine twenty p.m. You did it much earlier." Cordova motions toward the hallway with his gun. "Back bedroom."

"Why?"

"Move. Now." Cordova doesn't wait for her to reply; he heads down the hall to the room where CSU brought Denise Morrow the night of the murder to process her and her clothing.

Although Denise is in the living room and could easily flee out the door or pick up her phone and call someone, he knows she won't. He knows she'll follow him; she can't help herself.

She needs to know what he knows. A moment later she proves him right. He's standing next to the bed when she appears in the doorway, her hands clasped behind her back. Her cat is behind her, rubbing against the backs of her legs and purring loudly.

"Did you grab a knife? I'd be disappointed in you if you didn't."

Her left hand drops to her side, and he sees she's holding a seven-inch santoku. "A girl's gotta defend herself," she says, "and it looks like you found my twenty-two."

"You don't need either," he tells her. "This is just a—"

"A chat," she says. "An exchange of information."

"Exactly."

To reinforce that point, Cordova slips his gun into the holster on his belt. He can get to it fast enough if he has to. Right now, he needs her to listen. "We found trace amounts of wool on David's body. It was on his clothing, mixed in with the blood. That didn't make sense. Nothing about this case made sense when I first looked at it, but that in particular, it's been nagging at me. So when I broke in here tonight, I took a good look around."

The bed is neatly made. He pats the thick duvet. "CSI set up shop right here, covered this bed with equipment. They probably spent six hours in this room. I can just imagine what was going through your head as you watched them. So close but completely unaware."

He grips the duvet and tosses it aside, revealing a copper-colored wool blanket. He runs his fingers along the edge until he finds a power cord; it's tucked neatly behind the bed frame. It's not just a wool blanket; it's a *heated* wool blanket. Cordova stares at it for a moment. "I bet there's trace on here, but we never bothered to look. Why would we? No reason to. Not in that initial search, anyway. By the time the medical examiner found the wool on David's body, Geller Hoffman had circled the wagons; there was no way we could get back in here. No judge in his or her right mind would sign off on the warrant—not after that debacle at your arraignment." He brushes the material, then looks at his fingertips. "I'm honestly surprised you kept it. Then again, with us unable to get back in your apartment for a second search, this might be the safest place for it." He straightens up and faces her again. "After you killed David, you covered his body with this heated blanket and left it on him until you got back from the bookstore. That kept his body temp high enough to throw off the ME."

She gently rotates the knife, her fingertips brushing the polished handle. "If that's true, how did I kill David without getting his blood on me? Your people checked."

The corner of Cordova's mouth twitches. "At first I thought you'd handed off whatever you'd been wearing to Hoffman at the bookstore when you changed into the clothing he wore when he killed Mia, but that wouldn't work. Stabbing someone is a messy business. There's spatter. It doesn't just get on your clothes—it gets on your skin, in your hair. CSI would have found that on you. Something would have been visible on the bookstore video footage. I watched it a dozen times and found nothing. Then I thought back to Declan. He'd been up here around six thirty p.m., right after you killed David. In the video we pulled from the subway station, Declan can be seen stuffing something into a trash can. It's hard to tell for sure but it looks like one of those cheap plastic rain slickers they sell in the museum gift shop across the street. You know, the kind that folds up small enough to stuff in your pocket. He throws away a package of wipes too, blue and white — Clorox, I think. Again, it's hard to tell. The footage isn't very clear. The city really needs to replace those cameras. Doesn't really matter now because we didn't pull the trash; it's long gone, lost to a landfill somewhere. The video isn't conclusive and the evidence is gone. The rain slicker — it covered up your clothing, had a hood to protect your hair, and the wipes took care of the rest." He smirks, nods at the knife in her left hand. "Nice touch, stabbing David with your right. That must have been tough for a lefty. You were quick about it too, not a bit of hesitation. David didn't have a single defensive wound."

Denise Morrow is quiet for a long moment. "Nobody will believe I killed David for cheating with Jeff, Mia, or anyone. Nobody will believe any of this."

"You killed David for a reason as old as time — it was cheaper than divorce."

"We had a prenup."

"Your prenup covered the assets you both had when you were married, which amounts to nearly nothing. It didn't cover earnings while you were married. And let's be honest — your book sales were shit until Mia Gomez started selling you intel, and you'd been married for years by then. You had millions of reasons for wanting David dead. Hell, even though he was a doctor, with the discrepancy in your incomes, he probably would have gotten alimony."

There's a flicker in her eyes, a crack; small, but there.

Cordova presses on. "You killed David, Geller Hoffman killed Mia Gomez, and it was your idea to mix up all the

evidence. Three-card monte, Declan called it. You had Hoffman wrapped around your little finger—he was more than
happy to help. Sounds like he was obsessed with you. I bet you
didn't even have to sleep with him; you just planted the notion
that you might. Guy like that, it's enough to string him along.
The way we found him . . ." The words trail off as the image of
Hoffman's body in the closet comes back into Cordova's head.
"I'm guessing it was a *You can watch me and I'll watch you* sort of
thing. He'd go along with that, right? Perfect for you—no
touching, no DNA." Cordova taps the center of his chest. "The
medical examiner found a small round bruise on Hoffman's
chest, right here. I'm thinking you got him in that closet, got
the belt around his neck, and stepped on him with one high
heel when he was in the heat of things. You kept the pressure
on until he suffocated. When he was dead, you spread the
photos around to lock in your story with Lucero. Then you got
dressed and left."

She's been drawing closer as he talks, and she's only a few
feet away now. Her grip on the knife tightens.

"Look, I'm a cop, so I shouldn't say this, but I'm gonna say it
anyway: I don't care that you killed Geller Hoffman—he was
a shitbag. Sounds like David took advantage of you, so maybe
in some twisted way, he had it coming. If Mia Gomez tried to
blackmail you, she made her own bed too. Hell, even Declan.
Dec decided to play with fire. He was a big boy. He knew what
that meant better than anyone. I've been in this game far too
long to get all sanctimonious. People do bad things; bad things
happen. I just need to know one thing." He looks her square in
the eye. "Lucero ID'ing Hoffman—that was bullshit, right?

You set it up? If I'm going to wash my hands of all this, I need to know Declan and I put away the right guy."

"You want to know if you *planted evidence* against the right guy," she says flatly. "Isn't that what you really mean?"

He stares at her for a long time, then finally nods. "We're all a little dirty here. I need to have a clear conscience before I get out of the game."

Denise Morrow sets the knife down on the nightstand by the bed. Soundlessly, she goes out into the hall. Cordova eyes the knife, then follows. He finds her reaching for a framed watercolor of a purple flowering tree hanging near the bathroom. She takes it off the wall and turns it around. There's a sheet of paper taped to the back. She carefully removes it and hands it to him.

CHAPTER SIXTY-SIX

Log 11/04/2018 16:08 EST

Transcript: Dannemora, Clinton Correctional Facility / monitored phone recording

Present: Carolyn Douglas (attorney)

      Ruben Lucero (inmate)

[Ruben Lucero] When are you getting me out? I
      can't take this place no more.
[Carolyn Douglas] You didn't make bail, Ruben. I
      can't get you out. Not now, anyway.
[Lucero] Bullshit. You ain't even trying. Public
      defender. I need a real attorney.

[Douglas] When you're back in front of the judge
next week, we'll try and get your bail
reduced. Until then, you'll need to sit tight.

[Lucero] Sit tight? Are you kidding me? If you
can't get me out, at least get me out of
gen-pop. Have them put me in protective
custody. Isolation. Whatever. I don't care,
just get me someplace safe. I go back in the
yard, I ain't walking out. That's for damn
sure.

[Douglas] I've made the warden aware of your con-
cerns.

[Lucero] Yeah, I'm sure you lit a fire under him.
Did you at least pick up that box I told you
about?

[Douglas] I told you, I can't do that. It's outside the
scope of my job.

[Lucero] Your job is to keep me out of jail.

[Douglas] Not by destroying evidence.

[Lucero] I didn't tell you to destroy it, I just want
you to move it before the cops find it.

[Douglas] I won't do that either.

[Lucero] Of course not. You want to see me burn,
is that it? Give me some half-assed defense
so you can sleep at night but you got no
intention of getting me out of here. Fuck the
judge and jury, you already decided what
needs to happen to me. You're no better
than that bitch I put down. She was a prick
tease, and you're a—

[Douglas] Ruben, all calls here are monitored.
Watch what you say on—
[Lucero] It don't matter if I'm dead. You don't give a
shit about me.
[Douglas] If this call is being monitored, I want to
point out I'm this inmate's attorney and this
conversation is privileged.
[Lucero] Go get the damn box!
[*Call disconnected.*]
[*End of recording.*]

/MG/GTS

CHAPTER SIXTY-SEVEN

CORDOVA SHAKES THE PAGE. "You used this to keep Declan in line, didn't you?"

Denise says nothing, but there's a slight smile on her lips.

Of course that's what she did. It was Declan's Get Out of Jail Free card.

A goddamn carrot.

Cordova reads the transcript twice before he hands the paper back to Denise Morrow. "The box? The same box of photos found with Geller Hoffman's body?" It all makes sense now. "Lucero couldn't get his public defender to hide that box for him, so he told you about it. Instead of disposing of all the pictures, you used them to frame Geller Hoffman. You..."

His words trail off.

Of course she did.

Three-card monte.

There's not an ounce of remorse on her face. She had copies of the transcripts. She knew Lucero mentioned another man in the park during his initial interview. She built on that. Wove Geller Hoffman into the narrative. She did what all writers do: She created a backstory. Got Lucero to play along, made him think it would get him out.

David Morrow.

Mia Gomez.

Geller Hoffman.

Declan.

She played all of them.

Hell, Cordova thinks, *she even played me. I bought it like every-one else.*

He can't help but smile.

As twisted as it all is, she committed the perfect crime.

"There's a beauty to what you did," he says softly. "I respect that. I've been on the force for decades and I've never seen anything like this." He rubs his cheek. "Follow me."

He leads her down the hall to the main bedroom.

The terrace doors are open.

He steps outside and lets the sounds of the city and the cool night air wash over him.

When he broke into Denise Morrow's apartment, he'd found a bottle of champagne chilling on the kitchen counter. He'd brought it out here along with two glasses.

Denise appears in the doorway, followed closely by her cat. She eyes the bottle and the glasses on the wrought iron table near the railing. "Are we celebrating?"

"I've spent years wondering if I framed the right guy," he tells her. "You have no idea how much peace you've brought me tonight by telling me the truth. And you..." He takes a step back, appraises her. "The way you did this, the way you mucked up the facts, the evidence...even if it all comes out, you'll never see the inside of a jail cell. There's not a single piece of evidence that can't be discredited by even the most incompetent defense attorney. You've created so much reasonable doubt, any jury would let you walk. A month or two later, even the press would forget. You'll never be held accountable. It wouldn't stick. You covered everything. Fucking brilliant, if you ask me. I'm done. I'm throwing in the towel."

"You expect me to believe you're going to just drop all this and walk away?"

Cordova shakes his head. "Oh, I'm not walking away. With Mia Gomez gone, you're going to need someone to supply you with information. I think you and I can work out a deal of our own. That ADA you saw downstairs and my lieutenant, they want in too. You put the three of us on your payroll and we guarantee you'll receive back-channel data on the city's highest-profile cases. Homicides, kidnappings, financial crimes. Nobody will be able to touch you. You get to keep writing, I get to supplement my crappy pension, and Daniels and Saffi line their pockets. We play this right, it's a win for all of us."

"What about that guy from IAU, Harrison?"

"Screw Harrison. He's an idiot. We'll take care of him."

At her feet, the cat sends up a soft purr. Denise bends and scratches him behind the ear. "What do you think, Quimby? Should Mama work with this man?"

The cat eyes Cordova, then weaves around Denise's ankles

several times in a slow figure eight, hops onto a chair, and licks a paw.

"I don't speak cat," Cordova says. "Is that a yes?"

Denise straightens up. "It means I'll consider it."

More than twenty floors below, an ambulance races down Central Park West; the chirp of its siren cuts through the air, momentarily loud and then gone.

Cordova picks up the champagne bottle, carefully fills both glasses, and hands one to her. He holds up his in a toast. "To committing the perfect crime."

Although Denise holds up her glass, she doesn't drink.

Cordova finishes his in three gulps and grins. "Worried I'll poison you?"

"It crossed my mind."

He wipes his mouth and sets his glass down on the table near the bottle. "Poison is too easy to find in the autopsy."

Cordova drops low, wraps his arms around Denise Morrow's legs, twists hard to the right, and rises back up, lifting her off the ground. With a grunt, he heaves the writer over the railing.

CHAPTER SIXTY-EIGHT

MORE THAN TWENTY stories up.

More than two hundred feet.

Falling at a rate of thirty-two feet per second squared, she reaches the ground in approximately three and a half seconds. She screams all the way down and hits the pavement with a sickening thud. Her champagne glass shatters about six feet from her body, coating the sidewalk in glistening shards. A puddle of black blood slowly spreads beneath her.

"That's for Declan, you pretentious bitch."

Breathless, Cordova wants to watch what happens next but knows he can't; he can't risk anyone seeing him. As the first bystander's scream comes from below, he stumbles back from the railing and trips over Denise's cat, who's jumped off the chair and is now running around the terrace yowling, a god-awful noise.

He gets back to his feet, knowing he has to move fast.

His own three-card monte.

Cordova retrieves his champagne flute, takes it to the kitchen, quickly washes and dries it, and places the glass back in the cabinet where he found it. He's not worried about prints—he never took off his gloves. The only prints they'll find on the bottle belong to Denise Morrow and whoever handled it before her.

His heart is beating wildly.

He goes to Denise Morrow's couch and retrieves his cell phone—not his personal phone but the burner he bought earlier. His personal phone is currently in Harrison's pocket along with Saffi's and Daniels's phones. If anyone feels the need to pull their location data for tonight, they'll find all four of them at the Jets game. He powers the cell on just long enough to send a group text to the burners Saffi and Daniels are carrying—*Go Jets!*—then breaks the phone in half, slips the pieces in his pocket, and heads down the hall to Denise Morrow's office. The damn cat follows him the whole time, meowing in distress.

In the office, he finds Denise's MacBook powered on and beeping incessantly.

Beep!

Beep!

Beep! Beep! Beep!

"What's that all about?" he asks the cat, but the cat is in no mood to answer. He's staring up at Cordova with a look of hatred on his face.

Cordova opens a new Microsoft Word document and quickly types five words:

I'm sorry. I can't anymore.

Not his best work, but hell, she's the writer, not him. He makes the font a little bigger, centers the text, then clicks Print. Denise's laser printer hums to life and spits out the page. He'll leave the note under the champagne bottle.

Beep!

Beep! Beep!

In a neat stack at the corner of her desk is the manuscript of Denise's latest book, *The Taking of Maggie Marshall*. Part of him wants to grab it but he knows he can't. It will be found here as she left it. Most likely it will be published post-humously. Most likely it will sell better than all her earlier books. Isn't that what always happens when a writer dies? He can't help wondering what that book will mean for Declan's reputation. Is he still the villain of her story or did she update the book to put it all on Geller Hoffman? Is Lucero some twisted martyr?

"Doesn't really matter," he tells the cat. "One news cycle and the world will forget."

Beep! Beep! Beep!

"Christ, what the hell *is* that?"

With each beep, a small message box appears at the top right corner of the screen but vanishes before he can read it.

He moves the cursor up and over and manages to click on the message, which brings up an open browser window. A page from Denise Morrow's website. It takes Cordova a second to realize what he's looking at, and when he does, the world diffuses; traffic sounds are muffled, everything is underwater. He reads the top of the website page.

Welcome to QuimbyCam!

For the next 48 hours, see the world through the eyes of my cat!

There's a video feed directly below that, and in the frame is his own face. He's being filmed from the side, the image bouncing and jerky.

Cordova slowly turns to the cat, who is perched on a corner of the desk staring at him. Dangling from his collar is a small black box—a camera no larger than a sugar cube.

Quimby offers a long meow; his green eyes narrow to slits.

On the screen, directly below the live video feed, messages fly by.

[Wimbly823] Did he just kill her?

[TheGrimPeeper] No way, it's some kind of publicity
    stunt.

[Bud4Me] That was no stunt!

[TwistedRead] Who is he?

[Wimbly823] Please don't let him hurt the cat!

[TheGrimPeeper] It's fake! That didn't even look like
    a real balcony! They're on a set somewhere.
    Hollywood bullshit 4sure.

[MosleyBear] Doesn't she live at the Beresford in
      NYC?
[Deb Alta] I know that guy! He's been on the news.
[MosleyBear] Channel 4 just reported a jumper at
      the Beresford...

ABOUT THE AUTHORS

James Patterson is one of the best-known and biggest-selling writers of all time. Among his creations are some of the world's most popular series, including Alex Cross, the Women's Murder Club, Michael Bennett and the Private novels. He has written many other number one bestsellers including collaborations with President Bill Clinton, Dolly Parton and Michael Crichton, stand-alone thrillers and non-fiction. James has donated millions in grants to independent bookshops and has been the most borrowed adult author in UK libraries for the past fourteen years in a row. He lives in Florida with his family.

J. D. Barker is the international bestselling author of numerous books, including *Dracul* and *The Fourth Monkey*. His novels have been translated into two dozen languages and optioned for both film and television. Barker resides in coastal New Hampshire with his wife, Dayna, and their daughter, Ember.

Also By James Patterson

ALEX CROSS NOVELS

Along Came a Spider • Kiss the Girls • Jack and Jill • Cat and Mouse • Pop Goes the Weasel • Roses are Red • Violets are Blue • Four Blind Mice • The Big Bad Wolf • London Bridges • Mary, Mary • Cross • Double Cross • Cross Country • Alex Cross's Trial (*with Richard DiLallo*) • I, Alex Cross • Cross Fire • Kill Alex Cross • Merry Christmas, Alex Cross • Alex Cross, Run • Cross My Heart • Hope to Die • Cross Justice • Cross the Line • The People vs. Alex Cross • Target: Alex Cross • Criss Cross • Deadly Cross • Fear No Evil • Triple Cross • Alex Cross Must Die • The House of Cross

THE WOMEN'S MURDER CLUB SERIES

1st to Die (*with Andrew Gross*) • 2nd Chance (*with Andrew Gross*) • 3rd Degree (*with Andrew Gross*) • 4th of July (*with Maxine Paetro*) • The 5th Horseman (*with Maxine Paetro*) • The 6th Target (*with Maxine Paetro*) • 7th Heaven (*with Maxine Paetro*) • 8th Confession (*with Maxine Paetro*) • 9th Judgement (*with Maxine Paetro*) • 10th Anniversary (*with Maxine Paetro*) • 11th Hour (*with Maxine Paetro*) • 12th of Never (*with Maxine Paetro*) • Unlucky 13 (*with Maxine Paetro*) • 14th Deadly Sin (*with Maxine Paetro*) • 15th Affair (*with Maxine Paetro*) • 16th Seduction (*with Maxine Paetro*) • 17th Suspect (*with Maxine Paetro*) • 18th Abduction (*with Maxine Paetro*) • 19th Christmas (*with Maxine Paetro*) • 20th Victim (*with Maxine Paetro*) • 21st Birthday (*with Maxine Paetro*) • 22 Seconds (*with Maxine Paetro*) • 23rd Midnight (*with Maxine Paetro*) • The 24th Hour (*with Maxine Paetro*) • 25 Alive (*with Maxine Paetro*)

DETECTIVE MICHAEL BENNETT SERIES

Step on a Crack (*with Michael Ledwidge*) • Run for Your Life (*with Michael Ledwidge*) • Worst Case (*with Michael Ledwidge*) • Tick Tock (*with Michael Ledwidge*) • I, Michael Bennett (*with Michael Ledwidge*) • Gone (*with Michael Ledwidge*) • Burn (*with Michael Ledwidge*) • Alert (*with Michael Ledwidge*) • Bullseye (*with Michael Ledwidge*) • Haunted (*with James O. Born*) • Ambush (*with James O. Born*) • Blindside (*with James O. Born*) • The Russian (*with James O. Born*) • Shattered (*with James O. Born*) • Obsessed

(with *James O. Born*) • Crosshairs (with *James O. Born*) •
Paranoia (with *James O. Born*)

PRIVATE NOVELS

Private (with *Maxine Paetro*) • Private London (with *Mark Pearson*) •
Private Games (with *Mark Sullivan*) • Private: No. 1 Suspect
(with *Maxine Paetro*) • Private Berlin (with *Mark Sullivan*) • Private
Down Under (with *Michael White*) • Private L.A. (with *Mark Sullivan*) •
Private India (with *Ashwin Sanghi*) • Private Vegas (with *Maxine
Paetro*) • Private Sydney (with *Kathryn Fox*) • Private Paris (with *Mark
Sullivan*) • The Games (with *Mark Sullivan*) • Private Delhi (with
Ashwin Sanghi) • Private Princess (with *Rees Jones*) • Private Moscow
(with *Adam Hamdy*) • Private Rogue (with *Adam Hamdy*) • Private
Beijing (with *Adam Hamdy*) • Private Rome (with *Adam Hamdy*) •
Private Monaco (with *Adam Hamdy*)

NYPD RED SERIES

NYPD Red (with *Marshall Karp*) • NYPD Red 2 (with *Marshall
Karp*) • NYPD Red 3 (with *Marshall Karp*) • NYPD Red 4
(with *Marshall Karp*) • NYPD Red 5 (with *Marshall Karp*) •
NYPD Red 6 (with *Marshall Karp*)

DETECTIVE HARRIET BLUE SERIES

Never Never (with *Candice Fox*) • Fifty Fifty (with *Candice Fox*) •
Liar Liar (with *Candice Fox*) • Hush Hush (with *Candice Fox*)

INSTINCT SERIES

Instinct (with *Howard Roughan, previously published as* Murder
Games) • Killer Instinct (with *Howard Roughan*) • Steal
(with *Howard Roughan*)

THE BLACK BOOK SERIES

The Black Book (with *David Ellis*) • The Red Book
(with *David Ellis*) • Escape (with *David Ellis*)

TEXAS RANGER SERIES

Texas Ranger (with *Andrew Bourelle*) • Texas Outlaw (with *Andrew
Bourelle*) • The Texas Murders (with *Andrew Bourelle*)

STAND-ALONE THRILLERS

The Thomas Berryman Number • Hide and Seek • Black Market • The Midnight Club • Sail (*with Howard Roughan*) • Swimsuit (*with Maxine Paetro*) • Don't Blink (*with Howard Roughan*) • Postcard Killers (*with Liza Marklund*) • Toys (*with Neil McMahon*) • Now You See Her (*with Michael Ledwidge*) • Kill Me If You Can (*with Marshall Karp*) • Guilty Wives (*with David Ellis*) • Zoo (*with Michael Ledwidge*) • Second Honeymoon (*with Howard Roughan*) • Mistress (*with David Ellis*) • Invisible (*with David Ellis*) • Truth or Die (*with Howard Roughan*) • Murder House (*with David Ellis*) • The Store (*with Richard DiLallo*) • The President is Missing (*with Bill Clinton*) • Revenge (*with Andrew Holmes*) • Juror No. 3 (*with Nancy Allen*) • The First Lady (*with Brendan DuBois*) • The Chef (*with Max DiLallo*) • Out of Sight (*with Brendan DuBois*) • Unsolved (*with David Ellis*) • The Inn (*with Candice Fox*) • Lost (*with James O. Born*) • The Summer House (*with Brendan DuBois*) • 1st Case (*with Chris Tebbetts*) • Cajun Justice (*with Tucker Axum*)• The Midwife Murders (*with Richard DiLallo*) • The Coast-to-Coast Murders (*with J.D. Barker*) • Three Women Disappear (*with Shan Serafin*) • The President's Daughter (*with Bill Clinton*) • The Shadow (*with Brian Sitts*) • The Noise (*with J.D. Barker*) • 2 Sisters Detective Agency (*with Candice Fox*) • Jailhouse Lawyer (*with Nancy Allen*) • The Horsewoman (*with Mike Lupica*) • Run Rose Run (*with Dolly Parton*) • Death of the Black Widow (*with J.D. Barker*) • The Ninth Month (*with Richard DiLallo*) • The Girl in the Castle (*with Emily Raymond*) • Blowback (*with Brendan DuBois*) • The Twelve Topsy-Turvy, Very Messy Days of Christmas (*with Tad Safran*) • The Perfect Assassin (*with Brian Sitts*) • House of Wolves (*with Mike Lupica*) • Countdown (*with Brendan DuBois*) • Cross Down (*with Brendan DuBois*) • Circle of Death (*with Brian Sitts*) • Lion & Lamb (with *Duane Swierczynski*) • 12 Months to Live (*with Mike Lupica*) • Holmes, Margaret and Poe (*with Brian Sitts*) • The No. 1 Lawyer (*with Nancy Allen*) • Eruption (*with Michael Crichton*) • The Murder Inn (*with Candice Fox*) • Confessions of the Dead (*with J.D. Barker*) • 8 Months Left (*with Mike Lupica*) • Lies He Told Me (*with David Ellis*) • Raised By Wolves (*with Emily Raymond*) • Holmes is Missing (*with Brian Sitts*) • 2 Sisters Murder Investigations (*with Candice Fox*)

NON-FICTION

Torn Apart (*with Hal and Cory Friedman*) • The Murder of King Tut (*with Martin Dugard*) • All-American Murder (*with Alex Abramovich*

and Mike Harvkey) • The Kennedy Curse (with Cynthia Fagen) •
The Last Days of John Lennon (with Casey Sherman and Dave Wedge) •
Walk in My Combat Boots (with Matt Eversmann and Chris Mooney) •
ER Nurses (with Matt Eversmann) • James Patterson by James
Patterson: The Stories of My Life • Diana, William and Harry
(with Chris Mooney) • American Cops (with Matt Eversmann) • What
Really Happens in Vegas (with Mark Seal) • The Secret Lives of
Booksellers and Librarians (with Matt Eversmann) • Tiger,
Tiger (with Peter de Jonge)

MURDER IS FOREVER TRUE CRIME

Murder, Interrupted (with Alex Abramovich and Christopher Charles) •
Home Sweet Murder (with Andrew Bourelle and Scott Slaven) •
Murder Beyond the Grave (with Andrew Bourelle and Christopher
Charles) • Murder Thy Neighbour (with Andrew Bourelle and Max
DiLallo) • Murder of Innocence (with Max DiLallo and Andrew
Bourelle) • Till Murder Do Us Part (with Andrew Bourelle
and Max DiLallo)

COLLECTIONS

Triple Threat (with Max DiLallo and Andrew Bourelle) • Kill or Be Killed
(with Maxine Paetro, Rees Jones, Shan Serafin and Emily Raymond) •
The Moores are Missing (with Loren D. Estleman, Sam Hawken and Ed
Chatterton) • The Family Lawyer (with Robert Rotstein, Christopher
Charles and Rachel Howzell Hall) • Murder in Paradise (with Doug Allyn,
Connor Hyde and Duane Swierczynski) • The House Next Door (with
Susan DiLallo, Max DiLallo and Brendan DuBois) • 13-Minute Murder
(with Shan Serafin, Christopher Farnsworth and Scott Slaven) • The River
Murders (with James O. Born) • The Palm Beach Murders (with James
O. Born, Duane Swierczynski and Tim Arnold) • Paris Detective •
3 Days to Live • 23 ½ Lies (with Maxine Paetro)

For more information about James Patterson's novels,
visit www.penguin.co.uk.